Happy Endings
Sleepover

Happy Endings Sleepover

By

Cade Jay Hathaway

Happy Endings Sleepover

cerulean
s k y

PRESS

Publisher's Note:

This is a work of fiction. Names, characters, places, and incidents either are the product of the author's imagination or are used fictitiously, and any resemblance to actual persons, living or dead, some business establishments, events, or locales is entirely coincidental.

LIBRARY OF CONGRESS CATALOGING-IN-PUBLICATION DATA
Hathaway, Cade Jay
Happy Endings Sleepover / Cade Jay Hathaway 1991—
p. cm.
ISBN 13: 978-1511559669   ISBN 10: 1511559667

1. Contemporary Gay Life—Fiction. 2. Life in Denmark—Fiction.
3. CIA / Espionage—Fiction. 4. Contemporary Teen Relationships—Fiction. I. Title

Printed in the United States of America
Set in Palatino Linotype
Book Designed by Wilson Rushbrook

10 9 8 7 6 5 4 3 2 1   FIRST EDITION

Author's note:

Certain characters in this novel speak various European languages. Whenever a character is heard speaking English as a second language, the writing reflects whatever limitations that particular character may have with grammar, accents, or pronunciations of certain English words and phrases. However, if the character is thinking any unexpressed narrative thoughts, those thoughts will reflect the usage of proper grammar and pronunciation as if the person is thinking in his or her native language.

For Lasse

1

There was Sander Lars Hansen, and there was me. I'm Johnnie Allen. At the time we met I was twenty and he was fifteen. He was quiet; not shy, just kind of quiet. Like 'in the background' quiet. I only noticed him because he spilled an orange soda on himself and everyone in the room laughed. Then he smiled, and we all went back to what we were doing. I can't remember now what it was—that's right, we were at a winter solstice party—but that's not so important.

I do remember that Sander came over the next day with Georg. I am an American and I was there to start school in Sander's country, a small country way up in the north called Denmark. They call it *Danmark* there, so I guess that's why they're known as Danes.

School was different there, as I would soon find out. A little more open, a little less rigid. I learned a lot and I would say my world opened up. It opened up really big. I can honestly say that I didn't know very much about anything, and I certainly didn't carry any kind of world view in my pocket—unless you consider 'I'm from America' and 'We're Number One!' as world views.

Georg was my best friend, Emil's younger brother and he became kind of a tagalong to everything we did, and that was okay. It was all an adventure to me, and 'The more the merrier,' I always say. Emil became my instant friend the day I landed in the little kingdom. I had taken the train from the airport, gotten off at the wrong stop, and since it was the last train of the day I figured I'd stay at a hotel and continue on in the morning. Then I walked through the town by myself and began soaking in whatever I could.

It was and still is a nice place. Odense is the town and it was where the fairytale writer, Hans Christian Andersen came from. I even saw his house. I was still internationally ignorant then, so I did what all good Americans do when they visit a foreign land: I scored dinner at McDonald's. It was exactly the same as at any McDonald's I'd ever been to, except it was cleaner and the helpers acted like they were happy and enjoyed their jobs. The girl who took my order even spoke English to me when I guess she got tired of me butchering her language. At least I tried, and she acknowledged as much. And her smile was real. The Big Mac was the same, and the fries were like they should be.

Wandering the cobblestone walkway led me through streets that appeared as though they were lifted from Disney World. The newest building was from 1862, and most were from two hundred years before that. It's weird to see a boutique clothing store crammed with teenage girls in a building that was erected about the time the Pilgrims landed at Plymouth Rock. It's even stranger to see a gay adult bookstore and movie arcade next door, in a building that's even older. I haven't mentioned yet that I'm a totally closeted, and very sexually active gay guy. I've known I liked guys since I was six, and I've been sucking dick since I was twelve.

My high school years consisted of nothing but unending days of frustration. I never had anyone to be with in high school. And not just sexually; I wanted love more than sex, and to have a boy I loved—and who also loved me back—would have meant everything. And imagine if he would have liked the sex part, too. And we could be together, and love each other, and hold each other, and make each other feel very good. But none of that ever happened.

Oh, I had plenty of sex, don't get me wrong. But it was usually from way older guys who would make eye contact with me in a store, or in a men's room, or on a city bus. It always happened the same way. Take the bus, for example.

I had to ride the number 49 bus to and from school, and one day I was sitting on the back seat when a guy who was about forty or fifty got on. He sat on one of the lengthwise benches and was soon glancing back my way. We made eye contact and he smiled. I smiled back.

The bus stopped and when everybody was getting on and off he got up and sat beside me. I got hard as he was walking over because, though I may have been only fourteen, I knew what was up. I remember he was nice.

The bus took off and he acted like the movement of the bus made him "accidentally" drop his right hand into my lap, where there happened to be a big boner waiting for him.

His hand didn't leave my lap. He began by lightly squeezing my insanely hard cock through my pants, and then he whispered to me: "Looks like you got something going on down there."

"Yeah," I replied.

He moved his hand so he could cup my ass. I acted like a bump in the road made me bounce up just high enough so he could slip his hand underneath, which he did. He squeezed my ass cheek and his fingers found their way to my crack, where they remained.

"You wanna play around?" he offered.

"Sure."

"We can go to my place, or we can get off at the park and do it there."

"The park's fine," I said. It wasn't that I didn't want to go to his house. It was that I couldn't wait.

We got off the bus at the entrance to Hill Park, a really big park that had lots of places where naughty boys could do naughty things. We instinctively headed to a little block building that contained a girl's and a boy's room. The cool thing was that they were singles, which meant the doors locked. Since it was early in the day, the men's room was even clean and smelled nice. The door was barely latched when we both started yanking off our clothes as fast as we could. I was still stiff as a board and the only bone of contention, pardon the pun, was who would get to suck the other one first. I won.

I dropped to my knees and took his cock into my mouth and started sucking like a guy five days in the desert without a drop of water. My hands grasped his ass, and he was as hard as I was. Then he kind of pushed my face away and he joined me on the floor, sucking me so hard that I thought he might forget to breathe. It felt so good. It felt like me. Like I could be *me* in those few precious minutes.

His hand found my ass and he began to move his fingers up and down the crack. One finger in particular found the hole and was playing a little more earnestly than the others. His mouth alternated between my dick and balls while his finger kept exploring. Then the finger hit The Spot. I thought I was going to pass out from such intense pleasure.

"Do that! Keep doing that, please... *God!*

"Pretty nice, ain't it?"

"Fuck! Oh, fuck, it's fuckin' great!" is what I think I might have said.

"Here, roll over."

I thought the obvious was about to happen. Then he surprised me again when he started to tongue my hole. That was definitely a new item on the menu for me. And I fucking loved it. I'd had a lot of sex before, but I never dreamed...

14

"Oh my fuckin' God!"

"You like that, do ya?" he managed, between the longest of licks.

I hunched up a bit so I could stroke myself while he did his business, but he took over and so I just laid my head on my crossed arms and enjoyed what Heaven surely must be all about.

"Lay off my dick a little cuz I don't wanna cum yet," I told him.

"Gotcha."

And then he got up on his knees and gently slipped himself inside me. I got on all fours and waited for the movement to begin. He started with the easiest of motions. Every time he would thrust inward he would brush by The Spot, and for the first time I understood why chicks moan and spurt all over themselves when a guy does her. God, this felt good. And as if it couldn't get any better, he guided me onto the floor and coaxed me into a spread eagle position.

"I'm gonna go a little faster," he whispered behind my ear. "Is that okay?"

"Are you fuckin' kiddin' me? Get a move on, bud!"

He chuckled and started a rhythm that resulted in the seeing of stars, and becoming as breathless as a marathon runner at mile twenty-six. I couldn't have talked if you had paid me. I just lay there, totally consuming the moment. Then I felt him reach around as he kind of turned me on my side. He was furiously plowing his cock into my ass, jacking me off at the same time. The explosion was going to happen any second, that was for sure.

"I'm gonna cum!" I sighed, very under my breath.

"I know. Go for it."

And at that moment I felt his thrusts turn to quivers as he filled me with his own.

"I'm cumming!" I bleated. Totally out of breath, I couldn't speak. And then I came in about half a dozen of the largest spurts I had ever seen come out of me. And I collapsed. It took me about five minutes to get to the place where I could just barely stand up. In fact, he already had most of his clothes on by then.

"Damn." It was all I could say.

"How old are you again?"

"Fourteen."

"Fuck... You sure got the moves for somebody fourteen," he said. "I hadn't even jacked off yet when I was your age."

"I think it just comes natural," I offered in all sincerity. He helped me pull my pants up and kissed my neck. He wasn't exactly handsome or anything, and he certainly had a couple of spare tires encircling his belly, but he wasn't bad looking either.

"Can we do it again?" I asked.

"You mean now?" he replied, incredulous shock in his voice.

"No. I mean some other time, maybe?"

"Sure, kid. I ride the same bus every day, so I'll see you again."

"Cool!"

He hugged me.

"Listen," he quietly said. "Let me leave first, then you wait a couple minutes before you head out, okay?"

"Yeah, sure."

He cracked the door open and took a second to look around and then he was gone. I never saw him again.

Back in Denmark now.

I entered the gay bookstore giving it the once over. I tried to get my point across to the clerk but I'm afraid that Rosetta Stone and Berlitz don't have any stock tourist phrases that work very well in a porno theater. I don't think 'Glory Hole' can be found anywhere in those books. For the second time that evening I was rescued by a bilingual Dane who spoke to me in English. There was no shame implied, either, as he pointed to the dark room, the little theater that showed gay flicks, and of course the booths with the glory holes—complete with wipe-ups for the inevitable spillage.

He explained how everything worked and then took my two hundred kroner—worth about thirty bucks. International transaction completed, I headed for the movie house. When I walked in I have to tell you that there was more going on in the room than was on the screen. It looked like Caligula's bedroom on a Saturday night.

There were about two dozen guys either paired off, or in threes, doing lots of fun stuff. And there were about ten others jamming the aisles just stroking and watching. So I dropped my drawers and joined in on the jacking, and within seconds there were two guys on me. One started playing with my cock and was soon on his knees worshiping it with his tongue. The other guy explored my ass as he jacked.

Two other guys joined us and I got my first taste of something called bukkake. Bukkake is a Japanese thing. A group of guys get together—the more the better—and they choose one guy to be the Bukkake Boy. It's the Bukkake's job to service the other guys. To suck them and to let them fuck him. Then, as they get ready to cum, they roll the Bukkake Boy onto his back and squirt it on his face. The Bukkake licks and tastes as much cum as he can, and the players say lots of domineeringly nasty things to him as they cum and cum and cum on his face and lips.

I was elected Bukkake Boy and never sucked so much uncut dick in my life. Danes don't butcher their dicks and then justify it as some insane and archaic Jewish tribal custom, like us Americans do. I really got a taste for Danish cock that night. And I got my ass plowed, too. All in all, it was great fun. This all happened the day before I met my friends.

The next day I asked the girl at the hotel desk how to find an apartment there. She circled a column in a newspaper and gave me the address of a place that rented them out. A nice lady at the apartment office found me a great place in a building with kids my own age, so that's where I landed. It was awesome.

When I pulled up in the taxi and grabbed all my bags from the trunk, two guys who were standing on the porch came over and gave me a hand. They were expecting the guy from the States because the lady who rented the apartment to me had a daughter who lived there, and she phoned her up and told her. Which promptly made its way through the whole place. Twenty-two apartments knew I was on the way.

The two who met me out front were Emil and Jonas. They spoke to me in English and made me feel really welcome. They were happy and exhibited a lack of worldly hardness that I needed so very much.

They led the way to my little apartment and I saw that the door was open. A cute old lady called Emma was finishing up some floor mopping and had wiped down all of the beautiful Danish wood with lemon oil. She smiled a lot and jabbered in Danish, of which I couldn't understand a word. Jonas stepped up as translator and basically passed on something to the effect that I was very welcome there, and that if I needed anything just call Emma.

If some days are diamonds and some days stones, this one was the Hope Diamond. I had been there less than half an hour, and yet it felt like I had already lived a whole other life. I'm enthusiastic by nature and I try to curb it whenever I can catch myself (because I can actually come off a little naïve sometimes), what with my rose-colored-glass-half-filled attitude. But I have to say that this was different. It felt like I belonged. It felt like I was home.

2

On the weekend, Jonas drove Emil and me to the Rosengård Centret which is their big shopping mall out on the edge of town. I was on a mission to get a television, a stereo, and some dishes and stuff. The mall was pretty cool and I found and bought the TV and stereo right away. Then came the Clown Show.

We rolled everything out to the car in an oversized shopping cart, and halfway to the parking lot something occurred to me: Jonas drove a Citroën 2cv. Now in case you're wondering about a Citroën 2cv let me say, first, that it's a French car that—no joke—is smaller than a Volkswagen Beetle. Second, if there is an uglier and more powerless automobile on the planet, I've yet to see it.

So here's the scene: Three tall guys with a twenty-seven inch, very heavy TV set that had to go ten whole miles (sorry, 16.1 kilometers). I guess the original thought was that we'd stuff it into the back seat and then squeeze the skinniest one next to the TV. No way that would work because the set was even too big for the car door.

By now bystanders started offering up their ideas, none of which could ever be implemented in a gazillion years. It was looking bad when Emil suggested that we cart the tube to the bus stop and wrestle it home on the city bus. We were resigned when a small girl, who was maybe eight years old, walked up to Jonas and calmly informed him that she possessed the answer.

"I know how to get that big TV home to your house," she said, with such an organizational authority.

Jonas smiled. "But the car is too small, just like you."

"You see," she continued without missing a beat, "your little top unsnaps so you don't have to have a roof when the sun shines."

"I know," said Jonas. "But how can that help? As

the TV still won't fit in the back seat."

"Aaaggghhh!" she growled, by now frustrated at the denseness of Jonas. (Emil and I were just as blank.) "You don't have to put it in the back seat. Open up your roof and drop the box into it crooked. The box can lean, but enough will be inside that you can hold on to."

It made sense. Emil opened the car top, and sure as shit it was going to work. I climbed in the back, Emil sat in the front and reclined the seat so more box could fit into the hole, and Jonas and the bystanders lifted up the precious cargo. It worked. Son of a gun, it absolutely worked.

As he maneuvered himself behind the steering wheel, Jonas reached into his pocket and pulled out a fifty-kroner bill and handed it to our little savior.

"Thank you, little girl."

"You may call me Susanne, and thank you very much," she said, as she pocketed the cash. "Good luck!" And off she went with her parents and brother, who were just as amazed by her as we were.

Oh... You thought *that* was the Clown Show, did you? Not even close.

Jonas went to fire up the mighty 2cv. Click, went the starter. Then click again. He had somehow bumped the headlight switch when he got out of the car, and the flashlight battery in that little junker had gone as flat as a pancake. But no worries, said Jonas. All we had to do was push-start the bugger and we'd be on our merry way. Since I was already squished in the back, Emil's straw was drawn and so out he went, standing ready behind our limousine.

"Hurry up! What's taking you?" Jonas barked. Emil trotted up to the window.

"You say something?"

"Push, man!"

"I was waiting for you to say *when*."

"When, already!"

"So I should push now?"

"Yes. Emil. Push. Now." Emil tried his best, but the car was entrenched.

"It won't move!"

"Push harder!" Which he did. And still the car stayed put. I offered a backseat suggestion.

"Um, Jonas... Does your car have a parking brake?" I could almost see the embarrassment fog up in the rear view mirror. Then he laughed.

"What's so funny?" Emil expelled in breathless frustration.

"I had the brake on. Sorry."

So without any further objection from the parking brake, Emil pushed the little car, Jonas popped the clutch, and she started up like a champ. Jonas had some fun driving in circles around Emil, acting like he was going to leave him behind. Some things are universal the world over, and leave it to goofy college kids to implement the dumbest ones.

Now that the car was puttering along, something more had to happen. It arrived in the form of a sudden deluge. I had no idea that raindrops could hurt. This downpour was so heavy that there was no way it wasn't going to soak through the box and ruin my new TV. So Jonas floored it. To about the maximum speed it could give us. Which was slower than the guy riding alongside us on his bicycle. Now it was getting embarrassing. Then I learned something that I think I'll never get over. It went like this...

The Clown Show was in full spectacle as we tottered down the road, when all of a sudden pretty blue lights flashed at us from behind. The long arm of the law had officially joined the Clown Show, now going on its second hour. Jonas pulled over, and of course I thought that he was going to get a big, pricey ticket that I would be happy to pay. But if Denmark was anything at all like the States, what I couldn't do was stop the ding on his insurance. I was so concerned that because of me, he would be stuck with an insurance increase, and there goes my new friend. The cops approached Jonas's window.

"Hey, men, that television will be ruined in this rain. You can't leave it up there!"

What was I hearing?

"Let's put it in our car and we'll follow you home with it," the second cop said as he started to lift the TV out of the hole in the roof. The first cop helped Jonas snap the top back into place, while Emil and copper number two loaded the set into the police car.

"Where do you live?"

"On Kochsgade, not far from the railway station," Jonas replied.

"Okay. Lead the way."

And with that, we were off. The curtain was lowered on The Clown Show. I still couldn't believe what had just happened. And what really put it over the top for me was when the *Politi* helped carry it in to my apartment. They shook hands, bid us a good evening, got back into their car, and drove away. The guys must have sensed my shock when Emil quipped, "Haven't you seen a policeman help somebody out before?"

"No." That was as plain as I could put it. No, I had never remotely witnessed the likes of what I had just seen with my two own eyes. It'd happened. But I still didn't believe it.

I had about a week to kill before school started, so I spent most of the time with people from my building. Everyone went out of their way to make me feel welcome, even an eccentric British expatriate called Wilfred. He had moved to Denmark from England over twenty years before, was married and had two girls, but there was a divorce. And rather than return to his native land, he stayed in Denmark so he could be close to his girls while they were growing up. He also had dinner at his ex-wife's at least twice a week.

Wilfred came off as kind of a know-it-all, and there wasn't a mirror anywhere that he didn't like—he fancied himself quite the ladies man—but he was lots of fun and always good for a laugh, whether intentionally or not.

We got the TV hooked up and it was great. There were all of five channels to watch, but I learned that half the shows on the Danish television networks are from the States, Canada, England, and Australia. I could watch the subtitles—Danish television never dubs programs; all are shown in their original languages with Danish subtitles—and so I began to connect Danish words and complete sentences with the English words that popped onto the screen. It was all rubbish for a while, but I would begin to make some sense of it all soon enough.

It's Tuesday of my first week 'In Country'. There's a knock at the door. The kid from the party who spilled the orange soda smiled as the door creaked open.

"Sounding scary."

"Huh?"

"Your door sounding...uh...like from a scary movie." (It sounded like he said MOOO-weee. But his English was definitely better than my non-existent Danish.)

"Well, at least the door works," I retorted. "What's up?"

"Uh... Has you sees Georg? He's is Emil's broder oh... He say I meets him here."

I understood every word he said, believe it or not. The thick accent and the fact that a kid his age could speak any foreign language at all amazed me to no end.

"I don't know where Emil is, or his brother," I told him. "But you can wait here, or use the phone to try and find them."

"Tak!" he said, and he made himself at home. He tried to track his friend down by phone, but came up empty. "No good lucks for me," he said, a smile growing across his very handsome face.

We talked—well actually, I asked—about Denmark. I was the one on the learning curve, and he obliged me as much as our mutually limited linguistic skills could muster. I had no idea how the country worked, or how things were done. You know, the day-to-day stuff that everybody takes for granted if you're from there. Sander was a smart kid, well educated, very well-mannered, and completely self possessed. He seemed to take whatever came and, as friendly as he was, he obviously had a certain amount of street smarts in him. In time I would learn that this was pretty much the way it was in the rest of the world. Americans, for all that we have and supposedly know, are fairly sheltered people, and it's halfway through college before maturity really shows itself.

"Hey, hey!" It was Emil and Georg. They'd gone to the bakery and saw my door open as they passed. "Look what we have here!"

They pulled rolls and pastries out of the bag and plunked themselves down on the floor. "Hey, thanks," I said. "You guys want something to drink?"

"Beer is good," Emil chuckled.

"You're kidding, right?"

"I never kid about beer."

I didn't know where to go with it, because I sure didn't have any beer in the fridge. "Will milk or soda do?"

"No. Got any coffee?" Emil asked.

"Afraid not," I admitted.

Faces fell. Disappointment wracked the awkward stillness. Diplomatic relations were teetering. Unlike coffee, the only thing brewing was an international incident of my own making.

"I get us some," Sander chirped. "Come, Georg, you helping me whit coff." Then he turned to me. "I needs monies for the coff." Okay, I said, and they were off for the coff. Emil clucked his tongue: "No wonder everybody hates Americans."

3

It's here that I should make a very big confession.
While everything I just told you is as true as it
goes, there was a specific reason I moved to
Denmark and it wasn't for the pastry. Or the cute
guys. Or school. I was there on assignment. I guess I
drew the lucky straw because I was less than ninety-
six hours in the country and I was already in love
with it.

The assignment? I was a spy for the CIA. Okay,
I'll pause a few moments while you laugh. And I
hope you weren't drinking *coff* right now because
your book is probably very wet from spitting it all
over the page when you just read this.

The CIA. The Central Intelligence Agency. The
Spook House. The most despised branch of the

United States government in just about every corner of the globe. Yes, I was a spy for the CIA. A Gay Spy. Funny, that.

Did I mention that you're not supposed to be both gay and a spy? Which is odd to me because whenever I want to get the dirt on anyone, anywhere, I just ask the first gay guy that comes flittering down the lane and, lo and behold, can gather enough intelligence to fill a file cabinet. Anyway, I'd better explain myself before you throw this book against a wall in disbelief.

When I left high school I wanted to do nothing, and everything. I have a huge range of interests, but none of them can really be translated into a job for money. So I decided I would try something that would bring in some dough while I figured out what I wanted to do with myself.

I like to travel, and I like the conveyances that make the travel possible. Things like ships, airplanes, trains, buses, cars. Everything but bicycles. I thought about joining the Navy, but I figured that the gay thing would out itself—at this point I should let you know that I appear very straight. No lisp, no girlie moves, I don't wear heels, and this wrist ain't limp, fella. I would have had no trouble lying to Uncle Sam and getting a bunk on any missile cruiser or destroyer this side of the Brooklyn Navy Yard. Thing is, I didn't want to destroy anything and the only cruising I probably would have done is in the shower room.

But I found out about something called the merchant marine. The big cargo ships, tankers, and passenger liners are crewed by people in the merchant marine. All I had to do was get a seaman's card from the Coast Guard, go to the nearest shipping hall and register, and wait for a ship that needed entry-level crew members.

I chose the steward's department because I had experience cooking from a previous job I held, and within weeks I found myself on a cargo ship sailing out of San Francisco—yes, I get the irony—bound for Asia. I took to it quite well. In fact, I loved it.

When you're on a ship you would think that friendships would be in line with whatever rank you hold. In other words, oilers hang out with oilers, officers hang with officers, and cooks and stewards would do the same. Not so. I learned this truth about my fourth week aboard the ship.

We were sailing off the Indonesian coast, bound for Surabaya, when a deck hand took very ill. We had to take him off the ship and put him in the hospital so he could recover enough to fly home. This left a night watch that could only be filled by another crew member who wasn't already a regular watch stander. That meant the replacement had to come from the steward's department. Since nobody wanted to stand watch from midnight to four o'clock in the morning, and since I was the new guy, I drew the short straw.

This meant that every day, seven days a week, would be spent working from six in the morning to seven at night. Then taking a nap from seven until midnight, when I would then fulfill my watch-standing duty from midnight until four. Take a quick nap. And then be back at it two hours later for a repeat performance. Talk about the days running into each other.

Usually someone in the steward's department only interacts with the captain on paydays, when signing on or off the vessel, during disciplinary actions, or while serving him in the officer's dining saloon. Once I pulled the night watch that all changed.

Captain Jefferson 'Jap' Logan was a very quiet fellow. Tall, in his late fifties, perfect officer's physique, and with his close-cropped hair definitely erring on the saltier side of the salt and pepper scale, he liked to spend time on the bridge in the wee hours. He would often spell the quartermaster and the third mate, allowing them to go down to the mess and have some night lunch. As long as they brought him a Fresca and a turkey sandwich when they came back, he didn't care how long they took.

It was his reflection time. I would watch him from my post out on the bridge wing and wonder what was going through his mind. He would light his pipe and I would smell the sweetness of the tobacco as it mixed with the brisk winds that had followed the late evening squalls.

One particular night as I gazed across the moonlit horizon, I was startled by a darkened form standing mere inches from me. Then I saw the orange glow of the lighter as it touched the bowl of his pipe.

"Good morning, Mister Allen," he said between puffs. "It's a bit on the chilly side for this time of year, especially for the China Sea."

"Yes, Captain."

He stood there for the longest time, and then we talked politics. World affairs. Geography. Ships. All sorts of things. And then my watch was over and I headed for my cabin.

The next night we picked up where we had left off.

And the next night.

And the night after that.

I truly admired him. Logan was a smart cookie, which should be obvious. I don't think the steamship lines are in the habit of giving a guy a 20,000 ton liner, with a cargo that's worth ten times the cost of the ship, unless he's got something going on upstairs.

Over the course of that voyage aboard the *S.S. Stargazer* of the Limerick Steamship Line, I learned more from that man than I had ever done in my twelve years of school. Then, almost as quickly as it had begun, we returned to American shores. We tied up in Seattle and the trip was through. It was back to the shipping hall to find another job, and I didn't know if I would ever ship out with any of those guys again. Oh well, it was nice while it lasted. I just hoped my next trip would be as good.

The Union Hall is a grimy place. Think of the worst county government office, but add the overpowering stench of cigars and cigarettes warring over whatever oxygen happens to be left in the room, and you get the picture. Add some fading linoleum floors, half dead potted plants and crappy magazines so old that

Gutenberg himself might have printed them.

What a sorry, dreary atmosphere. And it was here that I would have to wait every day, from eight in the morning until six at night, if I would ever stand a chance of catching another ship. Lowest man on the totem pole equals longest hours spent in the Union Hall waiting for a berth.

The phone behind the dispatcher's desk rang— yes, *rang*, as in dingalingaling—followed by the squeal of the P.A. system. He called my name.

"Pick up the call over there," he glowered.

A cheap, white phone minus a dial—like the kind they have at cab stands in the old black and white movies—gurgled a weak jingle.

"Hello?"

"Johnnie?"

"Yeah, who's this?

"It's Captain Logan. We're sailing in about an hour and our second cook hasn't shown up. You want it?"

A half an hour later I was climbing up the gangway and into the cabin I had vacated barely forty-eight hours earlier. I quickly signed aboard and reported to the chief steward; I was back in the saddle, and ready for another trip to the Far East.

"Say Allen," Eddie Ty, my boss, chuckled. "You

gots the Cap lovin' whatchoo do, damn!" he smiled. A skinny little black guy shaped like a pencil with glasses, Eddie was straight up. He knew his business, and his reputation at sea was bar none. Everything I learned about keeping a crew happy at the dinner table I learned from Eddie Ty.

"What are you on about, Eddie Ty?"

"Well, son, it's like this, see..." Then he paused his gravelly voice for effect. "You know Munson, the fuckhead whose job you replaced while he was on the beach?"

"Yeah?" I kind of stammered.

"Well, as you may or may not know, everybody aboard this piece of shit, rust bucket, fuck tub, *hated* that mu'fucka's useless ass, knowhatimsayin'?"

"I guess so..."

"So that mu'fuckin' captain say, Eddie Ty, what we gon' do 'bout that mu'fuckin' Munson mu'fucka!"

"Yeah?

"Damn straight. So's I say, Cap, you know what we mu'fuckin' got ta do, so he do it."

"What?"

"Munson drag his big ol' racist Dukes-a-Hazzard ass up the gangway and Cap say, Munson, you fired, so getdafuckout!"

"Yeah?"

"If I'm lyin' I'm dyin'!"

Seems like the Chief Mate discovered some "contraband" in Munson's cabin. Funny thing was, his cabin had been my cabin up until the moment I signed off the ship when we landed in Seattle. And I know I didn't have anything bad stashed away anywhere in that room. So I guess that poor Munson had been side slammed. On account of little ol' me.

"Wow!"

"Wow, my big black ass! You be the best mu'fucka for the job, that's all. Fuck Munson, that white-sheet-wearin' mu'fucka! Fuck!"

So I was back aboard, ready for at least another hundred days of this loony-bin-of-the-sea.

"You gon' just stand there, you mu'fuckin cracker-ass fuck! Gitcho ass ta work, son. What, you think this is, the mu'fuckin' Love Boat? This ain't no goddamn cruise to no Bahamas!"

My God, it's hard to keep from laughing your ass off when Eddie Ty's on a mu'fuckin' roll!

Somewhere off the Philippines.

We're supposed to be pulling in to a private island owned by the Dole Pineapple Company.

We're picking up tons and tons of pineapples, and there's a company town called Bugo that has, of all things, a Shakey's Pizza Parlor and a Kentucky Fried Chicken stand.

We're steaming slowly off the island, looking for the pier that's supposed to clearly jut out from the pineapple processing plant. We can see the plant, and can smell a mixture of pineapple and fried chicken, but there's no pier to be found. And because this part of the P.I. is so remote, there aren't any harbor pilots to help guide us in.

Captain Logan is afraid to go too far in because it's kind of hard to turn a six-hundred-foot liner around if we make the wrong approach. He decides to stop the ship and drop anchor and think up a solution to the mess we're in.

"The chart says here's where the pier is, and we're *here*, so what in Sam Hill is goin' on here?!" Logan spews, more to himself than anyone in particular. "Can't we get those pinheads on the radio?"

"Radio?" Sparks laughs. "Smoke signals, maybe!"

"God damn, I don't wanna have to launch a boat and go on a fuckin' expedition to find the place, but I guess that's it."

And off he went to round up the bosun and go

on a little boat ride. I headed back to the galley after I collected all of the coffee cups from the bridge and got started on lunch. When I got to the galley, Eddie Ty and all of the off-duty crew that were hanging around the crew's mess wanted to know why we'd dropped the hook. I told them what I knew and got busy lighting the stove and pulling ingredients from the cold lockers. Sailors travel on their stomachs. And whores and booze. But that's another tale.

About the time supper was ready, I heard the putt-putt of the ship's launch buzz past. A puff of diesel exhaust wafted through the galley porthole, and about a quarter of an hour later I could feel that we were moving. It wasn't much longer before we felt the gentle bump of the hull kissing the pier. The hollering up and down the deck to the linesmen signaled that we were in. About dessert time the throbbing of the engines stopped and the big ship was ready to take on her full load of pineapples. I made a mental note to divert a few of them to my cabin.

Later that night, long after the ship made port, I took a stroll out to the fantail. Dave, a cute guy fresh out of college who was on his first trip, forgot to bring the flag in. Aboard ship a flag goes up at 0800 and comes down at sunset. I hauled it in and gave it a nice roll and planned to walk it up to the bridge and stick it in the flag locker so it would be there in the morning for the bosun. No need for Dave to get his ears boxed for such a little thing as this.

"Good evening, Mr. Allen. It's a bit on the warm side tonight, isn't it?" It was the captain.

"Yes, Captain Logan. It's really tropical. Like in movies and stuff."

"Look over there," he pointed at the horizon. "You see what looks like flash bulbs going off?"

"Yeah. Kind of spooky lookin'. Strange, anyway," I said. He stepped over to the railing.

"Well, enjoy this warmth because by morning we're in for it."

"In for it?" I asked him. "In for what?"

He said that a whale of a monsoon was heading straight for us and that it would be a very warm rain. He said we wouldn't know if the water dripping down our faces would be from the rain or from sweat.

"Make sure that you dog your portholes tonight before you turn in," he warned. "And don't just leave 'em even a tiny bit open cuz when it hits, the wind can slam your port open and you'll have a cabin full of glass to deal with."

"Aye, sir," I replied in my best sailor-speak. He

stood there for what seemed the longest time and changed the subject in a way that, if I didn't know any better, felt more like a job interview than one of our usual conversations. He asked me where I was from, what my political and religious beliefs were, and then he asked me the damndest thing I ever heard.

"Johnnie, what would you do if I dropped you in the middle of a market bazaar in Cairo or Bangkok with nothing but a quarter in your pocket?"

"I dunno... Cry?" I chuckled.

"No, man, I'm serious. If you were dropped in the middle of the asshole of the earth somewhere, with nothing but the clothes on your back, what would you do? How would you get home?" he asked. I figured he was just making conversation, or maybe it was some kind of word game or math problem. I played along.

"Well, Cap, I guess I'd make sure that I wasn't in any immediate danger, then I'd figure out where the people who speak English are."

"Go on..."

"Maybe I'd look for an American hotel, like a Hilton or something. Then I'd ask the dude at the front desk if there was a consulate or embassy near there and get myself to it, I guess."

"Pretty good. Then how would you get home? And remember, you can't call for anyone to send you any dough from the States. You gotta get home under your own steam. What do you do?"

I thought a while and came up with the most dumbshit idea. I told him I'd find an American ship and stow away on it. I'd check the sailing board and see where it was bound, and then hop a ride.

"Right answer," he smiled. "I mean, there's a lot of ways to do it, but that's a real good one. Just make sure it's a merchant ship, though," he cautioned. "Those navy squids are pretty hard ass and they'd probably drop you off at the first port and tell you to go fuck yourself," he grinned.

"That's pretty cold," I said. "I'd think they'd wanna help, ya know?"

"Yeah, but them's the breaks," he said. "I know a guy who tried it and they put him in the brig on bread and water, and then the bastards had him arrested when they got to Guam. Bunch of serious characters, those squids."

What had started as flashbulbs on the horizon was turning into full-on sheet lightning. The wind was definitely blowing the storm our way.

"I see you've got the ensign," Logan pointed at the rolled up flag. "How come?"

"Bufkin forgot to bring it in. I did it. I was gonna take it to the bridge when I was done out here," I told him.

"I'll take it," he said. And he turned and headed for the ladder to the boat deck. "Great gumbo tonight, by the way," he said, over his shoulder. "I do love your gumbo. Keep up the good work, Mr. Allen. See you in the morning." As he climbed the ladder I felt the first raindrops hit my face. The red sky from the morning was right. By midnight, the decks would be awash and the overhead in my cabin would sound like a tin roof on an Arkansas farm house in a summer storm. What an adventure.

Dave Bufkin was—is— a great looking guy.

Just a couple months younger than me, he had a pixie face accentuated by white-blond hair, and he was perfect in every way. Physically, that is. Otherwise, he was a complete dick. And of course I would have gone to bed with him in a fucking second. I tried everything to point him in that direction, but there was no interest, which I had to respect. Isn't it funny how standards can be swept aside if somebody looks as cute as Bufkin did, but somebody who is a great person on the inside, but is a dog on the outside never gets sought after, and seldom—if ever—gets laid.

Personally, I'm a really good looking guy by anyone's standards. And I happen to be nice, too. How that happened is anybody's guess. But ever since I was a little kid, I always backed the underdogs. I just wanted to be friends with everybody. I think Bufkin's dickishness was a straight guy thing. I really believe, deep down, that as shallow as a lot of gay guys can be, they really are some of the kindest and most thoughtful people in the world. Straights are brutes, pure and simple. So why do they always have to be so fucking cute?!

I noticed that the crew became a little standoffish towards me after I threw out the hints to Bufkin. Well, it's happened plenty of times before, starting in junior high school, and all the way until now. But you have to take a risk in this closeted life or you'll get nowhere.

One of my best friends and lovers, Larry Davis, worked beside me at a dishwashing job I once had. He was 'religious closeted', a closeting of the very worst kind, and if I hadn't made the first move it would have been no Johnnie and Larry. So it's a fifty-fifty proposition on the best of days.

I knew what was coming next. The homo-haters would talk shit and avoid me, and the closet cases would make their own pitches to me. Which is exactly what happened.

This old bedroom steward, Santiago, was about as closeted as they come. He was in his late fifties and was married, Catholic, and had a neighborhood full of children that all could be traced genetically in some way back to him. And he was a closet fag.

I was leaning against the rail on the sea side of the ship when he saddled up next to me.

"So, how goes it?" he offered.

"Great. Just hanging out."

"I'll say," he said, checking out my package. "Do you like messing around?"

"Yeah."

There was no risk for him because Bufkin had already blabbed, so he knew I liked dick. "I got the keys to the ship's infirmary. There's no one down there, and I've got the only keys. Wanna go?"

"Sure." That fucking Bufkin had outed me in the crew's mess and Santiago's ears must have prickled up, well, like his prick. This was basically going to be pity sex, but the old guy deserved some fun. And as long as he did most of the work, I was okay about it.

He was so excited that he could hardly get the

keys in the lock. We entered the darkened room and he started stripping everything off. I was only at my shoes and socks, when he walked over to me as I sat down on the bed. He was a little guy, so he didn't have much in the way of cock and balls, but he was earnest. He started unbuttoning my pants and, believe it or not, pulled them off in a very seductive way. Then he asked me to lie face down on the bed so he could give me a massage. Okay, this was getting good.

He stood inches from my face, his uncut dick twitching from the excitement of it all. And damn, could he give a great massage.

He started at my neck and, I'm not kidding you, he relieved about six months worth of tension in those moments. He rubbed my back, and then he started rubbing down my butt cheeks through my underwear. He was really turned on by the fact that I was still in my tighty-whiteys.

He spread my legs so he could drop his hands down from my butt to the back of my balls, and then he began running his fingers lightly up and down the crack. I was rock hard by then.

After a very long while he gently pulled my underwear down, and I really thought he was going to bust a nut when he saw my ass. Side note: I will say that I have an awesome ass. I always have. When I look at pictures of me from when I was a kid, I had a really cute butt. And my balls and cock are just as awesome. I wish the parents would have left my dick alone, though. Like ninety fucking percent of dumbass American moms and dads, they had it mangled up with that circumcision bullshit. Fuck them for that. But as circumcisions go, it was a good one. I've seen some of my friends and theirs don't look so good. So for that I'm thankful. But fuck, leave a kid's cock alone, why don't you?

Anyway, Santiago really started kneading my ass once it was flying in the breeze. I'm practically hairless except for some pubes around the base of my cock, so I knew he was going into major fantasy overdrive, what with my smooth legs, hairless chest, and my even more hairless ass. Let the old perv have his fun, I figured.

Things heated up when he started spitting into my hole and explored deeper and deeper. Then he climbed on me and stuck it in. Despite the fact that his dick was so small, it actually felt pretty good. He was a really good fuck, too. I mean, he knew what to do with that little dinger of his.

He was moaning with so much pleasure that I thought he would cum any second, but instead he rolled off and rolled me over and started sucking my cock like a major dick fiend. And, boy, could that man suck cock.

We were ten minutes into that when he started deep fingering me as he alternated between sucking my dick and licking and sucking my balls. This was getting pretty intense. I was going to cum any second, and it was going to be a mother lode.

I felt it reach the end of my dick; the point of absolutely, positively no return. I think I pumped out about six or seven squirts—big squirts—and he lapped up and swallowed every drop. Then, while I was as hot and as turned on as I could possibly be, he rolled me over and started pounding my ass with that tiny cock again. Even though I already came, that act of him furiously pushing that cock in and out kept things going for me. And even though I was dry, I was still getting these little orgasm spasms.

I felt him tense up and then the warm, pleasurable sensation of receiving a hot load up my ass took over and I reached down and started jacking off as hard and as fast as I could. He finally slowed, and then stopped. But he stayed inside me as I furiously jacked my dick.

I actually squeezed out more; just a little batch of spooge. Not much, but enough to make it worth it. I came on the blanket, and without missing a beat he pulled out of me and scooped my cum up with a couple of fingers and stuck it in his mouth. I've got to say, I've never really had a bad sexual experience. And even though Santiago would never have qualified as my first choice, after tonight I was determined to keep him on my dance card. At least for the remainder of the voyage.

Next morning came a knuckle rap on my cabin door. "Turn to, Cap'n wants to see you," came the raspy voice of Arnold, the Chief Mate. I pulled myself together and headed for the Captain's office up on "A" Deck, doing the best I could to not leave shoe prints on the freshly mopped linoleum.

"You wanted to see me, Captain?"

"Come on in. Take a seat. I gotta ask you something," he remarked, not looking up from the cargo manifest he was checking. You ever have a feeling like you're in trouble—bad trouble—even though you know you haven't done anything wrong? Well, that was me right then. Call it a case of *principal's office-itis.* I've got nothing to worry about, right?

"Go ahead and close the door," he ordered. Okay, *did* I do anything wrong? I mean, technically I shouldn't be getting butt-fucked by the bedroom steward in the ship's hospital, but if that had been the case, and I was now somehow busted for it, the bad news would have come down way before this. Shit. What was the deal?

"So I guess you probably wonder why I asked to see you?" The thought had occurred to me. A lot, in the last one hundred and twenty seconds. "So I wanna talk to you about something that you might find very agreeable to you, if I've in fact made the right call."

Okay, this was really starting to freak me out a little. Now I was completely lost. But, hey, at least it looked like I wasn't going to be in any kind of trouble. So that's something. I didn't say anything yet. Better to let him do the talking for now.

"Before I can tell you what it is, though, I've got to have you read this document and sign it," he explained. "And if, after you've read it, and decide that you'd rather not sign, then no harm, no foul. We just forget this meeting ever took place, and you'll be paid an hour's overtime."

The document was, to make a long story short, a government secrecy pledge regarding an interview for some kind of secret clearance job. I shrugged and signed it, pushing the fancy paperwork back across his desk.

"I gotta warn you," I chuckled, "that if you're trying to recruit me for submarines I'm about eight inches too tall." He smiled and just shook his head. He filed the paperwork, and then he became even more serious.

"So here it is," he began. "Do you know what the Central Intelligence Agency is?"

"Yeah, uh, it's the CIA," I stammered. "Spy stuff, and secret agents, right?"

"Well, that's the James Bond version which, for the most part, doesn't really exist." There was an awkward silence, kind of like when you're getting lectured by somebody and they can see that you're not quite getting it. He leaned back in his big chair, fingers interlaced behind his head.

"Of course CIA is an intelligence gathering agency of the United States, pretty much everyone would agree with that, yeah?"

"Yeah," I nodded.

"So do you have any idea what goes on there day to day?"

"If I'm being honest, not really," I admitted.

"Good. It shows me that I'm on the right track with you," he smiled. "See, most folks try and act like they know more than they do, usually to their own detriment," he explained. "So if it's okay with you, maybe I could fill you in on some stuff."

"Sure, sounds interesting," was all I could think to say that would come off at least halfway intelligent. Considering that what we were talking about had to do with intelligence.

The captain gave me a thumbnail sketch of what the CIA was all about. How that only a tiny part of it did all those spy missions that you see in movies. And that most everything they did was fairly mundane. He also explained how important the analysts were to the whole shebang, and that by that point in my life I probably knew at least a dozen people who were in some way involved with the Agency and that he was the thirteenth. That had my attention.

"So what do you do?" I asked.

"I do what you see me do every day. I'm the master of a United States-flagged merchant vessel," he said. "I sail these liners all over the world. And that, my friend, is my value to CIA."

He told me that with all of the access he had in so many port cities around the world—even ports that belonged to hostile nations—he could report ship movements, cargo placements, and just generally keep his ear to the ground when dealing with the shipping world in other countries.

"You have no idea how much valuable intel I can provide that is nearly in real time," he explained. "And don't forget, we share the deep blue sea with naval vessels from all around the world, too. So I guess they figure that if they have a guy who can report what he sees, well, then that's a good thing," he said. Then he said something that was really cool: "Of course, my biggest job is field recruitment. Are you interested?"

What? The fuck I know. But it was intriguing, to say the least.

"So now, I leave you to think about it. I want you to really consider what we've talked about today," he said, rising from behind his desk. "I don't want an answer either way until we've left Yokohama for Seattle, okay?"

"Yes, sir."

"And another thing," he cautioned, "I want your word that you will not breathe a word—not a fucking word—of this to anyone on or off this ship, understood?"

"Yes, Captain."

"Good. Of course I trust you, or we wouldn't be having this conversation in the first place."

"Thank you, sir. You can rely on me."

"I know it, Johnnie. And one more thing," he

said. "If anyone asks—and they will ask—why you were called to my office, it's because I wanted to let you know that your relief trip has been changed to a permanent berth because the guy who had your job's not coming back, okay?"

"Yeah, sure."

"Now that you've accepted the job," he motioned, in a yadda yadda yadda way, "we'll let the Mate know to sign you on again after Seattle, yeah?"

"Sounds good, Captain."

"Okay. Until *after* Yokohama, then."

And with that, I left his office not knowing what the fuck had just happened. But whatever it was, it sure didn't sound boring. And I thought of everybody I'd gone to high school with. They were working at fast food joints, car washes, and doing yard work with guys named Amelio. I already had it one over them just with the job aboard the ship. Now something else was headed my way, and I couldn't have predicted it for all the pineapples in Bugo.

4

*A*re you a homosexual? Hmmm. Difficult question, that. *Have you ever had a/multiple homosexual experience(s) when you were younger, below the age of eighteen?* To lie or not to lie, that is the question.

Describe the homosexual encounters you have experienced. Please be specific and include all details. Use additional paper if necessary.

Additional paper? How about two reams of paper. So, it is a government form, and bullshitting on it is punishable by a $5,000 fine and/or up to one year in prison. Oh, what the fuck. I ticked every NO box, and wrote N/A on every line. I'm standing on the fifth amendment. If I'm to be incriminated, then the fuckers will have to do the work themselves. And if I do wind up in prison, well, I'm sure I'll make lots of new friends. So either way, it don't matter.

It took me two goddamned days to fill out the application for the CIA. Wow, what a trip. That's right up there with having an astronaut application form. Weird. That done, I sent it in the ugly yellow-brown envelope provided—postage paid if mailed within the United States of America, Guam, Puerto Rico, or the U.S. Virgin Islands—and off it went to Langley, Virginia. I'll probably get outed by a past friend-with-benefits who supposedly woke up one day "craving" pussy instead of cock, and he'll of course change the story to reflect his total straightness.

> *"Yeah, I spent the night at his house in the eighth grade and he begged for me to let him see my dick, and then he told me that he wanted to suck me off. Of course, being the ever vigilant All-American Straight Boy that I have always been, I slugged him in the mouth, called him a faggot, and went straight home... Emphasis on STRAIGHT home!"*

That would be the report from Ronnie Huffman. The Huff played every sport in creation, was the jock of all jocks since kindergarten, was always juggling at least five girlfriends at once; oh, and he was the biggest closet flamer I had ever met. Here's how it really went down with The Huff.

So one day I walk into the locker room to pick up a stack of video tapes of the football games from the coach's office. I had two periods of audio-visual class, and I was responsible for the tape library.

The door to the boys' locker room was rusty and squeaky, which always served as a warning to any kids who might be doing something they might not ought to be. But on this day, the door was propped open. So I sauntered in.

I heard the shower going, so I thought I'd walk innocently past on my way to the coach's office and, you know, take a peek at some naked boy, hoping that it would be Mike Abbott who, in my opinion, was the reigning fox of South Junior High School. It wasn't Mike. It was The Huff. Only the hottest looking and most popular kid in school. And he didn't see me. *And he was jacking off!*

He was moaning very softly, and I could tell that he was about to cum because his legs were getting kind of wobbly, and his upper body was doing that *jerk, jerk, jerk* thing. And right then, he looked over his left shoulder and we met eye to eye. He froze. He was terrified. Petrified. Well, at this point he was just another kid pounding his cock like every other boy in school. I didn't want him to yell at me (or worse), so I started playing with myself through my pants, and I already had a boner so it worked.

Huff slowly began stroking himself and he gave me a little *wassup* nod. I dropped my pants, kicked off my shoes, ripped off my socks, and was tossing my T-shirt on the floor as I reached for the water spout next to his. He checked out my angry rod and then looked back at my ass. Then I knew.

We were both at full jack when he reached behind me with his left hand and placed it on my butt. As he pumped his cock he felt up my butt cheeks and I soon sensed about three of his fingers exploring my crack. He half whispered, "You wanna fuck?"

This was something I hadn't done before, but I had sure thought about it often enough.

"Yeah, how do we..."

"Just bend over; put your hands against the wall tiles," he stuttered. He was nervous, but I think it was because he was really turned on.

"Soap it up first, okay?"

"Yeah," he breathed.

I felt the cool liquid soap line my hole, and he poked in a little bit with his forefinger. Then he saddled up behind me and slowly pushed his throbber into my waiting anus. I was so turned on that I actually forgot how to think. It's like my brain had to reset.

His dick was about the same size as mine, but he had a ball sack that hung really low. He was cut like me, but the head of his dick was really big. It really had that mushroom shape. So as he guided his cock into me, the thing I remember the most was how good it felt because of that mushroom head. And when he would pull in the out direction, I swear if I had any socks on I would have jumped right out of them, it felt that good.

"Wait a minute," he said, still breathless, "I gotta stop for a second or I'll blow too quick. Just let me stand here, okay?"

"Yeah, sure." Then he reached around and started playing with mine while he just stood behind me with his cock inside me. God, it felt good. Then we both heard the door close. Someone else was in the room. Huff pulled out and turned away, and I faked that I was itching my elbow. We missed the coach seeing us by about five seconds.

"I'm locking up the place, you guys need any towels?"

"No, coach, we're good!" Huff said as cool as a cucumber shaped like a big green dick.

"All right. Turn out the lights when you go. See ya Monday." And he bailed.

I figured that my luck was up at that point. Maybe Huff was only messing around because I'd caught him when he was really horny. I figured he'd make the usual threats, say how disgusted he was, and then hate me for the rest of the school year.

"You wanna finish it up?" he smiled. And. We. Did.

That summer, after school was out, I hung out with Ronnie Huffman just about every day. And every day that we *did* hang out, well, things hung out. Like our dicks.

First would come the *You wanna mess around?* talk. This was followed by mutual sucking. Then, after about a quarter hour of mouth-on-cock action, his clarion call of ultra horniness would be spoken into my ear, his warm breath carrying my three favorite words: *You wanna fuck?*

Of course, you know the answer to that.

I would ask him how he wanted it—it was one of four ways: doggy style (my favorite); spread eagle (okay, that's my other favorite); me on top (that way's fun, too!); or on my back, legs in the air. And then we'd be off to the races. Depending on the day, he was either very slow and loving, which would then build up to the final cumtastic frenzy. Or he was Mad Dog Horn Dog and he'd fuck me like a fucking machine. I was good with it either way, just as long as it ended with his warm cum shooting into my hungry ass. For the record, I'd swallowed his load quite a few times, and I loved the taste and the warm feeling of his cum dripping down my throat. The problem was, the second The Huff blasted off it was all over. So there I'd be, with a hot ass, waiting for the cock that would never make its plunge. Unless he was spending the night. Then he'd be revved up again in a couple of hours, and we'd start *that* session with a good ass fucking.

We were good—inseparable, as a matter of fact—until about the second month into our freshman year of high school. That's when he met The Pussy. And it was all over. He didn't so much as even acknowledge my existence from then on. We even went to Kids Kamp over spring break that year, and I think he said hello to me one time that whole week. So I could just imagine the heap of horse shit he would tell the government goons when they came-a-callin' in search of a reference for me. *Oh, that guy? Yeah, he was the class fag. Everybody knew it.*

So it was all out of my hands now. I'd just have to wait and see what would happen. In the meantime, I'd just hang out between ships and enjoy some vacation time. I was officially On the Beach.

5

ear Mr. Allen, the letter began. *The Security Services of the United States of America, Central Intelligence Agency, is pleased to offer you a position of employment commencing on...*

I made it! I couldn't believe it. I'm in, despite the fox-in-the-hen-house-homo thing.

Wow. I'm a government operative. I'm gonna have clearances, and probably get to wear a secret agent spy coat. Burberry catalogue, here I come!

First thing I did was call Captain Logan. He already knew I'd made it, and he acted like it was nothing but a thing. He asked when my report-for-training date was, and then he wished me good luck. I had a lot to do before heading to Virginia, but I was amped. Close down the apartment, sell my car, get my plane reservations, clothes shopping for cold weather stuff. And I had less than two weeks to do it all. But it was exciting.

I also had to check in with my next-of-kin info because I wasn't allowed to tell anyone where I was going; nothing about the job at all. So if something happened to me, or if I went AWOL, they could fill my folks in on what I had been up to.

> *Good day, Mrs. Allen, this is Josephine Blow calling from the Central Intelligence Agency to inform you that your son, John, has been lost and presumed executed as a spy while on assignment in the Congo. Please accept our thanks from a grateful nation. Your flag will arrive within the week.*

I do go on, don't I? Well, it's not like I'm really gonna be anybody important, but it's fun to think about, anyway. And even if I was just the janitor there, my mom's jaw would still drop because even though I made twice the money she does just by working on the freighters, she still has it in her little narrow mind that I'm basically unemployable. Well, Uncle Sam obviously doesn't agree.

To the mall! I forgot I've got to get some decent luggage, too. A boy can't travel with a grocery bag!

Your Johnnie Allen became a member of the Mile High Solo Club today. I beat off in the bathroom on the airplane. I can report that jacking off in an airplane restroom is not the most fun I have ever had. But at least I've crossed it off my list.

Plane lands. Guy picks us up in non-descript shuttle van; van is a nice shade of government white. Arrive at training place after dark. Eat good cafeteria-style food. Go to sleep in dorm room for four. The next day, rise and shine and go to orientation.

"Good morning, ladies and gentlemen. Welcome to Camp Peary. This is now your home. You live here, you train here, you work here, and you do not leave here," said the lady with the funny glasses. Reminded me of a pent up English teacher sorely in need of a big, fat...

"And your name?" She was looking right at me.

"Uhmm..."

"Well, Mr. Uhmm, welcome to the Central Intelligence Agency. With answers like that we're certain to win the hearts and minds..."

Just ten minutes in and my mind was already wandering. Something about me and schools just don't click. Much laughter ensued. Oh, well. The school calendar and clock had started. I would be a little government cog for the next sixteen weeks, and what after that I had no clue. But one thing for sure, it was never boring.

For those wondering if life in the CIA is all cloak, dagger, and drinks ordered shaken-not-stirred, well, let me pop your balloon. It's basically a whole lot of boring. If you like life in an insurance office, that's about it for ninety-five percent of everyone with a valid ID schlepping along the hallways of the Langley campus. But it's that other five percent that keeps Hollywood and the publishing industry fed with the spy stories and espionage epics that we all grew up on. And I must admit, there are a few instances when I had my brushes with some Bond antics—more about all that later.

Other than the occasional toilet stall jacking session, sex was way down the totem pole during my training days. Either I was just so overwhelmed by the never ending training schedule, or they put salt peter in the food. I really can't recall a day off, either, because even the purported free days were crammed with assignments and sleep. Oh dear, sweet sleep.

Better than any drug sold on an urban street corner could ever be.

Weeks and weeks and weeks and weeks and then it was over. Had a final test of sorts; they dropped us, separately, in some butthole foreign country without any personal resources and told us to find our own ways back to Langley in seven days. Or else.

I was deposited into a friendly middle eastern country. Since there's only one American ally there, you can probably figure out where I was dropped. Actually, I think I fared better than my classmates who found themselves in South America. They might have thought they had an advantage, those countries being connected by land mass to the U.S. and all, but they were wrong.

And now, two years later, I am in Denmark. I live here. I have an assignment. My job is weird, and I'm tasked to make it work. And for that they pay me.

6

Hello it is me, Sander. I have a story to tell and it is my best story ever. I met a new friend today and he is very nice. He comes from America and came to a house party at Georg's brother's apartment building. It was very fun and we watched movies and played music. And I met Johnnie Allen when he saw me spill appelsin vand all over my clothes. Everybody laughed. I liked him right away.

Johnnie is older than me, but I think we are alike in many ways. He is a joker. He is very tall and sporty and I think we'll be great friends. But maybe not; who knows? We will see.

Maybe Johnnie thinks I am not old enough and he only wants to be friends with Georg's brother,

Emil. But I like it when he talks with me about America. I want to see the Disney park and see New York City and Hollywood and the Grand Canyon. And maybe Hawaii, too, because the only island I have ever seen is Fanø, and it was very cold and windy there. And there was definitely no hula dancing like Hawaii has. Only very stern fishermen that seldom smile.

I will write about my times with Johnnie. It is a good tale to tell and I think everybody wishes they could have such a friend. And we are good friends together.

It is three months until school is back, so I have promised myself to have fun this summer. I want to do new things because I am old enough to do them. Perhaps I'll make time for some fun with Georg, but I will have to be number two in line behind Grethe. Grethe. Grethe. Grethe. Georg and Grethe. Grethe and Georg. This is how it has become since the last school year. I am happy he has a girl but there is more in life than just Grethe, Grethe, Grethe. I don't think she is so Georg, Georg, Georg all the time. She goes out with her girlfriends to places because I see them in town.

Well, Georg has it bad I think. I wouldn't want to have a girlfriend so badly that I don't like to swim or sail or ride on motorbikes anymore. But there it is. There is plenty of time for all of that later when you are old and your friends don't want to be with you anymore because they are old, too. Then you can get a Grethe and spend every minute of your life thinking about Grethe, Grethe, Grethe. Poor Georg.

So I got a job at the pølser vogn next to the train station. I make lots of things that people eat when they go to the trains. There is ristetpølser and hot dogs and the bread. Mustard and ketchup and red beets and all kinds of stuff. And Jolly Cola and Coke and of course, applesin vand. That is where I got the one I spilled at the party. I borrowed it and took it to the party with me.

I make the food and collect the money and sometimes my boss sells newspapers, too. I make eighty kroner every hour. But sometimes I get extra tips, especially from the American tourists in the summertime.

One day I got 500 kroner from a banker from America. He was to take the train to Copenhagen for his airplane and wanted to get rid of his Danish money, so he bought two pølser and said for me to keep the change because he didn't want to worry about changing kroners into dollars.

I was very happy, as you can imagine, so I gave

him a free Coke and maybe I forgot to put the money into the cash machine. So maybe he got two free pølser and a Coke. And I got 500 kroner. Everybody's happy. Except my boss, but he's an asshole from Turkey and is not so very nice. And since he thinks that everybody is a thief, I did him a favor and made him happy by letting him think that maybe I'm a thief, too. The real thief is his brother, Devlet, who takes half the money and stuffs it into his own pocket. They will kill each other some day, I am sure.

I watch the television. I am alone. I see things that are sexy and then I think about sex. I am a little itchy down there. I move it to the left because it's getting bigger. I think about sex more. I reach into my pants and move it again. Okay, it wins. It has to come out and play before it goes crazy. I turn off the television. I put on my Toto CD and close my eyes and hold my dick and go up and down, very slowly at first. Then faster.

This is what I think about when I'm stroking myself off. Here is my list in the order that it comes into my head.

- Teacher at school; her name is Dorthe Hulle.

- Jennifer Lawrence's tittes.

- My friend, Lars Bo, is fucking Jennifer Lawrence.

- Lars Bo has a big dick and big balls and they slap Jennifer Lawrence on the ass.

- I'm watching Jennifer Lawrence.

- Dorthe and Jennifer Lawrence are licking their pussies.

- Lars Bo and Johnnie are kissing and I touch Johnnie's ass and look at his big dick.

- Johnnie is buttfucking Lars Bo whilst Jennifer and Dorthe lick those pussies.

- Lars Bo is cumming all over his own legs from Johnnie buttfucking him in the butt.

- I start to feel that my cum is about to explode all over me. I think about Johnnie. He is a tall and handsome American with pretty hair. I love his face. I am cumming. I am cumming!

- I came. I was thinking about Johnnie too much, I think.

- I was thinking about Johnnie some more. I smell my cum.

- Does Johnnie's cum smell like mine does?

7

It was about three months before my first direct contact came from my superior in Copenhagen. A simple letter arrived in the mail slot that told me to call a phone number between a certain numeric spread on a certain date. And so it began.

When I made the call a nice lady with a New England accent answered the phone. She put me straight through and I was instructed to take the train in to Copenhagen and attend a book club at the central public library there. They would do the rest.

It was a beautiful sunny day with the sky a shade of blue that I had never seen before. To say it was azure or cerulean would never do it justice. If ice were a color perhaps we'd be halfway there. And then the gentle breeze, mating to a perfect 64 degrees, was the final ingredient. The crispy clean smell of totally unpolluted air easily topped what any recreational drug could ever provide. And the clouds moving from the northwest with the texture of cotton candy were proprietary to the little kingdom. Nowhere else were they like this day.

I took the bus to the Odense train station with time to spare, and as I stepped off the bus I was surprised to see Sander pedal up on his bicycle. The surprise was definitely a pleasant one.

"Hey, Johnnie!" he smiled. I feigned surprise and gave him a little slug on his arm.

"Goddag, min ven!"

"Oh, you speaks Danish wery good I think," he said, hopping from his bike and walking beside me. "Do you go somewhere on the train today?" he asked.

"To Copenhagen," I said. "I have to see about a job there."

"That's far to go for a job. Will you move there?"

"No," I explained. "I just get my assignments there, that's all."

"What is assign..." He didn't know the word.

"It means they show me what to do. They give me the job there, but I do the job someplace else."

"Oh. Must be important. What will you do?"

"That's what I will learn today!"

Sander parked his bike and followed me into the station.

"Aren't you going to lock your bike?"

"What for?'

"What if somebody steals it?"

"They won't do that because then I wouldn't have a bicycle anymore. It will be okay."

I still wasn't used to how things like that worked over here. True story: I was in the park about two weeks ago and I walked to a little pond to watch the swans float past. There was a little kiosk with candy bars and various soft drinks. I noticed a price list, and a money box. That's it. If you wanted some candy or a drink you placed the money into the box and made your selection. Wow.

So Sander's decision to leave his bike unlocked in front of a busy railway terminal seemed to make sense in his world. But then why should anybody need to take Sander's bike when there were already about thirty free city bikes there for the taking?

In Denmark anyone can borrow one of the city bikes for free. Let's say you arrive in town and need to get to your hotel. When you leave the station you grab one of the big yellow bikes parked outside and ride to wherever you're going. When you get there, you just leave it in the bike rack and somebody else will eventually ride it to where they want to go, and so on. So I guess Sander was right in thinking that no one would take his bike. After all, if they did that, he wouldn't have a bicycle anymore.

"I have money, do you think I can ride to Copenhagen with you today?" Sander asked. "I will stay clear when you go for job." Of course, the answer was yes. Not only would I enjoy the company of a friend, but I would have me a ready-made translator for the day. And of course he was easy on the eyes. Very easy.

The train arrived right on time and we scurried into the coach and found our compartment. The trains in Denmark have individual compartments that seat six passengers on comfortable couches that face each other. There are three seats on each couch and a sliding door that opens to the corridor. Since it was a mid-morning departure, the train was light. We had the compartment to ourselves.

Sander drew the drapes on the compartment, and he opened the top of the window. Then he sat opposite me and the train rolled out of the station.

"I always am liking to ride the train," he smiled. "Ever since I am little boy I like to see the trains and to ride on them."

"Me too," I said. "I don't care where it's going, I

want to ride it."

"Do they has trains in America like this one?" he wondered.

"Well," I said, "they're a bit different. But on the whole they do the same thing. They take you where you want to go." And then we just stared out the window and watched the day pass by.

Okay, I admit it. I peeked. I looked. I dreamt. If I'd have been thirty years older I would have qualified as a full-fledged perv.

I let my eyes drift from the gorgeous scenery outside to the exquisite view inside the train.

Sander wore a pullover green and white striped rugby shirt, and tan cotton slacks. The perfect tan that outlines every crease, bulge, and shape hidden within those tan slacks. So I looked. Damn that Superman and his x-ray eyes. I was so jealous right then!

His legs were spread at just the right distance to see the shape of everything between them. I could see the ball bulge, and just above it, to the right (Sander's left), was the dick shape, as clear and as present as any danger could ever be.

I imagined what it looked like. Sander's hair was dark brown and so I figured the pubes must match. And of course I was sure he must be uncut because he's from a civilized society. And his nut sack was just awesome. Awesome! Perfect size. He also has the cutest little brown beauty mark on the left side of his neck. Then he had to go and get cruel on me.

About half an hour after I began my window shopping, the little shit goes and lays down on his side, facing the seat backs. Which gave me an eagle-eyed view of the cutest, roundest, most perfectly shaped ass I had ever seen. And I mean that with all the appreciation possible for guy asses the world over.

I had never in my life seen as perfect an ass as Sander's was. This was going to be a very long day.

"Just a moment, please."

The building was nearly four-hundred years old, and like all of the structures along Amaliegade it was as sturdy and pristine as the day it was built. The interior looked like it was pulled from the most modern design you would ever see paging through *Architectural Digest* magazine.

The desk from which Deanna Louw gatekept on behalf of the United States government had no legs. It was suspended from the ceiling by thin stainless steel rods. The cables for the computer and the telephone were hidden in the rods, and the whole affair bordered on the ridiculous. One thing, though: no one would ever guess the office, disguised as an agency for sculptors and modern artists, could ever be mistaken for a government office here or in the States. I guess good covers cost a few bucks.

Deanna, who would be my scheduler, soon pointed the way to Marguax Stuplemann's private office where I would finally learn exactly what I was supposed to do for my monthly stipend of $5000.

"Come in, come in, you are John, right?"

"Johnnie, actually. That's the name on my birth certificate," I smiled, as we shook hands. She waved at a chair from across her floating desk.

"Oh, Johnnie. You shall call me Marge. We will get along famously, I'm sure." Marge had a speech impediment, kind of like Barbara Walters, but a little more—how would I describe it—spitty. All in all she seemed nice enough.

"We have lots for you to do," she continued, "but first I want to get to know you a little better."

She went down my learn list from The Farm and

noted all the high points. Then she dropped a bomb as casually as Taylor Swift drops men.

"You're a queer. I've never run a queer before. Is that gonna be a problem?"

"What?" I half stammered.

"Oh, now you're deaf, too? A deaf queer. What am I gonna do with a deaf queer?"

"Uhmmm."

"Relax, already. Why do you think you're here? We *picked* you because you're queer."

"Can you stop that, please?" I exhaled.

"Stop what?"

"I hate that word."

"What? Deaf?"

I averted her eyes. My ears throbbed and I felt dizzy. I felt caught. In fact, it was the first time that anybody I respected had called me that. Images flittered past me; I felt so exposed. I slowly brought Marge back into scope and was mildly surprised to see the dopey grin that was plastered across her triangular face.

"Queer," I said. "I hate that word."

"Well, what do I call you, then? Should I get all antiseptic and refer to you as a practicing homosexual? Not that you need any practice, from what I know," she added.

"Okay, so, what, I'm fired, right? I'm twenty-one. I can be *queer* if I want. So kill me," I snapped at her.

"That's the thing about our type. We're always so damned dramatic. At ease, sailor."

"What..."

"You don't think I'd waste all my beauty on some guy who grunts like an ape and sticks things wherever he can shove'em, do ya? I seek out the feminine among us, laddie. So relax."

"But I thought..."

"Yeah, yeah, there's official, and then there's *official*, if ya know what I mean. Let's just say that you and me are, well, official. There are certain skill sets that folks like us have that Uncle Sam finds very useful," Marge chuckled.

"I don't get it..."

"You will soon enough. Look, what you and I do is very important. When it gets down to brass tacks it won't seem like so much, but as a whole what we do affects the whole world," she explained. "There are some personality types that really mesh with what it takes to pull off some of this stuff, and you and me fit that bill quite nicely."

"But I don't act queer, as you put it, in any way. Nobody's ever thought I was that way, somebody totally fucked this..."

"Exactly!"

"What?"

"Exactly. Nobody ever called you queer. You had'em all fooled," she said, suddenly more serious. "You've lived almost twenty-two years undercover and you didn't even realize it. Give yourself some credit," she chuckled.

"But I..."

"You are as gay as a church mouse, kid. You've had more ass than a toilet seat, yet up till now nobody's ever questioned 'who' you are. Don't you think somebody who's as good at keeping that kind of thing quiet in this day and age might be worthwhile to us?"

My mouth had never been that dry in my whole life. Again with the heat; I thought I was going to pass out.

"You okay there, Johnnie boy? Need a drink?"

I could only nod. She grabbed a bottled water from the little fridge in the corner of the room and cracked the top for me as she took a chair beside mine.

"Look, I didn't mean to make you feel bad," she began, "but if we're going to do great things together we have to approach them honestly."

Again I nodded, staring intently at the opened bottle of spring water.

"You like boys and I like girls and—listen to me, Johnnie—there's nothing wrong with that. Some would like you to believe that, but..."

"You mean like Uncle Sam?"

"...But it's not us who have the problem. Yes, our bosses wish we were all straight little foot soldiers but I'm afraid we're a little on the bent side." I couldn't help but smile. I loved this woman. I loved truth, and she spoke it.

"Look, Johnnie, we don't have to be liked or appreciated to do a great job. You and me and everyone else who are on our team will deliver what is expected of us, and all the while I intend to eat as much pussy as I can. I hope that goes double cocks for you," she laughed. I felt like eight tons of elephant had just been lifted from me. Who'd have thought that an American dyke in Denmark would be the first person to tell me that I was okay just as I am.

"Now, should we get down to the business at hand?"

8

"How goes it?" Sander chirped. "Have you a job now? A big job, yes?" He kind of walk-skipped beside me as we headed up the cobblestone lanes of the shopping district called the 'strøget'. We made our way past street performers (and a gaggle of Korean tourists) and ducked into an allé café.

"Well, yeah, I have a job. Sort of," I reported, as the waiter laid Cokes and pretzels on the birchwood table. "I'm kind of like a travel agent."

"What does that do?"

"Well, rejsebureau is what you call it here. I know because I looked it up before we came today," I said, downing a swig of the lukewarm soda. "What do you guys have against ice, anyways?" I added with a warm belch.

Sander chuckled, "It's too expensive." Which is funny when you consider that all of Scandinavia is one big ice chest. "What do we do now?" he asked.

"I dunno. What do you wanna do?"

"When have you to begin the working?" Sander continued. "Do you must starts right now?" Actually, I would be waiting for a specific assignment, I learned. I would just wait until they called me.

"I start sometime, I'm not sure when. So we're done here for today," I explained. "What *should* we do?"

Sander thought a bit and smiled when the light bulb in his head flashed on. "I know, Tivoli!"

Tivoli Gardens is the leafy amusement park by a lake and pavilion in the dead center of town. It's next to the central railway station and is the number one tourist attraction in Denmark. I heard it's where Walt Disney got the idea for Disneyland. Sure, why not?

"I will buy aftensmad when we go, yes? And then we can go on the big fast train coasting. It calls the roller coaster and the tracks is made from trees!" Sander exclaimed. Translation: My friend plans to buy our dinner and then we'll ride the wooden roller coaster. Fair enough.

We rode the coaster four times in a row and then ambled down the pathways through the Gardens to an outdoor café overlooking the little lake. The sun had long since cast its last rays of light as the coming night sky transitioned from the deepest of purples westward, to the steady cobalt blue of a summer's eve. Music and laughter mingled on the breeze and it felt as if we were anywhere but in the city center of one of the most cosmopolitan cities in Europe.

"Are you going to eat that?" Sander looked longingly at the meat and potatoes left on the metal plate served from the Viking-themed restaurant.

"What do I get in return," I joked, lustfully eyeing his aebleskiver. And, no, an aebleskiver isn't what you're thinking! It's a dessert.

"No deal, the aebleskiver stays with me!" he laughed. What a laugh. Sweet, not in the least bit overbearing. It's an honest laugh. He makes me want to laugh, and I do.

"Here, eat a dead cow," I said, sliding the plate his way.

"Do you know why cows are so soft?" my new love smiled. I fell for it.

"Why?"

"Because they are made out of leather."

"Well maybe it's softer than this steak it made," I snickered. We were truly friends. Deep friends, I knew then. I would—could—trust him. Now *there* was the pickle. I knew I could trust this beautiful lad, but could he trust me? What was it that I really wanted? Was it him, or just the vessel that carried him, as beautiful as that was. I didn't want to blow it; well, I wanted to blow *it*... Never mind. See what I mean? Just call me Gutterhead.

See, that's the fucking problem when you're gay. You just never know. For sure, anyways. Until it happens. And how would it happen here? What if I just let him make the moves, if any moves were ever to be made. But in the meantime, how could I be near him and not die from want? I don't know the precise moment that it happened, but I was hopelessly, helplessly, ridiculously in love with the boy. And I fucking lie: I do know the exact moment that I fell for him. It was how he reacted to the teasing when he spilled the orange soda at the party. Since then there were a thousand reasons. Since then I was finished, over and done with. Pathetic, how love tricks and traps you. And then the realization that, in every likelihood, he couldn't care less. In fact, I'm sure he had absolutely no fucking idea what I felt, and as progressive as Denmark appeared to be, you either are or you ain't. Sure, some guys fiddled around with each other, especially when they're kids. That shit happens the world over. But at this point each of us knew what we wanted, right? Thing is, he hadn't given me any idea about where he landed on the sexual curve.

True, until now I hadn't heard a thing from him about chicks, bitches, or ho's; nor did I catch him wolf whistling, even silently, at any passing female. But I'd been stupid and burned before when judging someone else's proclivity. With Sander, I vowed I would not make that mistake again. He meant too much to me.

The evening turned a bluer shade of chill and the swans in the tiny lake made for the reeds, paired off like they had just arrived courtesy of Noah. They were done for the day. So was I.

"What now?" Sander sat back in his chair as he pushed his plate away, inhaling the night air with a little whistle in his nose. "We are full of cows, so what shall we do?"

"I don't really know. It's kind of your town, yeah?"

"Not really," he smiled, "but more than yours, I guess." He got up and scooted over to the chair next to mine, bumping my shoulder with his as he plopped onto the cushion. "I gots a idea but you think it's maybe crazy, I think."

"No."

"Okay, then."

"No, I mean no, I don't--*won't* think it's crazy. Tell me!"

Okay, he's crazy. But it's okay. The idea sounds fun, provided we don't end up in jail before the night ends.

The friend's idea is to trick the Royal Palace Guards into saluting us. Yep, the joke is that he knows how to imitate the sergeant-at-arms giving a heads up warning to the watch, where in turn they will stop what they're doing—presumably guarding the Queen—and present arms in a royal salute. At one in the morning.

"There they are. See them?" Sander whispered. "No," I breathed. "Where?"

"Can you hear them? Listen!"

The light tap-clunk-tap-clunk, with a soft hint of an echo bouncing off the four mansions formed around the square that makes up the Amalienborg

Palace, breezed through the tiny alley by the colonnade. Yes, I heard something. And then my eyes adjusted and I was spooked by the sight of two seven-foot somethings that didn't register quite right. The confusion soon gave way to recognition. It was two of the Queen's guards minding their post, their heads topped with bearskin hats. I could see why they wear them. They're scary.

They halted at the end of the building, did some cool heel-snapping moves, and turned the other direction. Impressive.

"So now what?" I asked. "And what are they gonna do, anyway?"

"You'll see," Sander grinned. "Follow me. We'll just walk over there, and then turn by where the harbor is. That's our escape!"

"What do I do?"

"Just see what happen when I makes the noise and you will see what the guardmans will do. It's very militær," he chuckled. "Then all we gots to do is go that way and then not be catch by them. See?" No. But when you're in love you'll do anything.

"Sander, they have guns. Big guns," I reminded him.

"Aaaa! They won't shoot," he said dismissively.

"Nuværende arme!"

Sander faced the dark, inside corner where two walls of the palace met. It was like a kind of ventriloquism; it threw his shout clear across the courtyard and I swear it sounded like the it had originated a city block away from where we stood.

He told me later that he had given the order to Present Arms, which stopped the soldiers in their tracks. At once they swung around, facing the silent cobblestones lining the great plaza. A powerful cacophony of clicks, clacks, leather on frocks, and boots slamming on pavement was met by a thick silence. The sudden stillness was punctuated by the occassional sound of a bus spooling up from a corner stop, and a lone bicycle bell a whole street away. That's when the Queen's Own Guard realized that they'd been had.

The sergeant steamed out of his night office, barking the command to resume. He shouted at the first pair of guards he encountered, which was some thousand feet away from us, kitty corner from the mid-square statue. That was our cue to exit stage left.

"Now we go," Sander whispered. "Follow me to safety!" And we headed for the esplanade and the cover of the fountains that gave us sanctuary from our Royal transgression.

"Fun, yes?" he smiled. "We are now Royals. You are the King of Danmark and I am the Crown Prince. The guards just prove it so!"

"You should be the king," I pointed out, "because you are Danish."

"But you are older than me, and are smarter and better looking." *What the fu...? What did he just say?* "Try that again? I missed that."

"You are older than me...and look better—than me."

"Are you crazy?" *Okay, don't say the wrong thing... Don't fucking blow it now... Maintain, idiot!!!* "You are the best-looking guy—*person*—I've ever seen? Are you fucking blind?"

And he just laughed. We were walking fast down the esplanade in the direction of—of all things—the Little Mermaid. It's a statue.

"We'll mix in with the tourists and the kids with beers, that's why we go to the memraid."

"Memraid?" I laughed. "That's fucking funny! You should be king just because you're that fucking funny!"

"Why is a memraid fucking funny?" Sander asked.

"Because it's not a memraid; it's a *mer*maid. Look it up," I chuckled. "And besides, I think it'd be funny to see a mermaid fucking."

"Oh, ha-ha-hee-hee. I gets it. Why is a mermaid fucking funny... Look, there she is," he pointed. "See? Many peoples comes to see her. And drink many beers."

There were about fifty teens and twenties hanging around the shoreline and the walking path, drinking and drunk. Lots of kissing and ass-grabbing, too. Probably some hot straight sex going on nearby. Ick!

"So now what do we do?" I asked. "Will the cops be looking for us?"

"No, we're excaped from the caper! We're free birds!" he laughed. "So now what shall we do?"

"Should we maybe head back to the train station? Maybe go home? I don't know how late the trains go, but we should maybe think about home, right?" I knew it was the responsible thing. He was just a little bit younger than me, true, and I should be responsible, right? I mean, even though things are different here: parents don't hover like helicopters over their kids, and *he is sixteen.* He's not a baby. And why am I trying to justify... I don't even know what I'm thinking. What is there to think about?

But you are older than me, and are smarter, and better looking...

Why would he say that? What did he mean by it? Was it that he somehow missed his own point because of a language screwup? What he really meant to say was... Fuck it. I don't need to drive myself fucking batshit on the very day I start a cool job that will—hopefully—keep me in Sander's sphere for a very long time. Like forever.

"Hey!"

I snapped out of it as quickly as I could. "Yeah..."

"To the trains, then?"

We are alone in a compartment meant for six people. I doubt there are six people on the whole train. But here's the cool thing. I am facing forward, by the window. In straight world, the other guy would be sitting across from me, also by the window. In this compartment, on this night, Sander is sitting right next to me. Why? Even if he wanted to sit with me on my side of the compartment, if he was straight he'd put a seat between us, right? So... *Is... He...*

The door slid open and the train conductor stamped our tickets, gone as quickly as he came.

"It was a very fun day, I think," my friend said. "It was much better than making pølsers and selling Cokes for the Turk, yes?"

"It was the best day. It was... Just the best day ever." My heart was skipping beats like a school girl's. Like how I imagined my friend, Dennis, from middle school, who had a heart murmur. He never had to do P.E., and he could baby out of anything at school just by pulling the murmur card. And his dumbass mom would clod on down and collect him. *Mommy's here, DenDen!* And they'd go on home, I guess, where DenDen would murmur his way through some junk food and any TV shows that his murmuring little heart craved. Dick.

I gazed out the window and let the night rush by, the hypnotic motion of the train calming my heart while my breath formed a lake of condensation against the window. It was all I could do to not write my declaration of undying love in it. Instead I just wiped it away. I was just a fool to think he thought of me as anything but a friend. I was a fool to be me.

The big world doesn't like me. I'm a faggot. I take it up the ass. I'm defined by who I love, and it's just not acceptable—who I love, that is.

I suck dick. I drink cum. I tongue assholes. I finger myself when I jack off. And you don't want to know what I think about when I'm pounding my cock.

And if the world doesn't like you, I guess the only thing left to do is to hate yourself right along with'em. Cuz there sure ain't gonna be any love— true love, anyway—tossed out to a fag like me. Maybe a fist or a gaybash. Cuz people hate fags. So I'll promise myself that if I can't love Sander in the way I want, I'll just enjoy being his friend.

We... Oh, Oh, we... Oh...
All I want is to be in his movie
And not simply be a time from yesterday
All I want is to be in his movie
All I want is to be under his covers
And not simply be a time from yesterday...

We... Oh, we...
All I want is the warmth from his smother
and not just be frozen for an age.
Oh my longing to be bare on your knee
and not just be home from yesterday...

It's a song from The Hidden Cameras, a Canadian band. Every time I hear it I cry. And now it's Sander's song. Forever.

9

When I was twelve years old I had a friend called Anders. He is one year above me in school. He was a very nice boy, but he moved away before school started that year. He moved to Copenhagen and his mother got a new man, so he has a stepfather now. I haven't talked with him in a very long time.

One time he stayed at my house for two days while his mother went to Germany. We slept on a very big mattress up in the attic. I had my stereo there and my computer and my flatscreen. It is like my very own place, and I stay there sometimes — sometimes more than in my own room. All of my games are up there, too.

It started by talking about having sex with people that we both know, and then what TV and movies stars and pop stars we would want to have sex with. Then Anders said, "If you have to have sex with a boy who will it be?" and I didn't even wait before I answered him.

"You."

"What?"

"You."

"Really?"

"Really. You asked," I reminded him.

Then we watched some youtube videos from Shane Dawson and Charlie McDonnell. Pointing at every boy we saw on the videos he asked, "Will you have sex with him?" and finally I said, "No. Just only with you."

We are lying on our backs now. We are finished with the videos. The cars hiss past on the road behind the house, the windows are open because it is a warm summer night. It is still light outside even though it is nearly eleven o'clock.

"Sander, I want to... Well, I got a question for you, but you must be honest, yes?"

"Of course," I respond.

"If you wanted to have sex with me, what would we do? I mean, I'm only wondering because, well...

106

I have always wanted to be close with Anders. He is my best friend since we were in the nursery school together, and I always wanted to know what he looks like down there—and to hug him and to maybe kiss him, too. But I am afraid because you can't know if somebody feels the same way as you do.

"I guess whatever we feel like, maybe," I said. "I think I'd like to hug you maybe, and play with—it down there."

"Blow job?"

"Sure."

"Butt sex?"

I thought about it, but I don't really know how. But I think I can learn. Maybe he can try it on me first.

"What would *you* want to do? I mean, if we were gonna have sex?" I asked.

"I don't know—the same, I guess. *If* we did it."

We just laid there for awhile. Maybe ten of the longest minutes I ever spent. Then I reached for his underwear and found his cock. He was already half hard, but the second that I felt him through his shorts it turned into a hard rock. Like the café.

"Can I see?" I whispered. He nodded and together we pulled his red underwear down to his smooth thighs. And there it was. Just traces of hair around the base of his dick, and his really cute balls.

I shifted into a position that brought my face within centimeters of his now-throbbing cock; his head slipped past his foreskin, glistening in the fading light. I spent a few breathless moments getting my bearings. This was new, sure, but it was something I had been dreaming about and hoping for since forever. Before another thought escaped me, I found him in my mouth.

At first the movement was slow. His smell was so pure and clean, his penis fitting so perfectly in my mouth as I tasted my friend and gave him pleasure. He was already groaning, and his hands patted along my hair and landed on my back. He caressed me, as together we found our rhythm.

"It feels so good. Dammit, Sander... Shit, it feels good."

My tongue was all over his ball sack, and I lapped up the backside of his dick while I jacked him with my left hand.

"Wait! I don't wanna go yet! I will do it for you now," he sighed. I yanked off my shorts and revealed myself to him. "Fuck!" he smiled. "It's bigger than I thought it would be!"

"You mean, you thought about me before? What

I look like?"

"Yes," he admitted. "But I like girls too, just don't forget."

"It's okay to think about me, I guess." I relaxed, waiting for whatever Anders had in store. And then he just started, and I had never felt anything like it before.

His tongue darted past the end of my foreskin; he did this quick licking thing with his tongue, and then he suddenly pulled my skin back and focused his attention on my head. My feet were itching; it felt so good.

His thighs and ass were near my right hand so I began to pet and stroke that area, finally finding my way to his butt crack.

"Rub me there," he breathed, between moving his lips up and down my hard shaft.

"Where?" I asked.

"My ass crack. Rub it up and down." And I did. My fingers felt the way to his hole, and I started a circular motion with my middle finger around his butthole. He began moving his hips in sync with my hand and fingers, and he guided my finger into position. And I was in him. I could feel him, his warmth around my finger as his tongue showed my cock what it's there for. I wanted to suck him off so badly. I also knew I wanted to taste his cum; I don't really know why, but I just knew that I had to taste him—and *love* him—at that moment.

"Let me suck yours," I pleaded. "I need to suck you now."

"Sure," he laughed. "But I can't promise how long I can go."

I knew what I was doing by then. I alternated from the up and down rhythms of pulling his foreskin back and tonguing around his head, to spitting all over his cock while I sucked and licked his balls. I even fingered him as his hips writhed in our tandem motion. His fast breaths and twitching legs hinted that the end was near.

"I'm cumming now!"

And before the words had settled in the room I felt the warm and savory liquid that meant that Anders Nielsen—my longest ever friend—had filled my mouth. Heaven.

"What's it taste like?" Anders asked, as his stroking hand finished me off.

"Kind of salty."

"Does it taste good?"

"You taste good. Are you gonna taste mine?"

"I don't think so. Maybe another time."

And I felt it building. I closed my eyes, thinking

of what I had just done with Anders. His legs were beside me, his crotch so close. I could still smell his cum, and I could taste him. My dick was throbbing and I felt the pumping.

"I'm cumming, Anders!"

I heard the slappy, squishy sound of his grip filling with my cum. He kept jacking me until I couldn't stand it for another second, then one last blast spewed out. He slowed down and I could feel the cooling of my semen as it dripped against my balls.

"Whew! That was..."

"Fun," he chuckled, as he went on the prowl for a cum rag. "But you better not fall in love or anything dumb like that because I'm not your boyfriend."

That was my first time for sex, and my last time with Anders.

10

My first assignment arrived by regular mail ten months later. Almost a whole fucking year!

The plain brown envelope contained the instructions—or key code—for the cipher. The message was to be deciphered from a book that I would get from the Arnold Busck bookseller across the street from the Royal Acting Company Theater in the old part of town. It was an English trade paperback version of a Graham Greene novel called *Our Man In Havana*. How ironic that my first codebook is a spy novel.

The job would be easy enough. I just had to get

a man from the Polish border onto a Grimaldi Lines auto carrier in Antwerp, Belgium. His recognition code was a quick, innocuous exchange...

ME: Excuse me, do you happen to know if there are any good shows in town?

HIM: I'm not from here; look in the Warsaw newspaper, *FAKT*.

ME: But we're not in Warsaw.

HIM: And we never will be again.

Then it was up to me to get him to Antwerp and onto the ship bound for South America. Thing is, we would have to cross two borders—technically easy enough since the European Union came into being; but, all it takes is an over efficient customs guard and the whole enterprise could go belly-up. Not to mention that, assuming we got to Antwerp without raising any German or Belgian eyebrows, he'd still have to get aboard the ship and ride it for three whole weeks before finally landing in Argentina. Where he would have to get *off* the ship and clear customs there. Assuming he was legit and had documents and an entry visa. Nobody thought to copy me in as to whether or not this would be conducted on the up and up.

I would be riding the train to Ystad, Sweden, where I would pick up a car for the ferry ride to

Poland. I wouldn't be able to rent a car for two reasons. One, I wasn't twenty-five years old yet and, two, there could be no paper trail. Or electronic trail. Most people don't know that rental cars all have trackers in them now, especially in Europe.

I guess the big thing would be if the guy had a legit ticket for the ship. How do you hide a guy aboard a car carrier for nearly a month? Plus, he's gotta eat and use the bathroom. I wouldn't know any of the details until I met up with him.

The meet was set for the coming Saturday night. That would mean I'd have to take the *Polonia* to Świnoujście at 10:30 Friday night which puts me in Poland early the next morning. Plenty of time to meet my passenger and start the drive to Belgium.

I heard the squeak of running shoes on linoleum, followed by a bump on my front door. Then the metallic snap of my mail slot being slammed open. I hopped into the entrance hallway and was met with a pair of lips. Literally, lips in my mail slot.

"Johnnie Allen, you must comes to your door!" It was Sander.

"What the hell?" I chuckled. "Just a minute while

I pull out my dick!"

"Aaaaa! You win!" he cried, jumping back from the door. When I opened the door he stood in the corridor with the biggest smile.

"Hallo. I am Jehovah Vidnet and you want a Bible?"

"Fuck you!"

"Then can I borrow a hundred grams of sugar?"

"Still fuck you!"

"Then can I watch your TV whit you?"

"Okay."

The door was wide open and he walked past. His fragrance was delectable; one of the most beautiful smells I had ever encountered. It was like a combination of sky and water. That's the only way I can describe it. The way the warmth of his skin merged with the scent of the cologne he wore could only be described as angelic.

"Sander. Don't get the wrong idea, or anything, but you smell awesome!" I declared. "What in hell are you wearing?"

"Giacomo. My sister gots it for my birthday and now I wear it because I come here," he stated matter-of-fact. "I think she has tasty."

"Tasty?"

"Yeah. You know, she pick good things."

"Oh!" I got it. "You mean, good taste!"

"Yep. She know whats to get for peoples, and she get me this so I don't stinks, she says."

"Well," I said, "she sure picked out a great one for you. Dang!"

"What means dang?" he asked.

"Uh, it's like a nice way to say damn!"

"Dang!" he laughed.

We sat on the couch and zapped on the TV. I don't mean to drill it into the ground, but now I caught the smell of his hair. This had never happened to me before, but I swear I was getting a boner from the smells. Seriously!

"You want something to drink?" I offered. "I have soda and bottled waters. There's coffee, too, if you want to make it."

"Is a Coke okay?"

"Yeah!" I said. "You know where they are; bring me one, would you?"

When he sat back down he landed least a foot closer than before. Smiling, he stuck the Coke bottle between his legs like a cock and dared me to drink. What could I do? I took the dare.

I bent down and play acted like I was totally giving the best head ever. "Hey! No teeth!" he joked, laughing like we were kids at a camp. Keeping it going, I grabbed the neck of the bottle, putting my thumb over the opening. Then I jacked the bottle up and down a couple times and moved my thumb away. Of course, the soda spewed out like elephant cum. He laughed even bigger and jumped to his feet.

"Looks like I cum too fast!"

"Was it good for you, too?" I joked.

"What are you wearing?" he seductively teased.

"Are you playing with it?

"I go to the glory hole now!"

Glory hole. Glory hole, he said. How does he know about glory holes? Could he... *What if...*

"Get a towel," I chided good naturedly.

"But I not even jacked off yet!"

"It's for the soda on the couch and the floor!"

"Dang!" he chuckled.

Wait a second—he just admitted that he jacks off. Oh boy, more images for me to use when I jack myself off later. "You are a bad boy I think," I smiled, as he grabbed a dishcloth off the sink.

"Here is my cum rag!" he said, faux serious. "I not has washed it for six month so it stand up in the corner and waits for more cums."

In the space of twenty seconds he'd admitted to knowing about glory holes, that he has experienced masturbation first hand—sorry about the pun—and that he knows teenage cum rag etiquette. Is he trying to let me know that he would like it if I suggested that we... Oh for fuck's sake, who am I kidding? This kid is perfect in every way. I cannot find a single flaw in him. I mean, I know he must have something wrong—we all do, right? Why would he even *have* to be gay. Or bi. Maybe he's bi-curious? Or maybe he's just a fun person who grew up in a forward thinking nation without sexual hang-ups and he's just having fun with a friend. He could have anyone he wants, and if supposing he did want another guy, why would he want me? And even if he did, he'd just say something, right? He wouldn't feel the need to hint around or play games like this.

But he came over on a weeknight, dressed like a prince and smelling like the angels in the evening stars. God, I'm gonna lose it over this. I swear, I'm— It's not fair to become obsessed over someone *you will never have.* I want to stay in his world.

I don't want to sacrifice whatever friendship I can enjoy with him on the altar of horniness. Can't I just suppress these feelings? I've done it before. Done it my whole life. I don't have to be in love with Sander. I can love him; I can appreciate him from afar, like one does a work of art. You can visit the Louvre museum and gaze at the Mona Lisa all day long, but that doesn't mean that you get to take her home.

I can admire his body and dream of holding him and caressing him. I can imagine his lips on mine, the feeling of his tongue as we explore each other's soul. I can wish for his breath against my neck but keep myself in check, never breaking his trust in our friendship. I'd spent a little over a year building that trust and damned if I was gonna ruin it because of my infatuation. Okay, it's more than an infatuation.

I'm fucked.

Two films and a rerun of *Cheers* later and he got ready to leave. We had ordered in a pizza and had gone through a six-pack of Jolly Cola. That was the program for the evening, and we'd fulfilled it.

"Well, I go home now," he said, climbing into his olive green jacket with the reflector on the back. "What is you doing at the weekend?"

"You know my job?"

"The one from *København*— I mean, Copenhagen?"

"Yeah. Well, I got my first assignment and so tomorrow I will go to Copenhagen and stay the night before I leave for the job," I revealed. "It should be interesting."

"When will you be home again?"

"I think maybe Monday, Tuesday at the latest."

"Oh, well, I will miss you. I see you then, okay?"

And then he was off, his shoes squeaking down the hallway as he made for his bike. He shot me a little wave before rounding the corner to the breezeway.

"Dang!" he said, laughing. And with the quick blast of a northerly wind enveloping the hall, the door shut behind him and he was gone.

11

Travel days are always exciting for me. Getting ready to leave on a trip is called being Journey Proud, my grandpa used to tell me. I was a hundred percent Journey Proud today because I had all of the intricacies of my new job to look forward to. And I would be using at least three different modes of transport on the trip, which tickled me to no end.

I gathered up all the essentials and tossed them into my backpack, then headed for the bus stop. Hey! That makes it four modes of transport on this job! Cool! Only thing missing is a plane or maybe a hot air balloon.

The ride to the central station took less than ten minutes and when I got there I noticed that Sander's hot dog cart was closed. I'd hoped to see him one last time before the trip. I thought surely he'd be there after school like he always is, especially on a Thursday because that's the day that the stores stay open later.

Imagine my surprise when I saw Sander relaxing on a bench on the platform, smile alight as usual. Radiant.

"Well, well! Look what the cat dragged in," I said. "No hot dogs today?"

"No hot dogs ever; I quit the Turk," he reported.

"Odense station will never be the same without your incredibly wonderful, huge, long, hot dog. Hot dogs! *Dogs!* With an *'S'*!"

"Then too bad for Odense," he laughed. "This boy is out of the hot dog business."

"What made you quit?" I asked him. "I thought you liked the job—I mean, as far as hot dog jobs go."

"I need less time for hot dogs, and more time for my friends," he said, landing a guy punch on my shoulder. "Really, I'm having a 'prenticeship from my school at the automekaniker. So I will fix cars when they is broke."

"When does that start?"

"In the fall time, when summer is gone."

I slapped him on his thigh in what could pass as an 'attaboy', but we know that's not why I did it. For the first time I felt a fleshy area near his crotch. Sicko perv. You know you'll beat off about that thigh slap the first minute that you can. And as always, he smelled so fucking good.

"So," he wondered, "are you overnight in Copenhagen before the new job is starting?"

"Yeah. I don't want to rush tomorrow, so I thought I would stay at the hotel and then start fresh with whatever they want me to do in the morning," I said.

"Yes, this is very smart. Do you know what else?"

"What else?"

"I not haves school tomorrow for six weeks. It is six long weeks from school."

I congratulated him and we waited for the train to Svendborg to pass before we resumed our talk.

"I has a wery good idea, do you want to hear my idea?"

"Yes! Let's hear this wery good idea of yours."

"Well, I has about five thousand kroner whit me, and my is bag here too. And I think, what if I come to Copenhagen and we have wery much fun this night before you go for your job. Kind of like our party for—because you gots your dream job, yes?"

He immediately backpedalled with all of the polite niceties: *Don't say yes unless it's really okay. It's just an idea I thought of. I should have called first, I know. It's okay to say no.*

"Fucking hell, that's great! Fuck, yeah!" I couldn't say it fast enough.

"Fuck, yeah!" he parroted. "Dang!"

"Dang!"

"We go to Copenhagen!"

"Wait a sec," I stopped. "What about your folks? Don't you think you'd better call and ask them first?"

"I already did," he snorted. "They say, cool man. Has a good time and don't fuck the Little Mermaid up the ass!" We both let out bursts of huge, annoying laughter. The other travelers were not amused.

"They didn't say that!" I whispered. "You fuckin' loon!"

"No, but they *did* say I can go. So we go!"

"So go in the station and get your ticket, quick!" I warned. "Train's here in about fifteen minutes."

He reached into his pocket and pulled out a ticket and held it under my nose for inspection. "Is this what you mean?" Cheeky devil. He knew I'd say he could come. Why wouldn't I? He's my friend, right?

"What if I'd said that you couldn't go with me?" I asked.

"Then I push you in front of the train when it comes," he joked.

"Well, then. I'm glad the answer was yes."

A quarter hour later and the train glided into the station, the door positioned exactly where we sat. I mentioned the luck of it to Sander and he looked at me like I was from Mars. I was informed that the platform bench groupings are positioned to line up with each door on the train. "It's so the old people and the mothers with the babies don't has to walk a long time to the doors or slip on the ice," he said. Imagine that: public transport that actually considers the needs of the rider.

Again, we managed to get our own compartment in next to the last car, and just as the train pulled away from the station, Sander hopped from the seat across and planted himself right next to me. Our shoulders touched when he put his feet on the opposite seat, using it as a kind of ottoman. He slunk down a little lower in his seat which meant his upper arm brushed against my side, and his elbow ever so lightly touched the side of my ass.

What was going on? Please, someone! *Tell me what the hell!*

An hour and twenty minutes later the verdant countryside of the little kingdom gave way to the bustle of its capital city. The mix of modern-day Scandinavian design ethos contrasts with a world long since past; the days of cobblestone alleys and structures that have stood the test of time. Those buildings still stand, and the people inside of them carry the same dreams and hopes that cobblers, merchants, school pupils, and royalty have done since the 1600's. The more things change, the more they stay the same.

The pleasant walk from the main railway terminal to the harbor was rife with the most delicious aromas, a different restaurant representing the flag and cuisine of far flung lands greeting us on the afternoon winds coming in from Kastrup. It was truly the most delightful of days.

The beautiful old sailing ships tied up along the sailors' district of Nyhavn, past the Kongens Nytorv, provided the serenity as the sounds of ropes through blocks and the gentle kisses of the ancient wooden hulls pulling against the tethers that kept them where they waited for their next chance to run before the wind, these thoroughbreds of the sea. Their red sails wrapped against the many years and coats of varnish agleam in the sun. I cannot imagine for a moment this day without Sander. He was meant to join me and I so appreciated his being there.

"Where shall we stay when we is here?" he asked.

"It is a nice place," I told him, "and I stayed here once back when I first came to Denmark. It's called Nyhavn 71, and it used to be a place where they kept things for the old ships. But now it's a hotel," I said.

"Here," he offered, "I will pay for the place for us because you let me come whit you." He pulled the banknotes from his little pouch that hung on a lanyard around his neck. His lovely neck—soft—milky white, his knit collar brushing lightly against it with every step along the strand. I didn't know that someone could actually envision slow motion movement, but I did right then. Like the prelude to the very best love scene in a movie that might have changed your life.

Oh, stop, you idiot. Why do you do this to yourself? If he knew what you were thinking about him he'd hate your fucking guts; he'd probably take off in a full-on run just to get the fuck away from you. What are you thinking? Stop it! *Just Stop!*

"There it is," Sander pointed. "You're right, it's a

really cool old building. This will be fun because the windows look to the harbor."

"Yes, but they won't let you pay for the room. So you better put your money back in your pack."

"Why?" he protested. "This money is good; look, there are pictures of old dead people on it."

"It's because you come from Odense; this hotel is only for Americans, and I think they take Czechs.

"I have a check, too, so I pay."

"No, Czechs; like people from Czech Republic. Get it?" and I gave him another 'bud slug' in the shoulder just as an excuse to touch him again.

"I think you're stupid," he smiled. "That was a stupid joke—*take Czechs.*"

"I guess I'm saying that your money's no good here today, okay?"

"Only if I can buy the aftensmad and the Cokes, yes? I think maybe pizza, yes? Is we too soon for pizza again?"

"Deal."

The lobby was a study in old world charm— truly antique furniture; desks, ship's cabin settees, cooper barrels, a model of a Baltic trader suspended from the open beam ceiling.

The clerk welcomed us with the perfect mix of distant Scandinavian friendliness, and seemed genuinely concerned that he could only offer us a single king size bed — after all, he reminded me, that's what I had reserved.

"I will be happy to bring a rolling cot in for you at no charge," he offered. I left it up to Sander.

"Nej tak," he said to the man in their shared native tongue. I knew enough Danish to know that he had just let the guy know that he didn't want the cot. Then, turning to me Sander asked, "Is that okay whit you? That we can share? Because those bed are wery uncuntstable."

"Are what?" I laughed.

"Uncuntstable; you know, they hurt your back and stuff."

The desk man traded sentences with Sander and then suggested to me that my friend meant that the cot would be *uncomfortable*. I didn't care what he said because, first, I knew what Sander meant and, second, all I was processing was that we would be sleeping in the same bed together. That night. That very night I would be in the general, close proximity of the single human being in this whole world that I most wished to be close to.

Maybe I would feel his warmth. I could watch him breathe; maybe I would even feel his breath. I would watch his chest rise and fall. I would be near him. Mere inches away from Sander Lars Hansen, age sixteen, of Odense, Denmark. That is where I would be.

"Room twenty-two," the man said. "And the total for both will be fifteen hundred and twenty kroner, and includes a very nice breakfast for you in the morning."

He handed Sander two keys as I completed the transaction. That was it: signed, sealed, and delivered—such a grand day. Tomorrow my first assignment; tonight, a wonderful time spent with the best person in the world.

12

The big man left the wrapper on the second to last seat, right side, window, on the number 175 city ring express bus to the airport, not sure if the contact he was supposed to make would actually get it. It was a risk, mitigated by the fact that on this Thursday afternoon the route was running nearly empty. It was a bank holiday in Poland, and the usual rush of commuters that would normally be clogging the articulated coach—every seat filled, and a capacity load of standees—was clearly absent. Even the *przystanek*—bus stops—were void of waiting passengers. The vibrancy of Warsaw on a work day was definitely tempered, and with it the anonymity that the man would usually rely on when engaged in activities such as these.

Of all days for a bank holiday. Normally he would have purchased a ticket from one of the red and gray ticket machines near the metro station or opposite the main post office, but he had to board this specific bus at this exact time and both machines were down for maintenance. The ZTM Citi-Card he found in his wallet had just a single zone left on it, which would never get him all the way to Chopin Airport, and he knew that the ticket validation machine would spit it out if he dared try. Best to play Dumb German Tourist if the driver challenged him, or if a roving conductor came aboard.

If his contact would just give the signal that he received the message he could hop off and be done with it. But he didn't know where the guy (or gal) was boarding, so it wouldn't be over until it was over.

Then he saw a prospect. The bus stopped near the Muzeum Narodowe—they had already passed the Uniwersytet Warszawski—where a lone patron boarded and headed straight for the agreed seat. As the bus revved away from the curb, the passenger pocketed the wrapper, made deniable eye contact with the big man, and turned his attention to the view outside and whatever was playing through his earbuds. Information successfully passed, the big man pressed the chime strip on the pier panel beside the window and made for the rear door. Now deposited on the corner of the Park Ujazdowski, he hailed a taxi and began the circuitous route that would eventually take him to his flat on Sochaczew.

When Dimitri Petrenko began his work on behalf of the United States government, and therefore of a dozen other Western powers, it was for entirely selfish reasons. He wanted the cash, of course, but like a woman scorned, Hell Hath No Fury like a government employee who felt overlooked and underappreciated by his bosses.

Petrenko was a career FSB operative, a holdover from the old KGB days, but after communism went extinct and the USSR was officially added to the roster of failed states, the new regime reasoned that as a rookie KGB man—he had only been with the agency for eight years—they could let him stay. They could use him, and if it turned out to be a bad decision they still had gulags of a sort. Siberia hadn't changed much since the dawn of the new Russian

Federation.

By '94 he was a fully ensconced CIA asset. He first came to Langley's attention soon after the failed coup back in '93. He had a hand in wrecking the August Putsch—Vladimir Putin's coup against Gorbachev—in 1991, and since he had weathered both periods of unrest without so much as a whiff of internal suspicion against him, he'd caught the attention of the field operational division at the CIA.

They had instigated quite the outreach program, which at first he resisted. That was until his arrogant fuck of a boss twice passed him over for major postings and promotions. The last straw came when the prick awarded a nephew a post at the United Nations. He had always wanted to see New York; now, he decided, he would see it another way.

All was well. The money always arrived on time, and he had even gotten a raise. He knew that Americans were happy with any given something whenever they would pay more for that something. For him, they paid more. And they really didn't ask for all that much in return. Truth be told, he would have done it for free just to get back at that fucking Mitrokhin. What a shit he was. Well, thought Dimitri Petrenko, he'd pay. He'd pay large, and someday he'd let the old wanker know that his downfall had come from him. But for now, he'd have to play everything close to the chest.

He had four weeks of vacation due, and he had gotten it cleared. Right after that, he contacted his handler to let him know that Operation Mango could commence. He had just been delivered his marching orders on the bus.

His job thought he would be in Poland for the month—out of the country, but still close enough to Russia that his superiors weren't worried that he might do something stupid. Besides, what did he know anyway? Certainly nothing that could put anyone's cushy state job at risk, least of all Mitrokhin's. Chances were strong that nobody would even miss him—such is the condition for the perfect spy, and Dimitri would use that to his advantage.

The communiqué described the straightforward transport arrangements—he was supposed to meet his contact at Saint Florian's Cathedral in the eastern part of town. He was to take with him only one small suitcase; travel documents and currency would be waiting for him at the hotel in Warsaw. He was to meet his contact in the church nave between eight and ten p.m. Straight forward enough. It was a 'go'.

13

"You can have the last piece."

"No, you can have it," I insisted.

"Are you sure?"

"Yep. I think half a pizza is more than enough for me. Besides, we can go out for Burger King later if we want to," I joked.

"Eeehhh. Okay, but only because I am growing boy," Sander smiled. "It is wery good pizza, I think," he added, grabbing for the lone slice.

It was way past dark now, and we had talked about anything and everything for the better part of the evening. We exchanged opinions on favorite bands, movies that meant a lot to our respective lives, and had discussed all of the flawed family lineage memories could summon. It was a wonderful time.

It was past midnight when we agreed it was time to turn in. I brushed my teeth and gargled, wondering what the pajama protocol should be. I always slept in the buff; okay, I knew that was out entirely. But I didn't do pajamas, or even the typical sweat pants and tee shirt deal. I'd see if I could get away with underwear. If he didn't laugh, or wasn't all wrapped up in some kind of sleepwear himself, I'd stay in the skivvies.

I'd also let him pick the side he wanted to sleep on. Oh, boy. Here I go, being stupid. He's not your date, asshole. He's your friend, and he doesn't need you pining over the lump in his crotch.

I bent over the sink to spit the mouthful of Vitis into the drain, and when I looked up in the mirror I saw the purist reflection of beauty staring back at me. No, I'm not a narcissist; Sander had snuck in behind me.

"Boo!"

"Boo, yourself."

"I am here to removes pizza breath from mine huge mouth," he smiled. "Can I use some of yours toothpaste?"

"It'll cost you," I joked.

"Okay, but if you don't lets me then you has to

140

smell pizza whole night. And I makes sure that I will breathe your direction, I promise!"

"Here!"

Well, one question had been answered; he was in his 'Euro Shorts'. Picture those Speedo swimsuits and you'll have a good idea of what underwear for guys is like all over Europe. His were a sky blue with little black stripes. And they hid nothing!

This was going to be a difficult night.

Okay, I promised myself, I would get into bed, roll away from him, and go the fuck asleep. Yep. That's what I'd do. Yep.

"Race you!" he challenged, and ran to the bed, claimed the left side, butt-jumped on the mattress a couple times before swinging his legs over the eiderdown comforter. "Oh, you are such a loser! Danmark, ONE; America, NONE! I win!"

"That wasn't fair, and you know it."

"All is fair in love, war, and bed!" he said.

Oh really, I thought, climbing onto my side. Let the torture commence. Oh great! *I can smell him again! Godfuckingdammit!*

"Okay, you're the big winner," I conceded.

"What do I win?" he cheekily asked.

"What do you want?"

He turned his head to look me straight in the eye

and went all serious on me.

"I want to go with you on your job trip," he said. But before I could even process what he'd said, he quickly added, "But I know that is impossible. But you asked me what I want so I tell you anyways."

"I wish you could go," I sighed. The room went dead, the only thing to be heard being our mutual breathing and the ferry loading up for Norway just outside the window.

The minutes ticked by, punctuated by the sound of the mini-bar fridge kicking on in the corner.

"Are you angry whit me now?"

"Fuck no!" I expelled. "Absolutely not! You don't know how bad I wish you could go."

"Good. I was worry that you think I am so pushy to even joke about it," he said.

"Were you joking, then?" I asked.

"No! I would really come if it was possible, but you has to work and not be thinking about if I am there, see?"

"Well, I mean it," I said. "I really wish you could be with me."

"Yeah. That would be a good thing."

Another lull; the beeping of the forklifts running around the dock, and the reflections of their flashing yellow lights dancing on the ceiling.

Sander expelled a long breath, like he was reflecting on something significant to him.

"Something wrong?" I asked him.

"Not really. Just thinking about something is all."

"Do you want to tell me or not?"

"Well, of course I *want* to tell you. You're my friend. But I don't think that I should because..."

"It seems you got sad all of a sudden. I'm sorry that you can't go on the..."

"Oh no," he protested. "It's not that at all. Don't even worry about that."

"Okay," I said. "Are you all right, then?"

He nodded, staring up at the ceiling. "Beep Beep Beep Beep Beep," he mimicked the busy vehicles outside. "I think maybe the Roadrunner can gets a job down there on the pier," he quipped.

"I think the Roadrunner says 'meep-meep' doesn't he?"

"Not in Danmark he don't. Besides his sign that he holds up sometimes say 'beep-beep' I'm sure," he stated. "So there."

"Seriously, what's eating you?" I asked.

"Pizza," he said.

"No! I meant..."

"I know what you mean," he laughed. "I pull yours chain."

"Okay," I surrendered. "I'm not trying to get all up in your business. I just wanna make sure you're not upset, or anything."

Again he nodded.

"Well, there is a problem, you know. But if I tell you... If I say what it is, can you promise that you won't be angry or something?"

"I could never be angry with you, Sander. Get real!"

"Well," he paused, "you say that now, but maybe what I say will not makes you so glad."

He had my attention now. Fuck, what was coming? Shit! I knew this was too good to be true. I come half way around the world and finally meet someone that—*knock it off, idiot! He's not your fucking husband!*

"Well, I'm all ears, and I promise I won't be mad no matter what, okay?"

The ticking clock. The fridge cycled off again. The yellow lights continued their shadow dance.

"I have this friend, and I really want to be much more than just a friend," he began. "Like, ever since I meet them I am always thinking when I can be there next, or what is the person doing right now, that kind of thing, Yes?"

"I follow."

"So I want to make the move, yes," he added.

"But there is the real number one problem, and it makes me wery sad sometimes."

"What is it?"

"Well," he sighed, "I know that there is no way that this person would ever want to be with me. In fact, I don't think that I will ever stands a chance."

"Okay," I began, "do you want my thoughts about it?"

"Is why I tell you. I am takes a chance to tell you, so as you can see I am wery serious," he admitted.

"Well if she has any kind of a brain at all, even the littlest, tiniest brain in the whole world, she will do anything she can to be with you every second of every day. If she did this, she would be the luckiest person in the whole world."

I thought about what he had said and how it was now official. He was in love with someone, and that was that.

He remained silent for the longest time. "Do you mean that?" he whispered.

"Yes," I returned the whisper.

"Really, do you *mean* what you just said?"

"I do... And why are we whispering?"

And he kissed me. He moved his body against mine and with his left hand he guided my head toward his, planting a kiss unlike any I had ever experienced. It spoke of love, passion, and purity—and my breath evaporated.

He pulled away, his head down so that my nose brushed against his hair.

"Please don't be angry whit me. I understand if you are not like me, but I cannot go more friends whit you if I cannot be who I am whit you," his words rushed out.

"Sander, I—"

"Please, let me say because I'm afraid if I don't I might never do..." He continued: "The person I tell you about is you, okay? There I say it. But I cannot have you dislike me because I am who I am. So if you want not to be friends any more I can understand because I know that—I'm sorry that I kissed you because it is not right for—"

"I'm not."

"What?"

"I'm not sorry you kissed me."

He met my eyes not sure if what I meant was...

"I'm not sorry that you kissed me, Sander, and I am what I am, too."

"What do you..."

"I love you," I admitted. "I am in love with you; completely, and totally in love with you."

He sat up, looking away, not quite believing what he heard.

"But..."

"But nothing," I said. "I can't believe what just happened. A dream came true just now. Sander, I love you."

Then came the tears. Tears of joy and of relief; it turns out the silent torture we had both endured those many months was, at that instant, forever eradicated and erased.

"Why have you not say this before?" he sniffled. "I am going crazy all these days, and—you love me like... You really love me like I love you?"

"If I understand what you're saying, and if that kiss is the example, then yes—I love you like you love me," I declared. And then he leaned over and hugged me with a grip that promised he would never let me go. I hoped he felt the same commitment from me.

He kissed my neck and I felt his warm breath as he moved his lips up to my right cheek. He brushed ever so gently past my ear and once again whispered his love to me. This was going to happen. For a moment I paused, wondering if this wasn't some kind of a dream, maybe even a psychosis. Since when does anybody ever get what they want the most? Ever!

"Sander," I breathed, "may I make love with you?"

He leaned back a little and looked me in the eye, and with a tender nod he laid back down on the eiderdown. He was already fully erect and I could see that his penis was throbbing in anticipation inside his shorts. This was the moment.

My right hand brushed and cupped his manhood and I positioned myself within inches of it, trying to catch my breath before laying eyes upon it for the first time. His gorgeous scent filled me with excitement as he raised up from the mattress a bit so I could remove the only barrier that remained between us. And there it was. Six and a half inches, and much thicker than I had imagined. And I had imagined it a lot.

His foreskin was retracted just below the head in its current state, and the first thing I did was lick the very tip, letting my tongue flitter around the underside. His hips rose up to meet me, and I engulfed my friend as deeply and as gently as I could, stopping at the base to affix the lightest pressure with my lips. Sander was inside of me, and our love story had begun.

To describe him as beautiful is such a massive understatement that a thesaurus would be of absolutely no use. There were and are no words...

We were in sync, his hips writhing in a gentle, rhythmic motion alternating from left to right, up to down, his breathing in time with the tiny thrusts meeting my lips and tongue. And ever gentle, Sander began to lightly brush my balls and the tip of my dick.

The fore and middle fingers of my right hand pulled the base of his cock to his pubes, while I used my lips to tease his foreskin over his head on the upward thrusts, and blew warm breath down his shaft, my mouth slightly open, as I went for each downward suck. Guess that's why it's called a blow job. It drove him to Nirvana, his toes curling and his inner thighs tightening up at the repetitive and steady action taking place.

"It feels so good—so wery good," he sighed passionately. "I love you so much, Johnnie. I can't believe this night."

With those heartening words, I rolled to position myself between his legs with my mouth by his balls. They hung low, the lower back area of his ball sack millimeters from his ass crack. I could see that gorgeous slice between the most perfectly formed butt cheeks I had ever seen, and the first thing I noticed was how good he smelled down there, too.

No hint of anything other than how he always smelled. This was going to be a full service session, I can promise.

I began licking and slurping his balls, every so often taking one into my mouth and giving just the slightest amount of pressure, enough to send an erotic signal throughout his entire body.

"God! Do that more... Oh, fuck!" he cried. The moaning was an even bigger turn-on than what my other senses were already providing. "How can this be so fantastisk?" he breathed. "I think it is a dream."

"Me, too," I agreed.

"Johnnie, please make this be for always," he sighed as my tongue ran up the back of his throbbing cock and engulfed his head and foreskin in a single motion that threatened to take him over the edge.

"I don't wants to cum so fast. Can I play whit you for a time?"

"For all time and forever," I smiled, as I lifted his right leg and rolled out from under him. "What do you want to do?" I asked.

"Can I make you a good massage for a time, and then maybe goes from there?"

"Sure. Where do you want me, then?"

"Just lay there; here, put this pillow under here and I do the rest," he offered. "And I will sit here like on a horse and start Sander's Thailand Massage for you!" He sat on my ass and I could feel his balls lying against my back as I exhaled and shut my eyes in anticipation.

"I go long time," he laughed. "I makes goody-goody massage for American tourist, only two dollah!"

"Fuck you!"

"Okay! But that cost three dollah!" And we shared the laugh together, his fingertips pressing up and down my spine. I learned at that moment that, indeed, some things are actually better than sex. He could have hung out a shingle and had folks lining up for blocks around. In my whole life I had never felt anything so hypnotically relaxing as Sander's tender massage.

He gripped my shoulders and squeezed with short bursts of intensity that transfixed me. I nearly felt like I was having an out of body experience and I let him know it.

"It feels good, yes?" he asked hopefully.

"It's the best," was all I could manage. My brain was firing off signals that it never had before. I didn't want it to stop. And then...

He scooted off my butt and slid down just past my thighs, still straddling me, and he leaned down and softly spread my ass cheeks. I felt the tickle of his breath as he blew lightly against my hole.

He dropped a trail of spit into the crack and then lowered his face and extended his tongue, starting a lapping and licking motion that repeated up and down the full length of my ass crack.

Remember when I reported that the massage was the best thing I had ever felt? Well, now it was the second best thing. This was truly the summit of every sexual experience I had enjoyed until then. He worked that area like a hungry wolf, and he showed no sign of slowing down anytime soon.

By now my ass was in rhythm with his motions and about every third or fourth pass he would brush a combination of fingers the entire length, stopping for milliseconds at my hole.

"Can I?"

"God, yes," I managed to say. It was hard to breathe, much less say anything. And then the bed shifted as he got into position and mounted me from behind. He entered me with such love and grace, so considerate of his lover. He would move in an inch or so then stop, wait a few seconds, and go a little farther until at last he was completely inside me.

At that point he just laid down on me, his breath flowing past the nape of my neck, his hair resting on mine. And then he slowly began the thrusting motion that soon graduated into a pleasant syncopation. We were one; we were now together.

The feeling was amazing because this, I recognized, is what love truly felt like. I had never experienced true love before feeling Sander deep inside me. I had enjoyed the physical aspects of sex many times, and I was grateful for almost everyone I had ever been with until now. But this was it. This was why millions of love songs were composed. This was what being human meant; to be in love with somebody without any reserve. This was the chemistry. It was the alchemy. And it was occurring in real time in a place I hadn't known existed a little over a year before.

"Johnnie, I love you so much," he said, as he increased the intensity of his thrusts. By now I was completely in his control. I was so overtaken by the many feelings and emotions that my whole nervous system was threatening electrical overload.

"Faster," I exhaled. "You can go as fast as you want!"

"You are so special to me," he whimpered. "I have not ever loved anyone like this."

"Sander, I love you. *Fuck me! I want to make you happy!"*

"I am so happy," he whispered.

"Will you cum inside me?"

"Do you want me to?" he asked, thrusting faster and deeper each time.

"Please cum in me," I begged. And then our world turned silent, save for the erotic noises of skin playing upon skin, and the heavy breathing of the boy atop me nearing climax—and the one who loves him about to experience his very first orgasm without having stimulated his own penis in any way. Wow, this was amazing!

He was really going at it now, deeper and faster, my ass hungrily meeting his every downward move. And then I felt the pressure building in my pubic area, my hard cock pumping on its own, matching Sander's steady movements.

"Johnnie, I'm cumming now!" was all he could manage before I registered the thick, warm feeling of his seed as it splashed into me in five distinct spurts. And then I was gone.

"I'm coming, Sander! You're making me cum!" and I felt the warmth of my own jizz as it pooled beneath my belly. I had never spooged so much before, ever. It was amazing.

Sander slowly wound down after he exploded inside me. He didn't just stop and pull out; instead, he kept the motion going and simultaneously slowed his movement while letting his dick go soft. Then he left it there for a good two minutes, both of us recovering, and finally pulled away and laid on his side. His chest was heaving, screaming for breath. I was completely spent and remained face down and enjoyed the feeling of his warm cum filling my ass while my own cum cooled against my body and the sheets.

"Wow," he said.

"Fucking wow," I responded. "Where did you..."

"Where did *you?!*" he laughed.

"Fucking hell!"

"Don't you mean Fucking Heaven?" he said.

"I was gonna suck your dick until you explosioned but I think you got a surprise instead, so I don't feel so bad," he grinned. "Have you do that before?"

"Never," I told him. "I didn't even know it could happen, did you?"

"No. I never see it in pornos even," he reported. "And if it not be in a porno then who knows?"

"It was the best orgasm I ever had," I said, "and I've had many."

"They better have be by yourself!" he said in mock anger. "Don't make me get jealous!"

We laughed again. The thing I realized in recent months is that whenever I am with Sander, I am beyond joy and happiness. Laughter doesn't just come easily, it's part of the fabric. That has happened since the day we met, and I've never met anyone who loves to laugh as much as Sander does. That can't be usual.

"Do you know what?" he asked.

"What."

"Can I tell you something?"

"Sure. Of course." Then he waited a few seconds, and scooted himself a little closer to me.

"You are such wery beautiful man," he said. "You are so kind to me, and I just wants you to know that. Okay?"

"Wow!"

"Dang!"

Thank you is all I could say in reply to his tender words. I was totally overwhelmed. "Now can I ask *you* something?" He nodded my direction and then rested his chin on his hand, his azure blue eyes glistening in the darkened room.

"Can you—will you tell me when you first fell in love with me?"

"That's easy," he replied. "Of course I was attracted to your sexy body..." I snorted out a *'yeah, right!'* in response, and he continued.

"Remember when I am spilling the soda all on me at the party where we first meet each other?" he said.

"Yeah. Of course I do."

"Well," he said, "everyone laughed at me—and that's okay! We're everybody friends—but you was the only one that instead goes to the kitchen and gets me a towel."

"That's it?"

"That's when I start thinking about you and can't stop it. So that means I'm in love. Now you."

"Huh?"

"When do you fall for me?"

"Well, okay... So I went and got the towel after you spilled the drink and I saw that you were laughing bigger than anybody else. At first I felt bad because I thought they were making fun of you in a bad way, but then I saw how everybody in the room loved you and..."

"So that's when?"

"Actually, when I completely and totally wanted to know you better was when I handed you the towel. You held onto my hand when we were drying you off. I won't lie, it turned me on... But what got me thinking about you, besides the big lump in your pants, was that I knew you were guiding my hand so that I wouldn't mess up my own clothes."

"Oh, I see..." he smiled.

"But wait, that's not the exact moment. That came when we rode to Copenhagen on the train that first time. You sat across from me and then you took a nap. *That's* when I fell in love with you."

"When I take a nap?"

"Watching you sleep. I fell in love with you when I saw you sleep."

"Then pretty soon you can fall in love all over again because I will have really good sleep tonight after all that," he said. "And we can call it our happy endings sleepover in wonderful, wonderful Copenhagen!"

We held each other close and he petted me every so often, his hand moving slowly down my arm, down my side, and resting on my hip. Every now and then he would reach for my hand and give it a squeeze. That was the last thing I remembered as I drifted away, the sound of his breathing marking the tempo of the day.

14

Petrenko had time to kill and, after all, he was supposed to be on a holiday. If the FSB fucktards actually had him under surveillance—impossible, he knew, *but still*—he reasoned that he might as well keep up appearances.

The Warszawska Opera Kameralna was running *Turandot*, and Puccini was just about his favorite. So a night at the opera it would be. The hotel concierge was a dear and arranged his ticket, and all that was left to do was enjoy a little rest before dinner and call again on Marek, the concierge, to arrange a taxi to the opera house.

At half eight he took his seat in the second box above stage left. His seatmates arrived after the overture had begun and he could tell that the middle-aged couple had been fussing about something on the way to the theater. Her face all but broadcasted their dirty linen in high definition, and the man merely seemed to be resigned to his fate. Petrenko couldn't help but feel sorry for the bastard, and smiled knowingly when he spied the telltale shape of a flask in the man's pocket.

The curtain rose on a beautiful set depicting the palace grounds, and Petrenko settled in for the three hour journey to China and all of the intrigue dominating the Royal Court. He had to admit that the treachery and senseless threats of death in Puccini's final opera were not unlike what he experienced every single day at the Lubyanka. He wondered why the FSB chose to stay in the same damned building after the fall of the USSR; the same one the KGB had occupied since the days of Iron Felix Dzerzhinsky. But he quickly answered his own question. *They stayed there because they never really changed.*

He awoke the next morning to a real gulley washer; it was pouring down rain so hard that it sounded like water over the falls, or at least a dam. Funny, he thought, it had been so clear and calm when he'd left the opera house. So clear that he even saw stars teasing the night sky despite the light pollution of the city. He hoped it wasn't a sign.

Breakfast was the usual fare: bread, bread, and more bread with some tired looking fruit, and cereal with milk much too warm to be of any use. Not worth the risk, anyway.

A fierce news junkie—especially anything with a political bent—Dimitri Petrenko was engrossed in an article about the pitiful Bulgarian economy when he was startled by a slap against his newspaper. Dropping the broadsheet he found himself meeting mischievous eyes belonging to a ten year old boy and his seven year old sister. His scrambled brain tried to make instant sense of this: he *knew* these children. But how? Who were they?

"Uncle Dimi! We scared you!" the small, black haired girl announced. "You jumped out of your chair!" The boy just laughed at him. Then it clicked. Holy shit! It was that asshole Kolya's brats. He was forced to bunk with the family at a two week training seminar a couple years back. His eye caught the parents, Kolya and Katryna, sitting at a table across the breakfast room, who both smiled at the big surprise. What was this? *No! It couldn't be!*

"Dimitri Nikolayevich! Come join us!" Kolya blasted across the room. "Fancy seeing you here!" Kolya's smile aped the fox's just before crossing the threshold of the henhouse.

"Kolya Ivanovich! Dear Katryna! How happy I am to see you! This holiday keeps getting better and better!" Dimitri grabbed his tea and a small brick of pumpernickel and crossed the room to their table. He made a special effort to acknowledge the children as he slid onto a chair borrowed from the adjoining banquette.

"What are the chances?" Dimitri smiled back. Kolya answered with a shrug and a grin. *We both know why I'm here, Dimitri, and I'm not above using my own family in this obvious deception.*

"I'd heard that you'd be out for the month, but I did not reckon I'd have holiday at the same time as you, and that we'd run into each other," Kolya lied. "But it is small world, as they say," he grinned, channeling the Cheshire cat. Now, thought Dimitri, was the time for all the training and tradecraft to kick in. He couldn't reveal anything. Not a single tic, or change in his pupils. He had to stay cool and jovial.

He had to be a man on holiday. A man with nothing to hide. Let the fucker follow him. Let him think he's mindfucking him. Give him nothing. Not a fucking goddamned thing.

"We should take the children to the zoo today," Dimitri offered. "That is, if you're not doing anything; it will be my treat."

"How generous of you, Dimitri Nikolayevich. I think it is a splendid idea, don't you, Katryna?" She nodded and smiled, keeping the children occupied and focused on their breakfasts. "If not today, then perhaps tomorrow, yes?" Kolya suggested.

"Whatever works for all of us. As you can see, I am a man of leisure!" Dimitri smiled, before excusing himself and returning to his room. "I am in room nineteen on the first floor. Just give me an idea what the plan is and I'll be available."

He casually walked the hall to his room and waved the keycard across the pad. The lock clicked open and he calmly entered the foyer and gently closed the door behind him. Although it was a long shot chance, he had to assume that the room was bugged; there would be no loud displays of emotion. It was then he had to laugh: he noticed the calendar diary opened on the desk. Today was Friday the thirteenth.

15

My favorite food, besides my mother's frikadeller and kartoffelsalat, is pizza. So when Johnnie and me talked about what to have for dinner, I thought pizza in our room was a great idea.

I took a big risk this morning. I told my mother and father that I was going to Copenhagen for the weekend with Johnnie, and I even got my sister to drive me to the station. I did this before I even knew if he would want me to join him on the trip. The risk paid off. Well, almost. I won't be staying the whole time with him. Just tonight. But I have enough money to stay in town if I want to, or I can just go back home and hang around with Georg or someone.

I've known Johnnie for a whole year, and in that time I think about him every day. It's getting where I wonder if there's something wrong with me. He's tall and he's really handsome. He's twenty-two years old, too, and I'm just a stupid sixteen-year-old teenager and kind of a nerd. So I wonder what he even sees in me. I wonder sometimes if he's just a nice guy and doesn't want to "make the kid upset."

I don't even know if he really understands how I think because, unlike how I'm thinking now in Danish—completely lucid, expressive, natural— every time I speak with Johnnie I have to slow my brain down. I have to consider every word and hope that it's the right one to say. And then I hope that when I say it, that he can understand me. How can you build a friendship as strong as I want ours to be when he cannot know my thought processes? How can he know how I feel about him if I can't even express words beyond what a schoolchild can say? Fuck it all to hell!

"You can have the last piece," I offered.

"No, you can have it," he said kindly.

"Are you sure?"

"Yep. I think half a pizza is more than enough

for me. Besides, we can go out for Burger King later if we want to," he joked.

"Eeehhh. Okay," I chuckled, "but only because I'm a growing boy." I told him I thought it was a real good pizza as I reached for that last piece.

We watched some things on the television, but if you paid me a thousand crowns I couldn't tell you anything about it. All I did was look at, and think about him. Watching him for that long without him getting wise to me was pretty hard, but I catalogued every centimeter of his body from head to foot, and I really wished I had Superman vision. At the very least I would have wanted to walk with him through the x-ray machine at the airport.

We talked about many things. If he only knew how much I just wanted to tell him that I love him. Real love. Like the kind of love when you stay with a person forever, and you know that they love you back.

The thing that I love about Johnnie is how fucking smart he is. He knows stuff. I don't think I have ever met anybody as smart as Johnnie Allen.

He's also so very kind to me. He remembers things, too, like my mother's birthday last March when he had flowers sent to her at work. It got my father into a little bit of trouble because he hadn't sent her anything. (I'll have you know that I made her breakfast and had gifts waiting for her from her son, Sander! Such a good boy she raised!)

I don't know what I should do about any of this, either. On one hand I could try and see if he might be like me. On the other hand I might insult him and even make him scared of me because I'm one of those homos! He might choose to stop our friendship right there, and I could never have that happen for any reason.

And what about tonight? I can't believe the luck that we get to share the bed, but it's like torture, too! How can I just lie there next to him and go to sleep?

The time comes. He's in the bathroom brushing his teeth. I strip down to my shorts and positioned my dick for the best possible viewing "just in case." Sneaking up behind him, he jumped a little when he caught my reflection in the mirror. "Boo!" I joked, and after my teeth were clean I monkey-jumped on the bed.

I watched him cross the room and sit down on his side of the bed. I caught just a little glimpse of his butt crack, and saw the lump in his shorts when he swung his legs onto the mattress. He was atop the eiderdown and I could see the shape of his cock and balls hiding in his undershorts. I was right. This was going to be a long night.

We'd just shared a joke with some typical guy humor—I thought it might get something going like it did my very first time with Anders. I'd dared him to race me to the bed, and I basically acted the fool. What the hell am I thinking?!

I had made a stupid dare, and he lost. So I acted like I expected to collect on it.

"Okay, you're the big winner," he said. So I asked him what I won.

"What do you want?" he asked. And that was the only opening I would have and something just took hold of me. All thinking went out the window and I just kind of stared at him. I was doing everything just to not cry. I felt like I might, so I just blurted out the first thing that came to mind.

"I want to go with you on your job trip," I said, "but I know that's impossible. But you asked me what I wanted, so I told you anyways."

"I wish you could go," he said. Then he kind of just stared up at the ceiling. I'd completely blown it!

"Are you angry with me now?" I asked him. And he told me that he really wanted me to go with him, but that I couldn't because it was a pretty important job he had to do. I made sure he knew that I was joking—*that* was a big fat lie.

"Were you joking, then?" he asked.

"No! I would really come if it was possible, but you have to work and not be distracted because of me."

"Well, I meant it," he said. "I really wish you could be with me."

I rolled onto my back and just sighed this long sigh. I hadn't meant to do it, but Johnnie got worried again.

"Something wrong?"

"Not really. Just thinking about something is all."

He asked me if I wanted to tell him what was bothering me.

"Well, of course I want to tell you," I said. "You're my friend. But I don't think that I should because..."

"It seemed like you got sad all of a sudden. I'm sorry that you can't go on the..."

"Oh no," I told him. "It's not that at all. Don't even worry about that."

He asked me again if I was okay and I just wanted to change the subject as quickly as I could, so I started making noises like the trucks outside. But he didn't let it drop. That's how Johnnie is; he was still worried about me.

"Seriously, what's eating you?" he asked.

"Pizza," I said.

"No! I meant..."

"I know what you mean," I laughed, confessing that I was only pulling his chain. Then, when it looked like he wasn't going to ask anymore I jumped into the fire, feet first.

"Well, there is a problem, you know. But if I tell you... If I say what it is can you promise that you won't be angry or something?"

"I could never be angry with you, Sander. Get real!"

"Well," I paused, "you say that now, but maybe what I say will not make you very happy. You might even be angry with me."

"Well, I'm all ears," he said, "and I promise I won't be mad no matter what, okay?"

Okay. So I let it out.

"I have this friend and I really want to be much more than just a friend," I began. "Like, ever since I met them I am always thinking about when I can be there next, or what the person is doing right then, that kind of thing, Yes?"

"I follow," he acknowledged.

"So, I want to make the move," I added. "But there is a real number one problem and it makes me very sad sometimes."

"What is it?"

"Well," I sighed, "I know that there is no way that this person would ever want to be with me. In fact, I don't think that I would ever stand a chance."

He asked if I truly wanted his opinion, and of course I nodded yes.

"Well," he began, "if she has any kind of a brain at all, even the littlest, tiniest brain in the whole world, she will do anything she can to be with you every second of every day. If she did this, she would be the luckiest person in the whole world."

"Do you mean that?" I whispered.

"Yes."

"Really, do you *mean* what you just said?"

"I do... And why are we whispering?"

I couldn't stop. I just leaned over and kissed him. And he kissed me back. *He kissed me back!*

"Johnnie, don't be angry with me," I pleaded, "I understand if you are not like me, but I cannot be your friend if I cannot be who I am with you," the words rushed out. "I can't be a liar."

"Sander, I—"

"Please, let me say this because I'm afraid if I— If I don't, I might never do..." I continued: "The person I tell you about is you, okay? It's *you!* There, I said it. But I cannot have you dislike me because I am who I am. So if you want to not be friends any more I can understand because... I know that—I'm sorry that I kissed you because it is not right for—"

"*I'm* not."

"What?"

"*I'm* not sorry that you kissed me."

I just stared at him; stared deep into his eyes. What had he just told me?

"I'm not sorry that you kissed me, Sander, and I am what I am, too."

"What do you..."

"I love you," he said. "I am in love with you; completely, and totally in love with you."

I sat upright. It had to be a dream. I couldn't have heard what I just thought he'd said.

"But..."

"But nothing," Johnnie said. "I can't believe what just happened. A dream came true just now. Sander, I *love* you."

Then I cried tears of joy, and of total relief. "Why haven't you said anything about this before?" I caught my breath between the tears running freely down my face.. "I've been going crazy for a year, and—you love me like... You really love *me* like I love *you*?"

"If I understand what you're saying, and if that

kiss is the example, then, yes, I love you like you love me," Johnnie promised. Again, I couldn't stop myself. I leaned over and hugged him to the moon and back.

As I held him close to me I kissed his neck and felt my face against his. I couldn't say I Love You enough, and then he asked if he could make love with me. Make love! Not *Wanna have sex? Wanna fuck? Want some head?* He loved me.

I looked him in the eye and lost my breath, then I laid down on my back and waited for him to make my dream come true.

He barely touched my cock, kind of laying his hand on my shorts. I was, of course, already very hard down there. I raised up and started to pull off my shorts and he just kind of helped me off with them. I kicked them onto the floor and there I was; I was all his, and I would have done anything he wanted.

He tickle-teased my hard cock with his tongue, just working around the head. He pulled my skin back just a bit, and then slowly moved it up and down over the head But then he just swallowed my whole dick, all the way to the bottom, and held there for a second before moving his tongue really fast all around, and up and down. I thought I was going to pass out!

I wanted to do something for him. I went for his shorts, but he had already kicked them off. So kind of by accident I was met with his swollen cock and his massive balls. His balls were so big that they hung down and almost touched the bed. And he was lying on his side!

His dick was perfect! I had never seen one that didn't have a foreskin, but his was so straight and stiff. And the head was shaped perfectly. It was, like the rest of him, completely beautiful. I lightly touched him and was going to roll a little on my side for some sixty-nine, but he was so incredible at what he was doing that I just couldn't move. I was frozen!

"It feels so good—so very good," I told him. "I love you so much, Johnnie. I can't believe this night."

Then he rolled himself over my leg and landed right between them. I looked down and our eyes met, and just as quickly I saw the top of his head as he licked my balls with such perfect pressure. I don't know how he could figure out exactly how hard to push against my balls with his tongue. And then he'd come up a little farther and lick and suck on my dick, pulling my foreskin down with his tongue and massaging my balls with the tips of his fingers.

"God! Do that some more... Oh, fuck!" I moaned. "How can this be so fantastic?—I think it is a dream."

175

"I think so, too," he said.

"Johnnie," I begged him, "please make this be for always." Then I asked if I could give him a little pleasure for a while. I was afraid I was going to cum too quickly if I didn't get him to stop. I asked him if I could do a deep massage for him, and when he rolled over I saw his gorgeous behind for the first time.

It was the most lovely shape, and his skin was so soft and smooth. I sat myself on his rear and started working his backbone with my knuckles from top to bottom.

Then, before he knew what was happening, I grabbed onto his shoulders and squeezed them as hard as I could. He let out a long breath and I heard the melody of his voice as he giddily reacted to the pressure.

"It feels good, yes?" I asked him.

"It's the best," was what he told me. I worked him for about half an hour, and my dick started to feel a little sore because it had been so hard for so long—ever since we started.

I slid off of him and without any conscious thought I found myself between his thighs, his manly scent taking me places that I never thought I would visit. The decision was made.

I started by lubing up his ass with my spit. And then I just found myself between his cheeks, licking and tonguing every centimeter of the length of my lover's crack. He was as clean as a Disney movie down there, and though I had never done this before I had sure thought a lot about it. Never more so than after I met Johnnie.

After another half hour of exploring Johnnie's beautiful ass, I couldn't wait anymore. I spread his cheeks and saw where I needed to be. I wanted to be part of him.

"Can I?"

"God, yes," he whispered.

I climbed up behind him and placed the tip of my cock against his crack and then slowly found his hole. He was so relaxed, and I just guided myself into him a bit at a time. I never wanted him to feel anything but complete and total pleasure.

I slowly began to rock back and forth and his moans told me everything that I needed to know. I cannot adequately describe how he felt to me. His warmth, the gentle pressure with which he matched every thrust—how my foreskin would roll back and forth as I moved, increasing the already intense and delightful feeling.

"Johnnie, I love you so much," I declared.

I couldn't say it enough. I could see he was enjoying it all as much as I was, and I wanted him to have the best experience of his life.

"Faster," he called. "You can go as fast as you want!"

"You are so special to me," I told him. "I have not ever loved anyone like this."

"Sander, I love you. Fuck me! I want to make you happy!"

"I am so happy," I said.

"Will you cum inside me?"

"Do you want me to?" I asked him. We were completely together at that moment.

"Please cum in me," he pleaded. Then something happened that neither of us could have ever expected.

"Sander! I'm cumming now!" was what I thought he said, and right then I came the biggest load of cum that had ever left my dick. But that wasn't the unexpected part. Anybody would have done as much, considering how fucking wonderful Johnnie's ass was.

The thing neither of us was ready for was when Johnnie came just as my final spurt entered him.

Johnnie came a huge lake of cum without even touching his cock once. The pressure and the motion had felt so good to him that all of a sudden he felt the cum building up inside, and then he just *went!* It was wonderful.

"Wow," I said.

"Fucking wow," he agreed. "Where did you..."

"Where did *you?!*" I challenged him.

"Fucking hell!"

"Don't you mean Fucking Heaven?" I said.

I asked him if he'd ever had that happen before and he was still shocked.

"I didn't even know it could happen, did you?"

He said it was the best cumming he had ever done. I was so much in love with him at that moment that I could hardly make any sense of what was happening around me.

"Do you know what?" I asked.

"What."

"Can I tell you something?"

"Sure. Of course," he said. I took that time to move even closer to him then I told him, straight from the heart, what a beautiful man I thought he was. "You are so kind to me, and I just wanted you to know that. Okay?"

"Wow!" he replied. So I gave him a big 'Dang!' and of all the things to say, he thanked me. Can you believe it? He actually thanked *me.*

We relived the moment and had a wonderful conversation—pillow talk, it's called—about the exact time that each of us fell for the other. Then we held hands. That was the last thing I remembered as I drifted away, the sound of his breathing marking the tempo of the day.

16

Rolling out of bed was going to be a tough order this morning. The city was spooling up for the last work day of the week, and a quick glance out the double-paned window revealed that the ocean liner-size ferry had cast off for Norway, and all points north. And all I wanted to do was draw the love of my life closer to me and hold him. *That* I would have happily done for the entire day. He was lying on his left side, his smooth back resting against a pillow pile he had erected in the night.

"Are you looking at my ass?"

"Good morning, my dear little Dane. And what if I am?" I quipped.

"Just checking." He rolled over and met me with his radiant smile. "I was hoping that you were."

"Now I'm looking at your dick," I informed him.

"Oh, I see."

"Now I'm *touching* your dick. See, I am making a little place for it to hide out of my hand. Kind of like a little doghouse," I explained. "For your hot dog!"

"I think maybe..."

"Yes?"

"Maybe... You should take the dog for a walk."

So I did. Right to the shower.

Dimitri Petrenko didn't have a handle yet on how the day, much less the mission, would play out. It was time for measures, he knew, but he also knew that one mistake at this juncture and everything would collapse like the house of cards that was already his life. He hadn't come this far to have it all go pear-shaped now. What had gone wrong? Why had he attracted scrutiny from his masters at this particular time? Had he always been under the microscope of FSB suspicion?

He had to let it play out, whatever the outcome. Maybe Kolya's appearance really was a coincidence. *No fucking way*, he concluded.

His options were limited, but he had options. The trick was to decide which one to choose. Time was the dictator in this scenario—he had about a day to get it figured out and implemented. He also realized that if he was indeed compromised, he could never return to Russia. This had just turned into a one way trip, and he didn't know how much *they* knew. Could Operation Mango still continue?

Time to issue a burn message. He had two burner phones waiting for him at the central station by the bicycle racks. He could use a public phone box. He also had a current list of dead drops that the American embassy checked twice a day. Better not put anything in writing until I find out more, he thought. Then it came to him. He strapped on his brass balls and headed for the breakfast room.

The Nyhavn 71 Hotel provides one of the tastiest breakfast spreads in all of Copenhagen, and Sander and I vowed to take advantage of it to the very best of our abilities. After all, we were just a couple of growing boys.

Now I faced a conundrum. Last night had totally changed my life. Over time I would know just how much, but I was feet first into this whole thing and I felt the need to make sure my prince and I were on the same page.

"Are you going back for more?" I asked.

"Of course," he answered. "I have to have my calories to make back those ones I used last night."

"I think we might have spent some calories in the shower, too."

"I know we did," he smiled. "What is your plan for today?" he asked.

There's a moment that you recognize when you know you're about to jump without a bungee cord. When you decide to make the jump anyway you have only yourself to blame when things turn out exactly like you know they will. I was on the bridge and about to jump and nothing or no one could stop me if they tried.

"About that," I began. "I was wondering if you want to come with me."

"But I thought..."

"I cannot be away from you right now. I know that's selfish. I can't expect you to just take off with me. And I know that I'm not supposed to do it; I could lose my job if anyone found out," I said.

"Then do what's the best thing. I'll go to Odense, and you will not gets shit from your boss, yes?" Sander said.

"You don't get it. My mind's not on the job anymore. I'd probably do a bad job anyway, so maybe I'll just quit and go home with you."

Sander sat back in his chair and studied me with those piercing blue eyes. He dabbed his lips with the linen napkin and mindlessly knotted it while gathering his thoughts.

"Since I am here with you all I want is to stay. But I think I want you to do the right deciding about your job," he said. "I know that you are wanting this job for many month and now you are here."

He was right, of course. Everything I had done since that day in Captain Larson's office led up to this moment. God knows how much the government had already spent training me and posting me to Denmark. If it wasn't for the job and everything I had accomplished to that point I wouldn't have even met Sander. I knew I was acting like a lovestruck chick, and of course I had to follow through with my assignment. That was obvious. Besides, the game was already in play; there was an asset waiting for me to collect and deliver him or her safe and sound.

"I have an idea," I told him, "but before it will work I have to tell you something very secret and I have to know that it won't go any farther than you."

"Do you have to say that? After last night I hope you trusts me on anything." He lowered his eyes. Had I hurt his feelings?

"Sander, I have to say that. Forgive me. When I tell you, I know you'll understand."

"You maybe should not say to me what it is, then," he said. "I will see you at home when you are finish." Pushing back his chair, he dropped the napkin on the table. "I can walk to the station whit you and I will go on my train, and you will go on yours and I see you on Tuesday, yes?"

No. I'd made my decision, wrong or right, and time had come to lay it all out. Yes, I trusted him. Yes, I knew what I was about to do was a crime punishable by far more than the loss of an exciting career. But there it is.

"Sander," I said, as we walked along the Rådhuspladsen, the town square nearly opposite the railway station, "can we sit over there for a bit. I need to tell you something."

We sat on the ground opposite a little jazz band playing for tips, our view blocked by a gaggle of Japanese tourists who were mesmerized by the runs the bassist was slapping up and down the neck of her standup bass. Another gorgeous day in Copenhagen.

"I'm just going to tell you everything, and I hope you'll understand how important you are to me for me to even be doing it," I told him.

"I know that already," he protested. "You don't have to do anything because of me. Do *you* understand *that*?"

"I do. But I don't just... I can't just say good-bye in some cavern of a train station and take off while you go the other way. I'm not that strong, and so that's..."

"So then say it," he chuckled.

Dimitri bypassed the buffet table and instead made a beeline for Kolya's table. Look at the disgusting bastards, stuffing their ugly faces with as much shit fodder as they can gobble, he thought, breaking into the toothiest smile he could generate.

"The happy family is together, I see," Dimitri

gushed. "Are we headed to the zoo today?"

The children took the cue, jumping and wiggling in their chairs at Uncle Who-the-fuck's good news. This was just another day in the life for a couple of spoiled Russian brats completely oblivious to their father's role in keeping their land's political and social oppression alive and well.

"Kolya, may I trouble you for your phone?" he asked. "Mine's up in the room."

Yes, brass balls were definitely in swing this morning.

"Of course, my friend. Please!"

Phone in hand, Dimitri called the emergency number he'd committed to memory six years ago. He never had cause to use it before; now he waited while the line hummed the steady one-two ring. *Buhmmm Buhmmm — Buhmmm Buhmmm — Buhmmm Buhmmm...*

"Hello."

"Uncle Vanya! Hello! It is Dimitri calling. How are you today?"

"Good, good! And you?"

"Change of plan, Uncle. We will meet tomorrow instead, as today I have promised two lovely children that I will take them to the zoo! Unless you would care to join us..."

He glanced at Kolya for approval and received a hearty nod.

"Uncle Vanya, we would love it if you can come with us today—if you feel up to it. We could pick you up in about an hour."

"No, nephew. Not today. But thank you for the call!"

"We'll see each other tomorrow, then?"

"That is good, Dimitri. Same time. Good-bye."

"Good-bye, Uncle."

Dimitri ended the call and handed the phone back to Kolya. He took great pleasure knowing that he had just contacted the station chief of the American embassy on his rival's phone. He basically had informed his colleague that he suspected that he might have been made, and by calling him on Kolya's phone, he hoped that the FSB would never suspect that he had just warned his American handler that possible trouble was at hand. In the meantime, while the CIA in Warsaw scrambled and kicked into overdrive, Dimitri would enjoy visiting the elephants and gorillas, and gazing at the long-necked giraffes at the Warsaw Zoo.

I sat alone in the train compartment, rolling past Swedish farm land, the Øresund Bridge—the link between Denmark and Sweden—a half hour behind.

The compartment door slid open and he sat down across from me.

"There is not more fun than take a shit a hundred kilometers an hour in Sweden, I think," Sander laughed.

"I thought you fell in," I joked.

"Fell...?"

"The toilet. I thought you fell into the toilet."

He laughed again: "No, I only leave some of me in Sweden, not all of me!"

Sander stared directly at my eyes, a bemused smile growing on his face.

"So..." he said. Moments passed.

"So..." I replied.

"You are a spy like James Bond," he whispered.

"No," I grinned, "nothing like that."

"I don't understand everything about it, but I thinks maybe your job is different than making hot dogs for the travelers," he said. "I like that I can goes whit you, but I hoping there is no trouble, you know?" he added.

"We're just two guys out on a road trip," I reassured him. "What can go wrong?"

17

uddies? Lovers? Mates? Husbands? Pals? Good Friends? Friends with Benefits? What do we call it now? The world has enough descriptive language to describe two guys in love. I won't trash up this journal with words like that. This young man means more to me than anything or anyone in my entire life, as short as that's been. That means that if all goes well, I will be waking up next to my dear Sander for at least six—maybe seven— decades to come. Imagine that! I guess now is as good a time as any.

"Hey, Mr. Hansen."

"Hey to you, Mr. Bond!" he smiled.

"Got a question for you."

"Shoot, cowboy!" He told me he heard that line in an old black and white western he watched on television when he was away at summer camp in Germany back in grade school. "Don't make me wait! This town ain't big enough for us two!"

"Two of us..."

"Yes. Two of us. Outs whit it, man!"

"Well," I began, "I wondered what we should call us now that we're together."

"Call us?" he questioned. "You mean on *telefon*? I has your telefon nummer already."

"No. I mean, what are we? Together. I mean, are we married? Like, do we call ourselves lovers, or husbands?"

"Aaahhh! I see whats you are meaning!" he said. "We can be whatever we wish, you know? If we want, we can get married, too."

"Really? I mean, you're not eighteen for another year," I said. "And what about your mom and dad?"

"What about them? They will be wery happy for us, I think. And mine mother will makes a wery good wedding for us."

"No way!"

"Sure. They like you much, and they trusts me, so where is the problem?"

I was speechless. What he said floored me. I shut

my eyes for a second or two and tried to regain my bearings. The soft clickity-clack of the train at speed and the occasional whoosh of the doors between the coaches were the only sounds playing at the moment.

"Wait!" Sander bolted upright in his seat. "There is one problem I do not yet thinks about..."

"What?"

"You did not ask me to marry you."

"HA! You are so awesome!" I told him. "Shall I get down on my knees?"

"Not so bad idea I thinks, because remember what happens last time you are on your knees?" he laughed.

"Sander, will you marry me? Can we be together always, from now on?"

"I think you will never ask!" he said. "Of course, I will marry you." And then he reached for me and enveloped me in the deepest hug, his lips reaching my mouth, his tongue against mine.

The compartment door slid open, revealing an older couple in search of seats.

"Pardon the intrusion," the gray-haired, nattily dressed gentleman offered. May we join you? We just boarded at Svedala. We don't mean to interrupt."

"Of course, please sit with us," Sander said. "We

were kissing because we are both very happy today," Sander later told me. He spoke to them in Danish; they replied in Swedish.

"It looks like you were very—yes, happy is the correct expression," the wife said.

"We are happy because we will be getting married sometime soon," Sander reported. "This is my boyfriend, Johnnie. He comes from America, and we met in Odense when he came there for school," he said.

They talked and laughed together for a few minutes, and I just looked kinda stupid. That's how it is when your friend—I mean *fiancé*—speaks with the locals, talking ninety miles per hour.

"Johnnie, this is Mr. and Mrs. Dahlström. They go to Ystad like we do," Sander said. "He is pastor of a church in Helsingborg."

"Oh." The day shifted from one of elation to...*this*. "So, do we make them sick? Are we going to Hell now?" I asked, growing angry and disgusted by the whole thing. Why did these ancient bluenoses have to barge in now?

"Heavens no, lad!" the wife said in perfect English. "I think it's sweet that you boys are in love. Oh, to be your age again!" she smiled. "Pastor is not so good with English; he barely understood your boyfriend's Danish," she chuckled.

"Can you tell him that we are both very much in love. And that nobody should ever judge that it's wrong. No one can say that what we feel for one another is any less important than what he feels for you. Will you say that to him?"

"I can say that, yes. But I will tell you, it's what he already believes."

Sander dipped his head in confusion; then in English. "Frau Dahlström, I goes to the church whit my grandmother when I am little. It is where I hear that who I am does not agree with the God they talks about. Johnnie is right when he say that church say we goes to the Hell for to be who we are. And I think that is wery wrong, I'm sorry."

I couldn't have said it better myself, in fractured English or Swahili. Then the old man smiled and gazed at the rainy countryside swishing past the window. "My fellows," he began, "I cannot speak for others in my profession." (Sander gave me the running commentary in his own endearing brand of English.) "But this I will say: Our son, Kjell, will soon be fifty-six years of age. He and his man, Gunnar, will be thirty years together this year. I could not be prouder of them if I tried. So we wish you nothing but happiness, and hope that you will leave some room in your heart for God. Because someone who loves you both very much brought you two together, and I don't think it was the competition!" he laughed.

As far as religion goes, I'm definitely out on the bench. I think it's a bunch of shit. I haven't spoken with Sander about my feelings about church and the whole Jesus nonsense. But if I was ever inclined to drink the Kool-Aid and toss all science and critical thinking onto the garbage heap of reason, I'd choose this old guy as my religious confessor.

"Thank you for saying that," Sander said. "I will tell my family what you say to us. It means wery much to Johnnie and to me." The old clergyman patted Sander on the cheek and gave my shoulder a quick squeeze.

"You two boys have a good life together, keep your promises to each other, and always be there when the other one needs you, and you will do well."

Our last view of our new friends was of them rounding the corner at the end of the platform. The two men who met them at the exit were certainly Kjell and Gunnar, this based on the gleeful hugs everyone exchanged before heading off to the parking area. "There they go," Sander observed. "They was such wery nice old people."

"We'll probably never see them again, and I doubt they'll ever know just how much what they said means," I said. "Why can't more people be like them?"

"There are more than you thinks there is," Sander replied. "And today we see two of them!"

Okay, pause for some Sander Love. Nobody, and I do mean *nobody*, could feel anything but joy and happiness while being within his sphere. He just makes you feel good—about yourself, and about everything around you. I often stand back in wonder at his positive take on everything. I appreciate his curiosity; his loyalty and friendliness is unlike anything I've ever humanly experienced before.

Sander is so smart; his humor is golden—I never laugh so damned much as when I'm together with him. But above all, his kindness and compassion is unending. My grandma used to say 'They broke the mold with that one' whenever she liked someone a lot. I get what she meant.

He's always the one who says 'Hi' first—to strangers, to little kids, to old folks in the supermarket (and on trains to Ystad!), and he doesn't have a conceited bone in that very sexy body of his, either. Come on! Everybody has faults! What are Sander's? Well, I've known him for way over a year and I've seen him on an almost daily basis, and I can tell you that if he has any faults, I sure don't know what they are. How is it possible?

I think I figured it out. I think I'm dead. That's gotta be it. I actually died in a massive airplane disaster on my way to Denmark, and like Bruce Willis in that movie with the kid who sees dead people, I'm—well—*dead!* I just don't know it yet.

But I must have been an extra good soul because I'm obviously in Heaven, where upon arrival I hooked up with an angel who goes by the name Sander Hansen. If you have a better explanation I'm all ears.

Speaking of planes to Denmark... A couple days before leaving on this trip—before I knew how much my life was about to change—I remembered the very first time I ever saw this little country that I now call my home.

I had a window seat on the left side of the plane and we flew in off the North Sea, making landfall over Skagen, Aarhus, and the lush island of Fyn, where Odense lies.

It was a very pretty morning, the sky so blue, and the cotton ball clouds drifting lazily over the countryside, imprinting shadows on the land below. The houses and shops appeared almost fairytale-like, and I could see the trains and cars scurrying to their destinations. My first thought was of how spotlessly clean the towns were. You could make out the cobblestones and could clearly see the church spires, and the parks with their walking paths and ponds.

It was my second thought that I really focused on. As I gazed down from the jet that had delivered us half way around the world to this magical place, I remembered thinking that—right at that very moment—there were new friends that I would soon meet.

I wondered who they might be; what might they be doing in that instant. Would I meet someone who would eventually turn out to be the love of my life? I got the answer to that question last night.

I remember from my days aboard ship that most harbor towns are smelly, rat infested shitholes. Not so, Ystad. What a pretty seaside town it is, and the port is as clean as a Mormon porno mag. The massive ocean liner that would carry us to Poland was tied up at the pier awaiting her passengers. In a few minutes we'd be off the train and meet with the contact providing the car for the job.

"That is a big, big boat," Sander said, excited for the crossing. "Is that the one we takes?"

"Can you see the name anywhere?"

"I see it. She is called *Polonia*," he said.

"Then that's us!"

The walk from the station to the Ystad Burger King on Dammgatan took just a couple minutes. We set ourselves up with some Cokes and Whoppers and waited for the car delivery. An hour later, and we had the keys to a dark blue BMW 528i. What a car!

"Fuck me!" Sander exclaimed when he saw the gleaming beauty. "I never think I can be in love whit a German! I loves *this* German!"

"It's not a Volkswagen, that's for sure," was all I could generate. "I'm afraid to touch it."

"Not me! Open it up!" Sander demanded with a grin. "Daddy needs new set of wheels!"

When we opened the doors we were met with the most glorious of odors and reveled in the intoxication of new car smell.

"Do you know how much time in Swedish prison for grand theft auto these days?" I asked.

"I don't know, but whatever it is, it's worth it. Do

you thinks they will miss it if we not bring it back?"

"Test drive?" I winked.

"Gentlemens! Start up your motors!"

We had some time to kill before the ferry began taking cars aboard, and we had a full tank of gas. The Highway 9 loop up to Brösarp and back past Tomelilla had us by the short and curlies, both of us being the natural motor-heads that we are.

"This is fucking great!" I screamed, Dire Straits' *Romeo and Juliet* blaring on the Bang & Olufsen sound system.

"If this is what your job is like, I'm wanting to be a spy like you!" Sander laughed.

"I'm not a spy, you knucklehead!"

"Whatever! I clean a pub toilet whit my dick to have a car like this one," he laughed.

"Ewww!"

"And you wouldn't?"

"Well..."

"Exact what I thought!" Sander declared, taking off his jacket and tossing it in the backseat. "You know, Johnnie Bond, there is something I always have want to do," he continued, pulling his shirt over his head. "Do you want to know what it is?" he said, unbuttoning his pants.

"What the fuck?"

"I always want to know what it is like to take a ride in a BMW whit no clothes on my hunky bod, that's what..."

Now his pants were off. The only thing left: shoes, socks, and... "Underwear! That's everything!" He looked at me and smiled, his eyes dancing up and down the whole of my body.

"You're kidding, right?" I laughed.

"The question, Mr. Bond, is if you are wanting a blow job when you is driving the big BMW before you goes to Polen!"

Have you ever tried taking off your shirt, pants, and underwear while driving 120 kilometers an hour down a motorway in Sweden? No? Me neither. Until now!

True to his word, he lowered his head into my lap and began sucking my hard cock while playing with his own. He soon fell into the perfect rhythm for both duties, handily jacking himself off while deep-throating all the way to the base of my throbbing love monster. (Love monster? *Really*, Johnnie? This isn't a Penthouse Forum letter!) Okay, already! I just hate the word, penis! That leaves dick and cock, which I've already used very much to excess.

So anyway, the love monster was really digging Sander's mastery of Oral Suckcockery, when I looked to my left and saw a co-driver grinning ear to ear from the shotgun seat of his semi truck. What could I do? So I shrugged and returned the grin.

Just before we closed in on Ystad I felt my load getting ready to erupt.

"Sander, I'm gonna cum real soon..."

He just nodded without missing a slurp or a beat. I could tell he was building, too. His hand doubled the pace; up and down, faster and faster...

"I'm cumming! Oh, fuck, Sander!" And it released into his waiting mouth, my lover greedily swallowing every drop. Then I felt his warm cum land on my thigh and leg, the sweet smell of his seed mixing with the fantastic aroma lingering in the car's cabin.

"God damn, man, how can you be that good?!" I exclaimed as I pulled over to the side of the road so we could recover from this latest adventure. He tossed my shirt to me, I found his left shoe...

"I can tell you the secret," he said, pulling his underwear and pants over his knees.

"Please do," I said. "I really want to know."

"It's easy... It's because I love you. I know what to do because I can feel you here," he told me, placing his hand over his heart. "Because of that... Because I love you, I can do anything."

18

X*-ray machines and metal wands at the zoo entrance? You're kidding me,* Dimitri thought, as he queued up for the ticket booth. The fear of terrorism had even found its shitty way to the gates of the Warsaw Zoo.

Kolya was certainly playing it cool, though, and either his little tribe were the best troupe of actors in the world, or Katryna and the two brats—Svetlana and Nikita—were completely oblivious to the truth about why Daddy had picked Warsaw as the family's holiday destination.

If all was a 'go', he knew that his contact was already on the way to him. All he had to do was play out the clock and—at the right time—ditch this fucker who spent all his waking hours pining for the good old days of unfettered KGB mischief and Soviet oppression.

The walk from his hotel to the pickup point at the cathedral would be the trickiest part of the plot. If he could do it without detection he'd have it made. The biggest barrier, other than the possibility of additional surveillance teams besides Kolya and Company, would be the traffic cams. In this post 9/11 digital age of zero privacy, all it would take would be an FSB agent monitoring his movements from the hotel lobby to his meeting point and the jig would be up. A grab team would swoop in, and off to the Lubyanka he'd go.

The ground options were limited; taxi drivers keep records of their pickups and drop-offs, the buses have cams on board and there's still the matter of the traffic cams at each intersection, and what if the taxi driver is in on it?

He had until tomorrow to mull it all over. In the meantime he'd enjoy the animals. He might even get lucky and watch little Nikita and Svetlana fall into the lion exhibit or get squashed by an elephant. The world would fare a little better minus Kolya's spawn.

Because it was Friday, the ship—and therefore the lines for the cars waiting to drive aboard—was full to capacity. Controlled mayhem made it all the more enjoyable for me; Sander just took a post-hot sex nap. He is so adorable when he's sleeping. His nose makes these cute little flares in time with his breathing, and he smiles when he sleeps.

The passport control officers each took a line and were slowly checking every car and its occupants before letting them... *Oh, motherfuck! Passports! I have mine, but what about...*

Tap, tap, tap on the glass and the little circular hand motion—the international signal to roll the window down. Shit!

"God kväll!" said the stocky blond port policeman. "Reser du till Polen ikväll?" I'm pretty good at conversational Danish, but Swedish is Greek to me.

"Can you speak English?"

"Yes, yes of course. Are you from Britain?" I handed him my passport and he gave it the once-over. "Oh, American!" he smiled. "Your Obama is a good guy. Much better than the one who came before," he stated emphatically.

"I voted for him. Obama, I mean... Not the guy before."

"Smart man! So who is sleeping beauty over there?" he kidded.

"Sander, wake up," I said, giving his shoulder a little tug. He woke with a start and was confused by the face leaning into the car.

"It's the passport man; he needs to see your passport." Well, this was it... We were either going to Poland, or not. The next few seconds would tell the tale.

"En sekund," Sander yawned. "Det är i min ryggsäck." And he grabbed his backpack from the backseat and produced the finest specimen of a Danish passport I had ever seen. "Varsågod," he politely added as he handed it to the guy. The man glanced at it for about a third of a second, and he was on to the next vehicle. Sander stuffed it into his pocket and promptly went back to sleep. We was Poland bound, yee haw! It took me half an hour to slow down my ticker, which had gone into crap-yer-pants overdrive when I thought Sander was without his passport.

"Dude, sleep when your dead!"

"I needs my beauty sleeping," he announced, eyes closed to the frenetic activity surrounding our luxurious ride.

"That's the one thing in this world that you do

not need," I said. "You're already too beautiful."

"Ahh, chucks."

"What?"

"I say, ahh...chucks. That's meaning that you embarrass me whit your nice words. Now I goes to sleep more, tak!"

"It's shucks... You mean to say shucks."

"I means to *sleep*, Mr. Allen. So fuck off."

I'm in a $60,000 car sitting next to the most awesome human being that I know, waiting to board an ocean liner sailing to another land, so that I can do a job that way overpays me, and perhaps have a tiny hand in keeping the machinations of global politics moving forward on behalf of the land of the free and the home of the brave. Damn! I think I'll take a nap!

At sea. Our cabin is on the starboard side just one deck below the nightclub. It's just past midnight. We're two hours out of Ysted and we're lying on our backs staring at the ceiling and listening to the muted *thump thump thump thump thumping* of the euro disco playing overhead.

"I think it's ABBA," Sander said.

"What makes you think that?"

"The beat goes whit the Mama Mia song. Listen..."

We started humming along together. Then the giggles started.

"You're right," I told him. "You some kind of disco queen?"

"Nah! You can fit any dance song to those beats. Just like whit hip-hop."

The view from the oversize window revealed the twinkling lights of ships passing in the night. We spooned there for the longest, peaceful time watching the moon become enveloped in the overcast.

"Johnnie, can you say exact what we do in Polen when we are there?" Sander asked.

"Well, there's a guy we have to get to where he needs to go. We're like a very expensive Taxi."

"A taxi for spies!" he chuckled. "We should drive like taxis in Paris do."

"How do they drive there?" I asked.

"They don't. They aim."

He leaned up on his elbow and took a swig from a Coke on the end table. "Want some?"

"Sure..."

"How do we know how to find this man?"

"We don't," I explained. "The asset finds us. With

a kind of code that everybody knows."

"Ass...what?"

"Asset. It's a fancy way to say spy."

"How come there's so many way to say things on English?" Sander wondered. "In Danish one thing mean one thing only. Not fifty words for one thing."

"If Danish is so easy, how come it's so hard to learn?" I countered. "Why'd you guys make the words so hard to say?"

"Not hard for me. There is three years old childs that talk just fine. I learn when I am little, and it's easy for me. Must be you."

"I think you guys just make it up as you go along," I joked. "Nobody can make those Danish sounds you make and be serious."

"Sutte min pik!"

"What's that mean?"

"Won't you like to know!" he grinned.

"What's it mean?"

"Say it and I tell you," he said.

"Say it again, then..."

"Okay," he said, "say after me... Sutte min pik!"

"Sutte... min *pik*?"

"Of course I will, since you say in Danish so perfect..." And then he turned around and dove un-under the eiderdown cover and took my cock into

211

his mouth, at first just quickly moving his tongue around the head. As it grew he sucked harder and pumped the base of that dick with his lips, quickly pulling back up and licking to the head again.

Even in sex his humor won over. The nightclub was really going strong. The music louder. The laughter of the crowd coming in little bursts. Another dance song began to play and Sander started sucking to the beat. I started laughing and he poked his face out from under the covers and said, "I am slave to the rhythm."

I totally lost it. Then he went back to work and I started to cross over to Sex Nirvana. I closed my eyes and marked the moment. I always want to remember this day, this wonderful time spent with the love of my life.

As he kept the great head going he surprised me with some fingering action as he pushed two, then three fingers into my relaxed asshole. By then he also incorporated the occasional oral foray to my nutsack, carefully licking and sucking my balls while pushing farther into my ass. Then his middle finger hit the spot. He knew right where to go, and the feeling intensified three-fold.

"Oh, God, Sander. Right there, man... It's incredible!"

We'd been at it for about twenty minutes and I felt bad that I was the only one enjoying the pleasure.

"What can I do for you?" I sighed in absolute pleasure. "Please, let me love you; what would you like me to do?"

"Can we kiss? I wery much wants to kiss and hold you for some time, okay?" he said. I scooted down the bed and met him with my trembling mouth. I felt his tongue explore me, and was taken by his soft caresses and his warm, sweet breath.

"I loves you so wery much," Sander said.

"I love you more."

"I don't think is possible," he said as he lightly blew against my neck, giving little kisses down to my shoulder.

I found his rock hard cock and began slowly and lightly stroking it, retracting his foreskin, making sure it would slide over his head, and then gently squeezed his shaft at the end of each downward stroke. His breathing intensified and I went down on him, filling my mouth with his perfect cock.

He was really into it, massaging my hair and rubbing my shoulders as I picked up the pace even more.

"Johnnie, please fuck me, okay?" he begged in passion. "I wants to feel you in me, please, Johnnie..."

"Sure," I said. "What way do you like it best?"

"Any way that you wants to do it. I just want to feel you deep inside there, okay?"

I repositioned as he rolled onto his belly. He laid himself onto a pillow and opened his legs in anticipation. I rubbed his butt cheeks and brushed the tip of my now throbbing cock near his hole. He instinctively brought his right leg closer to his midriff, which naturally parted his sweet, darling ass.

Mounting him now, he guided my dick right where it needed to be and waited for me to push ever so gently inside of him. He felt so warm, and I was really afraid that I might cum before I even started the main event because he just felt so damned good.

"That is so wonderful, Johnnie. You feel so good," he said.

"You, too!" And I slowly moved my hips left to right; right to left. He spun totally out of control.

"It's fantastisk!" he said. "I don't know about that. How do you do this?"

"It's easy. I just love you, right? You're very easy to love and the rest of me knows just what to do." Then I shifted from left to right, to up and down. That's when he began to moan in ecstasy. So now was the moment.

I pushed deeper inside him, held that position, and then slowly pulled back, my head just centimeters from pulling out. But then another slow thrust inward would make him moan again, and when it was as far inside as it could be, I pulled back a little faster.

Soon we were in sync, and the regular rhythm of my hot cock plowing in and out, in and out, threatened to send him spinning. Then he began to push his ass back against my inward thrusts, proving that he was as versatile as anyone could imagine a sexy young guy could be.

"Faster, Johnnie. Please, I want as fast and deep as you can do!" he whispered, as we both began to feel the peak of our excitement for each other.

"Does it feel good?" I asked.

"God, yes! Please, love me and make me cum! Make me cum, Johnnie!"

"I'm gonna make you cum. I want your cum all over me. Let me feel your cum, Sander!"

"Fuck me harder! Harder, Johnnie! Oooo... Ah, fuck, it's so good!"

I reached under him and took his cock into my right hand, jacking it with love and fury. I felt his ass tense against my cock. He was building to eruption, and I felt the pressure of my own pending explosion into my love's waiting ass.

"I'm gonna cum, Johnnie. I can feel it now!"

"Me too! I'm... I'm... Cum-cumming now, oh God!"

My dick pushed the hottest cumload into Sander, and at that instant, without warning, I felt my hand fill with his hot seed. We both moaned in such ecstasy that we would have bet they could have heard us up in the disco.

It took a couple of minutes for us to come back down to earth, and as I rolled off of him and onto my back, he laid his head on my chest.

"Did I tell you that I love you, Johnnie?"

"Say it again."

"I love you, Johnnie."

"I love you, Sander."

Our ship sailed on, the vibration of the engines muted by our beating hearts, our love beckoning us to dream. This was our time. Goodnight, Sander. Sleep well.

19

The *M/F Polonia* tied up at the dock in Świnoujście, Poland, on time to the minute. Within ten minutes of our arrival we drove the BMW off of the ship and onto Polish soil; the game was afoot. The mission countdown had started.

"Where do we go now?" Sander wondered. "This day is wery excitements I think."

"I have to check in with the bosses over here first, and then we'll know just what we have to do."

The drive from the port to the center of Warsaw would take about seven, maybe eight hours with stops for gas and grub. In no time we joined the S3 motorway and we settled in for the trip. I was happy because it would give us plenty of time to talk.

"Your turn to be the DJ," I said.

"I like what we was playing before. I know, how about Mark Knopfler, or maybe even Brooooooce..."

"Springsteen it is! But you have to hook the phone in and get it going."

"I can do that, Johnnie Bond!" Sander smiled, and got the tunes up. "I start with the best one." The opening harmonica strains of *The River* led into the American rustbelt tale of young people very much in love who were in the first act of their lives together. Much like the two in this car who were feeling the deepest soul stirrings that only true love brings.

"Will you laugh if I tell you that this song always makes me cry?" I confessed.

"Me too."

"Why does it make *you* cry?"

"Well," Sander began, "my mother say that peoples are the same everywhere. I think she is right, because when I hearing this song it tell a story of two who are doing best they can do with what they have."

"Do you know they are from a place in America where people are poor, and the jobs are gone?" I said.

"I think why I cry is because they still has hope and will try because they loving each other so wery much," he said. "If I am crying, it's not for being sad;

it is because I understand how they feels when only what they want is to be happy together, yes? That is why I cry sometime when I hears this one, and *My Hometown.* This is why I'm liking Bruce Springsteen, I guess."

This is an example of the heart I am connected to. As if I needed another reason to love him.

"Wow, are there any more incredible things that I don't know about you? You know, I just fell in love with you all over again," I said.

"Do you knows the time?" he asked.

"It's right there on the dashboard, banana head."

"Oh... I sees a minute have passed by."

"Okay... What's your point?"

"It's another minute that I fall in love whit you once more," he said.

What do I say to that? How can I feel any better about the day, about my life, about everything that's happened in the last year? My seminal year.

"There—another minute goes," he continued. "Sander falls for Johnnie once again, and loves him even better than the last minute before that one."

"Wow... Just... Wow."

"Do you understands now?" he said.

"I think I do."

Dimitri Petrenko was packed and ready to go. He was given the green light by the Warsaw CIA Station Chief to continue with the objective, and assured him that a watch team would be nearby in case of any FSB monkey business. He would ditch the crap family in the middle of dinner, and then duck out to a place he'd scoped the day before when returning from the zoo outing. Kolya might believe that he's all that and a bowl of borscht, but when it came to tradecraft nobody beat Dimitri Petrenko. Now it was time to chill out and wait for the right time. This he could do.

"Hey, Sandy—that's your new nickname, I hope you like it—can I ask you something?"

"Always, Johnnie Bond."

"What's your family like? I mean, you know I've met them, and all... I just wonder what it was like for you growing up with them," I said.

"Ah, so you wants to knows more about your in-laws, yes?"

"Well... Yes."

"There is Niels, my father; mine mother, who you know is called Magda; my big sister who is Ingrid and who have a crush on you, but that's her bad luck; and my smaller brother, Jannik, who think I am Luke Skywalker."

"Why?"

"He think I can do anything. Mother say to me I am his helten...uh, I think is hero the word?"

"Hero, yep. Well, I know what he sees in you," I told him. "Smart kid. How old is he?"

"He is nine years. Really good whit football. I think he might be something there someday. Maybe we goes to a football match to see him. We can make a barbecue party for us, for the family, you see? And then we can watch Jannik and his team kick some butts."

"Uhmm... About that, what will your family think? I mean, what are we telling them really?"

"That we is together, that you make the family bigger because you are my man," he said.

"Is it really that easy? Are they gonna be okay with...*us*?"

"Why not?" He seemed genuinely confused by my question. "You are the person that I love. We will be together for all time, so of course I tell them everything about us so they can enjoy to love you, too."

"Do they know that you're..."

"...That I like boys, not girls? Yes, of course they know. You are being joker now, right?"

"No, I'm serious... When did you tell them? *How* did you tell them?" I asked.

He shifted in his seat, turning to me and laying his head on my shoulder. "Johnnie, sometimes I don't know what I do whit you. But I tell you it all since you ask..."

"I really do want to know," I said.

"Okay, well, of course I always know that I likes mostly boys. When I am young I sometimes look at a girl, and I have a crutch on my teacher, but not so much," he began.

"Crutch? You mean crush?"

"When you like somebody a lot and wants to be their boyfriend or girlfriend, yes? That is crush?"

"Yeah... Go on..."

"Well, I falls for a boy called Anders who I know from nursery school, and one time we have sex. He is first guy I have sex whit. It was four years ago, maybe? So he move away to Copenhagen and I am wery sad and my mother ask why I am so sad; I even cry about it and she catch me crying. So I tell her that I love Anders and he move away, yes?"

"Yeah?"

"And so she gives me hug and kiss and say that she understand everything. But that every boy have a crutch—crush, I mean—on another boy sometimes but maybe I will like girls someday, too."

"So what happened?"

"What happen is I don't like girls for except friends, and I am here whit you!" he smiled.

"No, I mean, what happened after Anders?"

"When I am in klasse nine I meet a boy called Torben, and we falls for each other and so I bring him to my house for the weekend and we are at the table when my mother bakes some bread, yes? And we tell her."

"What did you say?"

"I say, *'Mor, jeg er bøsse'*—that means 'Mama, I am gay'. And I tell her so is Torben, and we are together."

"And that was it?" I asked.

"Yes. And shortly after my sister bring Jannik home from football—he was wery little then—and she tell my sister. In about a week, whole family knows; grandmother, grandfather, my two uncles and my aunt; my cousins. Then, when school start again, Torben and me tell our mates at school, so that's the big story. Pretty boring story."

"You're kidding, right?"

"No, that's what happen..."

"...No! I mean about the story being boring. That story is not boring!"

Sander shrugged and once again shot me an incredulous look; like, *what's the big deal?* I'll tell you the big deal: There is no way I could have ever done what he did with my family. They would have kicked me out and totally disowned me.

"Can I ask you another thing?"

He grinned and chuckled a bit as he fiddled with the music. The drawn, intense but gentle guitar plucks of Mark Knopfler's *Local Hero* became the new score to our life movie that was unwinding at a hundred and twenty kilometers per hour down the S-3.

"Anything," Sander said.

"What does your family think that we are... I mean, does your mom think that you and I are..."

"No, not yet," he said. "None of us thought you are even gay, which make the whole last year living in Hell for me."

"Me too," I quickly added.

"But I tell my mother and my grandfather that I wish that you and me can be together, but they say that it can only happen if you was like me. And even my sister says no way are you like me. But, after Happy Endings Sleepover and everything after that, she is wrong."

"Yes, I agreed, "she is very wrong. And I am very happy for that."

He sat back up and took my hand, giving it a little squeeze as we both contemplated this magnificent change in our lives. The motorway seemed never ending, the horizon always providing a few more kilometers of roadway as the cows by the side of the road grazed upon limitless pastures, contentedly ignoring the passing motorists and the noonday sun.

Late lunch. We're at a rest stop complex that sells gasoline, diesel, rooms by the hour, and the worst food I've ever smelled. It was egregious. Sander saved the day when he suggested that we just make our own sandwiches with ingredients bought at the little food market inside the gas station. It was fun! We loaded up on everything we needed, paid four times what it was worth, bought some sodas and tossed them into the—get this—built in refrigerator in the back seat center console. Oh, hail the Bavarian

Motor Works!

A full tank of gas later and we were back on the highway. More cows. Sun getting lower in the western sky. Sander making us sandwiches as the GPS ticked down the miles—er, *kilometers.*

"What was it like for you to grow up in Denmark?" I asked him, resuming our little heart to heart.

"Wery nice. My family are wery close, you know. Ingrid and Jannik is my best friends. My mother and father are so kind to us, and they is always works so hard for us. You know, it is a good life." Sander handed me a sandwich. "And now it is even better."

"I can't believe that they just let you go on a trip like this."

"Why not? I am not a child any more, and I never gives them a reason so they don't trust me," he said. "One time the summer before I'm meeting you me and Jannik goes to Norway for two weeks. So I think if they can trusting me whit my eight years old brother, this is nothing."

"They sound awesome," I said. "And soon they'll be my family, too."

"No, not soon," he said. "Now. We are your family now."

I became so overwhelmed by what he said that my breathing turned shallow. I hadn't considered the fact that not only had I merged my life with this amazing young man; I now had a new brother and sister, and what sounded like the best parents anybody ever had.

"How will you tell them? About us, I mean..."

"I show you." And he unplugged his phone from the car stereo and pressed the keypad. Before I could process exactly what he was doing, I heard...

"Mama, it is your favorite kid! I speaking English so Johnnie can hear, too, okay?"

He flipped on the hands-free and I heard her respond, *Yes, yes, of course, Hi, Johnnie;* all the words spoken in a very Danish rhythm. It's a kick to hear Danes speak English. Everything is said in such a laidback way.

"How are you boys today?"

"We have it good, Mama. We have news for you, too. Do you care to hear it?" Sander asked.

"Yes, yes, of course, what's the news?"

"Johnnie and me are together."

"Yes, I know that. You are in Copenhagen, yes?"

"No. I mean, yes, we went to Copenhagen; what I mean is, we are together."

"Ahhh!" She hit on what he was saying. "You are

really together. You are boyfriends, then." she said.

"Yes. Well, more than that, I think. Mama, Johnnie is the one, you know?" Sander said with the biggest smile. "Me and him are forever."

"Congratulations! I am happy for you both. *Til lykke*, Johnnie! You have a wonderful man, I can tell you."

"Tak, mor!" Sander said.

"Thank you—*tak!*—Mrs. Hansen. I love your son very much."

"I know you do. And Sander loves you. This we have known for a while now," she said. "And please call me Magda. My husband is Niels."

"I will."

"Or you can just say mama or pop, like the kids do," she said.

"I will, I promise."

"This is very good news, Pokey. Everyone will be so happy for you. Well, maybe not Ingrid," she chuckled.

"I know," Sander said. "I already say to Johnnie why that is, but I get even whit her now for when she bring Mads to the house! HA!"

"When do you come back from Copenhagen, boys?"

"Oh, yes," Sander began. "We will be back on

Tuesday, but right now we are in Polen and we off to Belgien tomorrow."

"Such a surprise! Is it your honeymoon trip?" she laughed. "Because I can think of better places than those!"

"No, no..." Sander replied. "It is for Johnnie's work. He just lets me comes, so I am sitting shotgun!"

"Okay, well be safe and see you at home on Tuesday, then. Bye-bye!" And he ended the call.

"And that, dear Johnnie, is how us Hansens do it. Live and learn, my boy! Live. And. *Learn*."

"Did I ever tell you that I think you're amazing... *Pokey?*"

"Yes, yes... Haves your fun!"

"So, Pokey, how come she calls you Pokey... *Pokey?*" I teased.

"Yes, well, that is a story, isn't it..."

"I'm waiting."

"We save the story for our year twenty-five anniversary, yes?"

"No."

"Ahhh..."

"Let's hear it!"

"When I am a wery little boy I never say Hey You, or Hello, I am down here, or such. Instead I go behind everybody and poke, poke, poke to get you to notice me, so you can ask what I want, see?" Sander explained.

"Poke means the same in Danish?"

"Well, no, in Danish it mean a little animal. So I guess my mother mean it like English, but also it means for a cute baby deer, or bear, or maybe even a elephant."

"So what if I say I want to poke you?"

"Then I say... *okay.* And I guess I bend over?" he laughed. "But maybe *I* want to poke *you!*"

"Just so it's like that first time."

"I am like sex machine whit you, yes? That never happens before. You bring something out of me when we are together, you know?" he said.

"Same here. I'm afraid that you are my drug!"

"I can't quit you!" he joked. "Do you likes my big humor? See, I'm your drug, can't quit... But then there is that cowboy gay movie where the man say *I can't quit you!* Get it?"

"I get it!"

"Danish humor is best, I think. I am like Danish George Carlin."

"Ha! Ha!" I chuckled sarcastically.

"You see? The laughing never stop here at the Sander Comedy Club."

Like with so many European cities, the transition from open motorway to downtown city streets is sudden and unexpected. Warsaw is no different. One minute you're tooling along like a crack express train, the next you see the lanes thinning down and up comes a traffic light.

We had a couple of hours to kill before the meet-up, so we made for a quiet side street about a mile from the action area and parked in front of a Doner Kebabs shop. The pleasant aromas of lamb roasting on the revolving skewer, and the fresh pita bread baking in the stone oven would lure us in soon enough. Right then I had to check in and report our successful arrival.

The phone picked up on the second ring.

"Echo sierra whisky, duty officer, how may I assist you?" was the greeting.

"Mango transport primary, report code five-five-kilo-oscar-charlie-hotel-sierra. End report.

"Mango transport primary, message received. Thank you. Good day, sir." And the call was ended.

Sander was looking at me in a way that said he was very impressed. Okay, I'm not above a little preening for the one I love. I have to admit that I did feel pretty cool doing the check-in protocol in front of him. So kill me.

"Wow! You really are like James Bond. See, I tell you before, you are sexy spy who want his cola shaking not stirring," Sander smiled. "So this is why I say you are Johnnie Bond."

"Whatever you say, Sandy Pokey."

"What all that means, anyways? And who is Oscar and Charlie? Must I be worry you cheat on me?"

"I'll tell you who they are, when you tell me about this Mads character," I teased.

"Oh, Mads..." he said dismissively.

"Yes, *Mads*..."

"Well, Mads is Ingrid's boyfriend and after Torben and me are no more, of course I am on lookout for somebody I might be whit. So Ingrid bring Mads to our house and, I tell you, he is wery handsome. He work in the magazines and on television as a model. So naturally..."

"Your sister is dating a model?"

"Yes. And every time he comes to the house or I am seeing him in a commercial I get frustrates because I know he is fucking Ingrid and not me. And the bad thing the most is that we can hear them when they does it in Ingrid's room."

"Your mom and dad can hear their daughter fucking in her room?"

"Everybody hears. Even Jannik! So you see, now I am whit you I get mine on Ingrid. Rewenge for all of those porno dates of Mads and Ingrid next to my bedroom wall," Sander laughed.

"Is she still with him?" I asked.

"No. They finish about six month ago. He make her get a bad disease down there, and so she have to go to the doctor and get fixed. But now she know that he was going whit other girls so she kick him to the curb."

"Wow. That sucks. What a way to find out you're getting cheated on."

"Exact," he said. "So a couple month later she's asking me everything about you. And of course I think that you are not like me, but I make excuse about you to her all the time," he said.

"Excuses?"

"Yes. She ask me your phone number and I say I forget. Or she ask if you see anyone and I say that you have a girl and you be married to her soon. Then she ask if you like to see a play because she have a extra ticket, but I know that she really buy the ticket for just you. So I tell her that you are in Germany on the time the play is at the theater. That kind of thing."

"I'm glad I wasn't interested in her. Man, with you around there's no chance."

"Exact! As it should be. Because Johnnie Bond is just for me and only me. So who is Oscar and Charlie?" he demanded.

"It's part of the nautical alphabet; it's how you say the letter 'o' and the letter 'c' when you are on the radio or on the phone and you have to be understood," I explained.

"Well, I don't understand that, I think."

"Okay... On the radio if I say the letter 't', maybe the one on the other end might think I said 'c' or 'p'. So each letter has a name. Like 'a' is alpha, 'b' is bravo, 'c' is charlie, and all the way up to 'z'.

"I get it! That's pretty cool. So what about 'æ', 'ø', and 'å'?" he asked.

"Don't have any. See, more proof that Danish is a crazy language."

"How do you say Fuck You in English?"

20

Orders of Polish-style appetizers were arriving at the table, and the room was electric with the excitement of happy diners, the room full to capacity.

"I think the food and service here is wonderful, don't you agree, Dimitri Nikolayevich?" said Kolya expansively. He could never stop holding court no matter the situation. It was part and parcel to his extreme arrogance. Dimitri was banking on that arrogance tonight. It was the key to the success of his mission. Dimitri believed that Kolya in his typical fashion could never conceive of anything less than total domination of the situation.

"This meal is fantastic!" Dimitri emphasized. "And the company is wonderful! What a glorious holiday this has certainly become," Dimitri added.

"What will you do tomorrow?" little Svetlana inquired.

"I will see my Uncle Vanya," he replied. "I have missed him for many years and tomorrow we will reunite! The first time since I was at the university with your papa."

"Are you old like Papa?" Nikita asked, much to everyone's surprise.

"Nikita Kolyaovich!" Katryna scolded. "Your manners! Dimitri is our guest!"

Not for long, Dimitri thought. In twenty minutes, just before dessert is delivered, I will be in a car bound for no place you know of, and will completely fuck up a moronic country's plan to derail the Americans' Iranian peace plan. Stick *that* in your Putin and suck it!

"She is just being honest, Katryna," Dimitri laughed. "Speaking for myself and for your dear husband, we are both crusted old horses not long from the glue factory!"

"My friend, I believe you are right," Kolya agreed with a paternal pat on Dimitri's back. "Why, just the other day Dimitri was telling me of those little blue pills he takes at bedtime!"

"Much like yours?" Katryna added with a hearty laugh. "Thank my lucky stars for the little blue pills!"

"Do you see how she treats me?" Kolya joked.

"Keep it up, Katryna! He deserves it!" Dimitri said. "Kolya, my friend, do you know of a men's room close by? I don't wish to go all the way back to my room."

"Yes. See that door right over there?"

"Ah, yes! Back in a moment." Dimitri pushed back from the table. "Don't you eat my dessert, you two! Your Uncle Dimi comes back shortly and I expect to see my tasty cake, yes?" he smiled.

The tradecraft kicked in the moment he locked the door behind him. The clock had started.

His disguise was hidden behind a waste paper container in the corner opposite the urinal trough. First the mustache, then the wig. A little red blush to flush out the cheeks. Change of trousers. Change of jacket after shirt is discarded in favor of a dark blue Warsaw University sweat shirt. So far sixty seconds gone. Stuff all remainders into the toilet tanks. Ten more seconds gone. Open pre-unlocked service closet which has an escaped-sized window over the kitchen services dock. Lock door from inside; bolster with a mop handle. Stand on overturned mop bucket and boost up and over the windowsill. The secure feeling of dropping onto the loading dock, free of the dining room and Kolya of the FSB. A bolt into the night, down alleyways and walking streets. A very successful getaway, indeed. Total time, one hundred twenty-four seconds.

"God, this tastes good!" I said, stuffing the last bite of a lamb and lettuce kebab into my mouth. "And the French fries are effing awesome, too!"

"Dang!" Sander exclaimed. "What a good food place. We shall come here again sometime, I think."

"Do you want a soda?" I asked, reaching for a Coke from the mini-fridge. "Nice and cold!"

"Sure. I can love one."

I looked at the clock on the dash; twenty minutes and we'd drive to the cathedral and get out of Dodge. We would be at the safe house at the old black site in about three hours. After a nap and a shower, it would be off to Belgium and a successful asset delivery. Job well done!

"So you know, you're not really supposed to be here," I said. "So listen carefully because this is what we'll have to do..."

21

Dimitri got to the pickup zone eight minutes after dropping onto the loading dock. He wasn't seen; in fact, there was a very good chance that Kolya still didn't suspect a thing. He maybe had another five or ten minutes before the alarm would be raised. Another five to get the dinner check signed, and have Katryna wrangle the brats back to the room. Add another five minutes to rally the FSB troops. That would mean a ten or twelve minute window of concern before the meet was scheduled. But he would only be concerned if he felt that the FSB thugs knew precisely where he was waiting. And how could they know that? Impossible. Not even they were that good, he thought.

"Okay, Sandy boy, let's roll!" I said, betraying the excitement I felt. "I can't believe this day has finally come!"

I fired up the BMW and threw it into drive, having no trouble pulling into traffic on that weekend evening.

"I can't believing that I am here whit you, too. It like a dream, I think," Sander said. I had rehearsed this part of the trip in my mind so often that everything around us felt familiar. Other than a tradesman's van that cut us off near the roundabout, the short drive was very uneventful and mundane.

"Look! That man have got his driving license in a Coke machine!" Sander hissed. "Don't he knows that Johnnie Bond is at work to save democratic?"

"Democracy!" I laughed. "And there are bad drivers everywhere."

"Just so he don't scratch our limo," he said in mock anger.

There it was... The street sign announced the name of the road that I had been anticipating since receiving the details of the assignment. I passed it by because this portion of the street was a one-way that led into the main ring road, so I would follow the corresponding one-way in the opposite direction and in a block I would be able to hang a right which would point us directly to the steps of the cathedral. Just like google earth promised, we landed opposite the alley where I'd planned to have the car hold while I made contact.

"Okay, my Viking amigo, we've arrived. You know what to do." I popped the trunk and Sander left the car, backpack in hand, and climbed in. He pulled the lid shut and curled up in the spacious cargo hold.

I tossed extra soda cans and lunch garbage into a bin by the alley and quickly crossed the road at the T-junction. The lights glowed low at the open church door reminding me of what it must have looked like in hundreds of years past. When I reached the entrance I could see why the lighting was so dim. The foyer and the nave and altar were awash in candlelight. The pale, yellowish flickering mixed with the aroma of lingering incense. Every sound was magnified, the echoes of my own footsteps on the stone paved floor met with the scattering of the pigeons resting on the oaken beams. Their disturbed screeches adding to the cacophony.

As instructed, I sat at the aisle end of a scrolled wooden pew, row fifteen, left side, and waited.

Within moments the metronomic clicking of shoes making contact in the cavernous sanctuary exchanged audio places with the birds. Per protocol the walker passed by and paused at the altar. He sat down mid pew, first row center, for precisely two minutes, then stood and made his way back down the center aisle..

"Excuse me," I asked him when he approached my row, "do you happen to know if there are any good shows in town?"

"I'm not from here; look in the Warsaw newspaper, *FAKT*," he replied

"But we're not in Warsaw."

"And we never will be again."

"Follow me," I prompted him. "Let me have your bag."

Down the steps and across the street. At the corner I triggered the door locks. then reaching the car tossed his bag on the back seat.

"You can take the front if you like," I said. "Well be stopping at a safe house in a couple hours to get a shower and some sleep. We're also picking up an assistant there who will ride the rest of the way with us."

We were in traffic now, bound for the main artery that would get us to the motorway and safely out of Warsaw.

"I am Petrenko," he said, extending his hand. "I am so relieved that you are here. Things don't always go as planned," he said. "We're off to a good start."

"Yes we are."

"Tell me... I'm sorry, your name, please?"

"John. Name's John."

"Yes, John... Tell me, is there food available at the safe house?"

"That I don't know. Would you like for me to stop and pick up something we can take with us? I imagine you're hungry," I said.

"Yes, that will be very appreciated. Anything will do."

Just before reaching the motorway I caught a sign for a Kentucky Fried Chicken stand and asked if that would do. Perfect, he said, and I dived into the tiny parking stall across the road from the shop.

"I'll just be a few minutes," I told him. "Anything you would like in particular?"

"Some fried chicken and perhaps some kind of salad dish, or vegetables. And coffee if they have any. Thank you."

I like movies, as you probably have guessed by now. One of my favorite things to do is go to the cinema with Johnnie, and then go for pizza or something afterwards.

I think one of the funniest things in a lot of comedy films is when somebody gets stuffed into the boot of a car. Well, here I am! Just like in the movies! I remember watching the Olsen Band movies on TV on Saturday nights with my family. In those films somebody always winds up in the boot.

Now it's like I'm in a spy movie with Johnnie. I'm in here so the guy that we picked up wouldn't think that anything's out of the ordinary. In case maybe he was told that only Johnnie would be picking him up and driving him to Belgium.

I heard them talking in the car. The guy's hungry so Johnnie stopped at a chicken restaurant to get him something to eat while we drive. When we get to wherever we're going, Johnnie said that he would tell the guy that I'm part of the rest of the trip. We'll get the guy to the boat, and then Johnnie and me will take a nice drive back to Denmark together. We might even stay the night at the German-Denmark border where they have a hotel next to all of the duty free shops. I don't know what we'd buy there, but it's something different to do.

The guy that we picked up at the big church is having trouble figuring out how to plug his phone into the great BMW. I wish I could help him. It must be frustrating. But it wouldn't do for me to pop into the back seat from the boot. He'd probably get a heart attack.

Oh! There he is... He figured out how to make his phone work.

Johnnie said it would take about three hours to get to the safe house. I took a pee before we left the kebab shop. But funny thing, I could pee like a waterfall and not have to go again for the rest of the day. But when you're stuck someplace where you can't get to a toilet... Is it me, or do you find that you have to go really bad in such a case? I hope that it won't hit me when we're driving. There's a couple of empty water jugs back here, but I'd have to pee laying on my side. If I was German I could get off by pissing on myself. It'd be a real treat! Thank the Lord I'm not German. Well, I'll just think dry happy thoughts.

The guy keeps trying to make a phone call but he can't get through. He should just send a text. Wait, looks like his phone wants to cooperate. Hurry up, Johnnie! I might have to pee...

"Sorry, they took forever in there," I said as I passed Petrenko's dinner to him. "I've got some drinks in the fridge behind you if you want something more than coffee. I can't guarantee how good it is, but it's hot."

"Thank you, John."

"My pleasure. Now let's get this trip started, whaddya say?"

"Excellent, my friend. I've got a long way to go."

Within minutes we were on the motorway bound for our respite at the safe house. But as excited as I was to be shepherding this asset to his destination, what I really wanted was to have Sander sitting beside me. I was upset that he was riding in the trunk despite his good humor about it. Just another story for us to remember when we're old together, I guess.

Three hours out of Warsaw and we were at the gates of the old black site in Stare Kiejkuty. There a time when this was one of the most secret places on earth. Now it was just another CIA way station. In a way it was the kind of open secret that says *fuck you,*

rest of the world. It's obvious that the FSB and every other intelligence service around the globe knows about the joint. But it was still secure enough for the purpose at hand, and I had done an awful lot of driving so I was definitely ready to crash on a couch.

Once I got the package situated in his room in the smaller house, I pulled the car around the back near the lake trail so it would be out of site for the immediate future.

"Knock knock... Anybody home?"

"Hurry!" Sander muttered through the trunk lid. A quick click and the trunk popped open revealing a very rummy looking Dane.

"How'd you do?"

"We have to talk private. Is wery much I should talk whit you but first I must pee," Sander said. "Wait here."

He bee-lined for a hedge and pissed like a race horse that just ran the Kentucky Derby. His face was drawn and he appeared troubled when he returned from relieving himself.

"We gots troubles, Johnnie, and it's wery bad," Sander began. "Where can we talk where there's nobody to hear?"

"You're scaring me. What happened?"

"In the car. And drive a little bit where nobody

can see or hear what I say. Do it fast as can be."

We parked about a quarter of the way around the little lake and sat quietly for a moment to make sure we were alone.

"Johnnie, I don't know what to do... You will know best, I think, but the man we are driving is not the one you were to get in Warsaw."

"What the..."

"He is a bad man. I hear him on the phone when you are in the food place. He call a place and say some of those words for letters—you know, those alphabet words. And then he say that his men get the one you are to drive and he promise he will stop... er... I forget exact what he say, but he is not the man!"

"Do you know who he called?"

"No. But he speak in English and he keep saying the name of a fruit. Ahhh... I can't remember. Maybe apple or... *Shit!*" he said, punching his forehead in frustration.

"Was it mango he said?"

"Yes! He say mango is finish. He will make sure, and then he say that you have no thoughts that he is the wrong man. He say that the man they steal will not like winter in Murmansk. That is place in..."

"Yes, Russia, I know. My God, if you weren't in the trunk there's no way we would have known...

Fuck, I'm glad you came," I sighed. "Do you realize..."

"Yes, but what now? Shall we call someone? Maybe police, or something? They kidnaps the man we are meant to drive to Belgien."

"Yeah. We just have to think this through. We won't have a second chance if we get it wrong."

"Shall we still drive tomorrow? What if he is a killer or we gets kidnapping, just like the first man?"

"For now, let's go to the house. We're in a different cottage than whoever the guy is. We'll park the car by the carriage house like we're ready to leave in the morning, and then just play it cool until I can figure something out," I said. "The main thing is if either of us come into contact with him we have to..."

"Contact? Like hitting him?"

"No, I mean if you or I see him, or if he asks one of us for something, we gotta act like there is nothing wrong. Absolutely *nothing* is wrong, yeah?"

"Yes, of course. Who do he think I am?"

"I told him that you would be riding with us from here to Antwerp, so he won't be surprised when he sees you tomorrow. No worries there, I think."

"I don't want him to know my name. What shall I do, Johnnie?" Sander asked with concern.

"Make something up!"

"Yes. I will think of a new name, but you has to call me that name, okay? Don't say Sander."

"I know! How does Pokey sound?"

"Fuck you, man!" he laughed. "I think I say my middle name, Lars. And my efternavn—I mean, my *family* name will be Sandersen. That way it is close; if we forget we can fake it."

"Sounds good. Go on inside and I'll call from the car. Maybe you can get the beds ready or something just to look busy; like you're supposed to be there. I'll see you in a minute."

"Right." Sander said, then he bounded up the stairs and entered the house from the side deck perched over the lake. I wanted to hug him so badly. Fuck, I thought, what if he hadn't been here?

The phone was answered in two rings.

"Marguax Stuplemann speaking," said the crisp and reassuring voice.

"Is your line secure?" I began.

"No. Hang up. I'll call you on your encrypted sat phone. Five minutes."

Three minutes passed and the creepy ringtone of the sat went off.

"Hi Marge, It's Johnnie Allen."

"Yes. So Johnnie, I know this isn't a social call, as much as I like you and all. What's the matter?"

"The package and the delivery are compromised in the worst possible way," I began. "I received actionable intel that our guy was picked up just before I was to meet him, and the guy we're driving is from the crew who took him."

"Who's *we*?" she asked. She doesn't miss a thing.

"I can't say right now, but he's a friendly. Anyway, the imposter was overheard talking to his contact, handler, whatever, in English, and he started the call with what sounded like a company code," I explained. "That makes me think that it might be inside, whatever it is. It's *gotta* be an inside breach. That's all that makes sense."

"So he knew the recognition code?"

"Flawlessly."

"Where are you now?"

"At the safe house in Stare Kiejkuty. We're scheduled to leave at seven in the morning and get him to the ship in Antwerp before nightfall," I said.

"Okay. Call me at six and I'll have a plan," she said.

"In the meantime?" I asked.

"Do what I won't get to do... Sleep." I heard her

chuckle as the line went mute, ending the call. Okay, Marge, I'm your willing servant. I hope you think of something.

One thing was certain, there would be someone besides Marge who wouldn't be getting any shuteye that night. How could I sleep when our asset had been compromised and was very likely in mortal danger? This is the part of the job that just sucks.

22

Rain usually makes me very happy. I love the coziness it represents; I often sit near a fire or heater and open the window so I can hear and smell the rain. The dawn broke rainy and was expected to last for a week. The weather nerds at the BBC World News predicted that many of the coming storms would produce thunder and lightning. What would have been great news on any other day—especially considering what stormwatching would be like with Sander lying naked next to me under an eiderdown comforter—would today just make things more complicated. Dang!

Time to get my head in the game. The car was refueled and the windscreen scraped free of insect corpses. Water and snack food was arranged, and showers were taken (mine without a certain Sander, damn it).

Sander, I also learned, is one hell of a cook! He prepared what amounted to a full English breakfast for the imposter, the maintenance staff, and us with what he found in the cupboards and refrigerator. The eggs were perfect, the potatoes seasoned with such savory spices that they were near perfect, and the bacon, beans, and fried bread tasted like they came from a pub in the British midlands. Sander gave me a little hip bump and snuck a morning smile into the mix as he carried plates to the oval oaken table.

"All right, Johnnie?"

"Fair enough, considering. Man, this looks great," I said, eyeing the repast in the heavy duty china plates. "What gave you the idea? And who knew you could cook, anyway?"

"My empty tummy gives me the idea, and besides, everybody should have a last meal," Sander quipped, throwing his gaze toward the imposter's cottage. "My grandmother teach me to cook ever since I am little, and I can bake wery tasty things to have, too. Like cake and pie and my family love my doughnuts I am making, especially Jannik," he said.

"Will you cook for us when we are together?" I asked him. He just smiled and waved his hands magician style over the beautiful breakfast he had cooked.

"I already do!" he smiled. "So have a seat, there's lots to eat!"

We enjoyed the short time we would have alone before the events of the day would dictate what would happen once we left the compound. I had about a quarter of an hour before Marge's call would come in and I was determined to spend every second of it with Sander. We didn't find it necessary to clog up that sweet interlude with conversation. Instead, we chose to listen to the rain blow against the kitchen window and just take the time to appreciate one another.

We heard the imposter climbing the steps and crossing the deck. The door quickly opened and shut, and the man's raincoat was hung on the wall rack as he stamped his feet on the mud mat.

"Good morning," he called from the little anteroom. "It is Petrenko here!"

He greeted us with a smile as if all was right with the world. I'm sure he thought everything in his world was okay. He didn't know what we knew, and I hoped to God Sander and I would be able to keep up the ignorant front until things got sorted.

"Good morning, sir," I said with cheer. "Breakfast

is ready. I hope you're hungry because our assistant just cooked an incredible meal."

"Looks marvelous," fake Petrenko gushed with the sincerity of a soap opera star. "I am Dimitri Petrenko," he said to Sander. "Thank you for the breakfast. And you are..."

"Lars Sandersen. I am helper for the rest of the journey," he said confidently. "If you are needing anything, please just ask."

Wow! My guy had really slipped into the role. This was very cool.

"I just have one bag so I'll be ready when you are," he said between wolfish bites of Sander's awesome meal. "When do we go?"

"I just have to do a couple things in the car; check oil and fluids, and report our departure on the secure line. Otherwise, we can leave when you're done."

"Excellent, my friends. I won't be long."

I excused myself and headed to the car and hopefully some news from Marge. Whatever happened, or whatever might happen, I knew that by the end of the day it would be over, one way or the other.

I also knew that I would probably be out of a job. I would have to report my failure to execute the one rule that can never be broken in this line of work: keeping one's mouth fucking shut.

By bringing Sander on the trip, not only was I putting him at risk, I was gambling the entire show. Sure, if nothing would have happened no one would be any the wiser. But shit did happen. And from what I can tell, some pretty big shit.

Yeah, it could be argued that having Sander along saved the day. We wouldn't have learned about the kidnapping of the asset, or that the imposter obviously knows everything there is to know about the mission. But that doesn't change the fact. At best I'll just get fired and take it like a man. But there's also the very real possibility that I might have broken some espionage law and be tried as an enemy of the Homeland. Crap!

"Hi, Johnnie here," I said into the sat phone when the call came through. "You're right on time!"

"Like a Swiss train," Marge said. "So here's the skinny... I requested an ident pic from the station chief in Warsaw and I'm forwarding it to you. Take a look. Is this your guy?"

In seconds the photo appeared on the little screen. It was the imposter, all right.

"That's the guy we got with us," I told her. "That's him."

"You're absolutely sure?"

"Definitely."

"Then we've got a bigger problem than we thought," Marge said with obvious disgust."

"What is it?" I asked.

"The only person I talked to about this is the station chief. He's also Petrenko's handler. He's the one who sent me the picture that you're looking at right now."

"So he's the one who compromised the whole shebang?"

"The very one. The big concern that I have is for the real Petrenko. Their little coup isn't gonna work, I can promise you that. I'll send out an alarm to all parties about the backstabbing job he did on us. I'm more worried about our asset," she said.

The battle order was that we would proceed as if nothing was wrong and Marge would have somebody waiting at the ship to take Mister 'X' into custody when we arrived. In the meantime, we'd have to maintain as if everything was fine. We'd have to play nice for eight hours then dump him into the waiting arms of the CIA in Antwerp. What a day!

"Are we ready to hit the road?" the imposter asked. "I have a boat to catch." *You're goddamned right you do; a boat to the moat of the Gray Bar Hotel. Enjoy your last taste of freedom for awhile, fuck knob!*

"All aboard!" I cheerfully said as I performed a quick walk around of the car. "We're just eight hours away from getting you where you gotta go!"

"Would you cares for front seat or rear?" Sander offered.

"The back is fine, my friend. You sit with the driver."

We soon left the safe house compound in the rear view mirror and joined the motorway west to Belgium. Sander tuned the radio to Sky Network and we sat back and settled in for the ride ahead.

What is his endgame, Marge thought, as she packed an overnight bag in anticipation of the scrambled days ahead. These things never work out as intended, she knew, and even when they realize that the jig's up the ones whose hands are deepest in the cookie jar always seem to want to play things out until the bitter end. Maybe they're counting on some kind of Hail Mary miracle to keep them out of the slammer. Marge's job today would be to toss a monkey wrench into anybody's plans to go to ground.

She sat on the utilitarian divan in her small bedroom overlooking the harbor. She had a dead view of the hippie colony at Christania, often smelling the odiferous mixture of cannabis, garbage, and body odor delivered by the onshore afternoon breeze. Still, she liked the building and its funky residents. And the rent was cheap.

Marge ticked off a list in her head. How high did the conspiracy reach? Who were the players—all the players? The Warsaw station chief had to be suspicious, she reasoned, because she had called him so late the night before asking him to send her a photo of the asset. So why did he send it?

If he wanted to plead ignorance and escape scrutiny he should have sent the true image. He had to know that his fraudulent replacement had been made somehow. Does that mean that Johnnie Allen was in even greater danger? Or even herself? And who was this trusted informant that Johnnie spoke of? Could the intel just be plain old wrong? Was the informant in on it? And how would she safely report whatever progress occurred to Johnnie? And this was supposed to be such an easy delivery...

23

Presently the radio switched over to a news break. Terrorist plot thwarted in Haifa, Israel; Some English footballer was caught with his pants down so his marriage is over; the International Monetary Fund would lose billions because Greece was planning to default unless they got better terms on their debt; Gay marriage is universal in the E.U. nations—even the conservative Catholic ones like Spain and Portugal.

"Listen to that shit," came the disgusted voice from the back seat. "I don't know why anybody tries anymore. Fucking butt faggots getting married like normal people. God, they make me sick," the Fake Petrenko spewed. "That's one thing the Soviet Union was good for," he continued. "They would at least disappear those pieces of shit and send them to Siberia where they could fuck each other in a snowy gulag!"

Sander stared straight ahead. He didn't flinch a muscle. Neither of us could say a thing due to the circumstances. Best we keep our eyes ahead and tune the asshole out.

"Can you believe two guys stick their cocks into their assholes? And the fuckers even kiss and give the blow jobs," he said with venom. To say he was a homophobe was like saying that Hitler didn't care very much for Jewish people.

"You seem to know lots about what they does," Sander replied, keeping his gaze affixed toward the horizon.

"Of course! Those butt fuckers are on the telly and in the newspapers every day throwing it in the normal peoples' faces. I'd kill every one of them if I could," he said, as though he'd thought about it often. "At least Putin's doing the right thing for his citizens. They won't be getting married in Russia anytime soon, that's for sure."

Sander's neck artery was twitching, his jaw clamped tightly. He closed his eyes and took a deep breath, but I didn't know how much longer he could hold out. One thing I've learned about my life mate is that he absolutely will not tolerate bullying or injustice of any kind. He even thinks the Vikings were complete jerks for what they used to do to outlying countries and villages. And he's a Viking!

"Can we take a stop for to use the toilet?" Sander asked as quietly and calmly as he could.

"We can use a break," I said. "There should be a rest stop in about forty kilometers. Can you hold on?"

He glanced at me with a sadness in his eyes and nodded. Thank the Lord the music resumed. If you are a believer in irony, the next song was Elton John's *The Bitch Is Back*, live concert version. Stick that in your hemorrhoid bedraggled corn hole, Fake Petrenko. Where *you're* going, you'll be on everybody's dance card. Though I shouldn't assume that your fellow cellmates are without standards. Even they probably wouldn't want sex with a loser piece of shit like you.

"Hey, assistant, I forgot your name..." the back seat belched.

"Lars."

"Yes, Lars. Where do you come from?"

"Denmark."

"Do you like it there? Nice place?"

"Yes, I loving it wery much. It is best place ever," Sander said.

"What's so good about it?"

"The peoples is wery nice and nobody go whitout food or a house. All is wery clean and nice, and the educations is wery good," Sander said.

"How'd you get this job?"

"I am good in the school, and so I am here."

"I mean, how do you get such job when you are not American? This seems unusual to me."

"Same as you. You are Russian but you work for America, yes?"

"But I am an asset. You're just a driver, yes?"

"Am I?" Sander replied with just the right hint of mystery and a smattering of subterfuge.

"Are you?"

"This is needs to know, and you do not needs to know. Please. We are at the rest place soon for toilet and walk around for stretching legs," Sander said with all the aplomb of a career officer.

"Yes, yes..." the Fake Petrenko said dismissively. Sander had bruised an ego nerve. Well played, Pokey!

"How about you, boss? Where in the States are you from?"

"California," I said with a clip.

"Disney!"

"Yes. Not far from there, actually."

"I have two children who would like to visit that. Mickey Mouse, yes?" he said, doing his best to be a pal. Whatever he was trying, it wouldn't work. But if it keeps him occupied, I'll play along.

"What ages?"

"Ten and six—I think so, anyway. Somewhere around that."

Thankfully the sign for the rest stop appeared. I moved into the exit lane and joined the slip road, slowed the powerful car, and glided into the parking area. I found a stall opposite some benches and a restroom building and shut off the engine.

"It comes not too soon," Fake said. "I see you in a while." He slammed the door and butt-pinch shuffled toward the toilets.

"His last shit he'll take as a free man," I joked, which caused Sander to break down in unrestrained laughter. "You sure handled him right," I said.

"What else can I do? I don't speak asshole so I do best I can," he said. "Shall we takes a little walk?"

It was difficult to speak with discretion with the backdrop of cars zooming past, but at least we knew our spoiled package couldn't hear us. So far so good; we would continue to act as if all was well. I was sure that Fake was getting off on his cleverness. Surely he believed that us stupe-ass CIA losers would do his bidding and remain clueless. We're just that dumb and unsophisticated, don'tcha know. We put ketchup on our steaks, remember. And go to the moon. And shit like that. So he had it all figured out.

"How will this end?" Sander asked.

"I don't know exactly, but my boss said she would put everything in place. My guess is that we'll get there and they'll have some agents waiting to take him to his new apartment," I said.

"The one whit the bars and the locks?" Sander smiled.

"The very same."

"Maybe they makes him wash the floors and the toilets."

"And peel potatoes," I said.

"Do you know something, Johnnie?" Sander began. "I know that this is really wery bad, and I'm sorry because maybe thing will not be so good for you whit your job... But... This is biggest adventure I ever have since I am born."

"You and me both," I admitted. "And you're right; I probably have lost my job. But it was all worth it."

"Yes?"

"Thursday night made it all worth it, you have to know that, okay?" I told him, ending with more than a fraternal hug. He leaned into my shoulder and reached his sweet lips to my cheek and kissed me. A whisper of a kiss, yet it sent chills.

"I loves you more than biksemad," he shyly grinned.

"Wait! This is serious! You love me more than Danish hash potatoes? Dang!" I said with mock glee. "Wow! Better than biksemad! I feel special!"

"Yes, and better than a Harley-Davidson, too. Just so in case you have any ideas, now you know, Johnnie Bond."

"Why, thanks, Pokey!" Then he took my hand and laid it across his chest.

"Do you feel this?" he asked me; of course, I felt his beating heart.

"Yes, I do..."

"It is wery happy. It is booming for you."

"Hey! Same as mine is...booming, too," I said, near tears. These moments were what I so looked forward to from now until forever. I thought I knew what love was. Now I know what I thought was love was just Tee-Vee love. The kind of love that you are expected to expect. What I had learned since the day I first met Sander was that love is truly infinite. There is no end to it. And each time I would be with him—even when I thought that we could be nothing more than friends—that feeling would expand, and it showed no signs of stopping or remaining in one place.

Yes, this was love. And no one would ever be allowed to step on it, quash it, diminish it, or take it from us—ever. That is one thing I would promise Sander Lars Hansen forever and a day.

I would live with him, live for him, honor him, and care for him. I would experience everything in life through our shared prism, and I would never again apologize for who I am. But more importantly, I would never apologize for who he is. In a flash of less than a dozen seconds this realization was completely affirmed at a rest stop along the A-2 motorway somewhere near the Polish-German border.

"Let's get back to the car. There's something I want to do for our friend," I said. When we returned we found him sitting on a bench smoking a Marlboro. Sander moved to his door and slid into his seat as soon as the locks popped. We bumped shoulders as we reached for our seatbelts; The Fake indicated that he'd join us once he'd finished his cancer stick.

After looking at a map posted on the side of the building, he sauntered over to the BMW and planted his fake ass in the backseat. Once he'd strapped himself in he sat back, expecting his limo driver to move on down the road. Of course I was planning to do that very thing. There was no way he was not going to meet his date with destiny on account of me. But first things first.

"Comfy?" I asked him, glancing into the rear view mirror.

"Comfy? What means this comfy?"

"Comfortable... Are you comfortable, sir?"

"Oh, yes, yes. Quite so," he smiled and nodded.

"Good, good. I just have to take care of one thing, then we'll be on our way," I promised. Then I unbuckled Sander's belt, did the same for my own, and leaned over to plant the biggest, longest kiss I had so far ever done with him. He gave as good as he got, swirling his tongue against mine, his right hand reaching into my lap. My fingers gently caressed his face, and I pulled away and found his loving eyes.

"Are you ready to go?" I asked Sander.

"What in the fuck is this?!" yelled the asswipe in the back.

"Nobody talks to you," Sander said, never breaking the lock of our gaze.

"Oh! You just wait! You just wait!" he barked, apoplectic and extremely distressed. "You are both so very kaput! *Do you understand me?!*"

I turned to my right and, over my shoulder, looked it directly in the eye and in my calmest, most serene delivery replied with a simple "No." Then I faced forward, restrapped my belt into the receptor as Sander tried his best to keep a straight face, pardon the pun.

"You are scum, do you know this?" the failure bleated from behind us. "You will both pay for your disgusting lives," he continued. "You know what I think of you?! Hurry up and get me to Antwerp so I can disinfect myself from you both!"

"I think he don't like us anymore," Sander quipped.

"And after that wonderful, tasty breakfast you made us this morning," I added.

"AIDS! AIDS is what you get, butt fuckers! You will see! You will see! I damn you to AIDS!"

Fake Petrenko was really wound up now. And then he made a very big mistake. He punched Sander in the back of the head.

24

Espionage, if it is going to succeed, relies on two ingredients most of all: friendship and trust. Marge was an old hand at this wacky world. She'd forgotten more stories than most in the business ever knew, and not only was she a respected member of the spy community, she was as close as being 'loved' by her peers as anyone could be.

She was going to have to milk the fact if she was ever going to get to the truth of what was happening to the Operation Mango delivery. She had a newbie on the field transport who had already likely done more than she knew to fuck it up. He'd already confessed to having invested his complete and total trust in some "friendly," as he had put it.

Everything was so far off the rails as to safely declare a complete and total train wreck of the situation. Now she had to back it all up from the destination and mission goal, to where it had all started. To do that effectively, she needed to know what Mango was all about.

The answer appeared in the form of her pal, Jens Jespersen from FE—*Forsvarets Efterretningstjeneste*—in English known as the Danish Defense Intelligence Service. Basically, Denmark's version of the CIA.

"Marge, my dear," Jespersen said, inviting her to sit on one of the plush Queen Anne wing chairs opposite his solid antique desk, "it has been much too long!"

"Jens, you know I wouldn't ask you to do anything untoward, but..."

"But you need me to forget a few rules, and talk shop with other shops about..." He paused for effect.

"What do you know about Mango?" she asked. "I have a fluid situation that could be everything, or nothing."

"Isn't that the way it always is?" he said, offering up a knowing grin to his counterpart. "What do you *think* is happening?"

"I have a virgin in the field doing what should have been a run-of-the-mill extraction and relocation. All indications were that he'd made successful contact, the package knew all of the recognition dialogue, and all was good..."

"So what happened?"

"I got an emergency sat call from him last night. He seems to think that the package was swapped with a hostile. Our guy's gone, and the one that we're moving is a false flag. Thing is, it looks like my newbie's got it right."

"You got corroboration?" Jespersen asked.

"Of a sort, yes. If this is truly going down badly, it looks like a station chief is pulling the strings." Marge said.

"Which embassy?"

"Warsaw. My newbie's about four or five hours away from his drop point. I can have a greeting party there and sort it all out later, but I don't know how far up the chain the dirt climbs," Marge said.

"Well, I do know about Mango. Of course, you know this or you would be darkening someone else's doorway, yes?" Jespersen chuckled.

"What can you tell me?" Marge pleaded.

"Nothing," he said, as he scribbled on a note pad. "Marge, you know there are some things I cannot do, even for a charmer as highly placed as you are."

"Can you at least point me in a direction? Any direction will do at the moment," Marge said.

"I really wish I could. You'll just have to wait it out. If your instinct says to have a party waiting at the delivery place, well, you would be wise to do that, I think," he said, quietly removing the paper from the pad. He held it up for her to read.

Meet me in 20 mins. at the Wessels Kro. Table in the back, left side.

"Well, anyway, thank you for your time. It was good seeing you," Marge said.

"Anytime, Marge. I wish I could have been of help. But you know the game as well as I do..."

"Think nothing of it, Jens... You have not if you ask not." And she left the office and headed straight for the tiny bodega pub. She understood that the little bar had been in the same location for over three hundred years. It was also a discrete place to conduct business of the sort she and Jespersen were engaged in. She knew he was risking more than a lot to even be seen with her off campus like this. That is what proved to her the massive scope that Operation Mango must be blanketing. It had to be big. Now her worry meter for Johnnie shot up by ten.

25

"Now, fucker! Get out!" I yelled, waving the Glock 17 nine-millimeter pistol at his fucking skull. "It's over for you!"

"Fuck you! Fuck you, butt fucker!" it screamed. "You can fuck yourself, do you hear?"

"Johnnie! I'm okay, Johnnie!" Sander cried, but I was there. I saw how hard the piece of shit clocked my man. The whole business was fucked anyway, so I figured in for a penny, in for a pound. "Johnnie, you can't!"

"Last chance! Get out or die where you're at!" I demanded. "I'm not telling you again!"

"Or what?! You'll butt fuck me to death?!" he sneered. "Get in and drive me to the next town. If you don't, I'll..."

BANG!

I shot the fucker in his left foot.

"FUCK!!!" It was scared now. It took me seriously. "What did you do?!"

"I shot you in the foot. Next time it's your head!" and I reached over his spastic leg and undid the seatbelt. Immediately I grabbed him by the collar and pulled his quivering mass out of the car.

The moment he socked Sander I left my body. Glancing at the speedometer I saw that we were passing a hundred miles per hour. Between threats and his pussy screams he managed to land two more hard blows on my mate.

In seconds we came to a little used road that had once linked collective farms back in the communist era. How I made the turn without rolling us is thanks to the design engineers at Bavarian; it was not because of my superior driving skills, I can promise you. Sander leaned forward, massaging his neck and head. And if I wasn't already way past enraged, I exploded in every fiber of my being when I saw that he was crying. That animal had brought him to a free flow of tears and anguish. That's when I pulled the gun from the center console.

The Fake was on the ground under the full weight of me and my Glock. "Sander! Open the trunk!" I called out, my heart easily beating twice its normal rate. "The boot! Get the boot!" Then the reassuring *thonk* of the trunk lid opening to receive the garbage it would hold for the rest of the trip was accompanied by the slide of a bullet entering the chamber.

"Get in!" I spat, stepping back to cover it with the optimal range from barrel to torso. Or perhaps slightly lower than torso. It stumbled from the ground, pulling itself toward the rear bumper. The waiting trunk had more than enough space to accommodate the loser.

"In! Now!"

"This isn't over!"

"Yeah, I know! You're still fucking breathing!"

I turned to Sander, who was by then outside of the vehicle and standing a little to my right. "Reach in and pull the tools out," I said, barely able to catch my breath. I was actually slurring my words a little, like a drunk. And no matter what I did, I just couldn't seem to keep enough air inside me to have any of my words make sense.

"Fucking amateurs!" the Fake expelled with such

hateful venom. "You are why your country is an embarrassment, you homo!"

Sander grabbed the tool kit and flung it on the ground. "Sander, find something to cut the trunk release cable. That thing with the handle, see it? That's gotta be cut!"

Sander dropped down and rifled through the sturdy bag, producing a pair of stainless steel wire cutters. Without prompting he reached over our detainee and snipped the cable, causing the taut wire to snap out of the guide and be forever lost into the space within the metal lid. He gave the handle to me.

"Souvenir from our holiday," he declared. The last thing I did was grab some heavy duty zip ties from the bag and make shithead tightly tie one around each wrist.

"You do the honors," I offered.

"What honors?" he asked.

"Take this big zip tie and thread it through each of the zips on its wrists. Then pull it tight as you can."

Sander complied then I slammed the lid as hard as I could, hoping that I blew out an eardrum or two in the process.

"I'm bleeding!" came the muffled protests from inside the trunk.

We moved under a nearby oak tree just as the rain started to pick up again.

"What do we do now?" Sander asked.

"I'll try to reach Marge on the sat phone before we leave. And I guess we'll still carry on to Antwerp until we hear something different."

"Will you be in the prison for shooting that man?"

"No. He hit you, he made threats, they'll know that if I really wanted him dead he'd be dead right now. If they don't fire me, I might even get a raise for that one!" I said.

"A gun... I'm not knowing that you has a gun, Johnnie, so I was scared."

"I want to look at his carry bag and see what he has in that way," I said. "Personally, I hate guns. But I'm glad we had one today. Truth told, that gun saved his life. I could have killed him with my bare hands for doing that to you," I said, reaching my arm around Sander's shoulders and drawing him near. Then for the next half hour we stood under the tree and wept.

26

Seedy darkness enveloped the cozy Danish pub, even at that time of day. The two intelligence workers found the table in the back as Jespersen directed.

"I'll let my eyes adjust a little," Marge said, pulling the chair from under the heavy table. "I'll try not to step on your foot, Jens," she added.

"You had lunch yet?" he asked. "You bought last time, so it's my treat."

"Sure. You pick."

The strikingly handsome man got the attention of the barman and conveyed the order.

"I got us something that is very bad for our

figures," he smiled.

"I was counting on it, especially today," Marge said. Anyway, how'd you know we'd get the table back here?"

"It's my table," Jespersen replied matter of fact. "I pay Søren monthly to keep it open for me so I never have to wait. I never know how much time I get in a day."

"My goodness, even the Queen doesn't have standing reservations at a pub," Marge chuckled.

"She has Amalienborg, I have Wessels Kro. Only difference is I have to pay the bill for both!" he laughed good naturedly.

"Who'd have thought royalty is relevant in the twenty-first century?"

"There's two ways to look at it I suppose," he said. "I can't imagine little Denmark without her royals. They kind of give us a steady, comfortable tradition that no politician ever could. And they're people that most everybody can agree on, though I wish her boys would quit siring so many little heirs! The crown prince has almost half a dozen including a pair of twins, and the younger one's got a litter spread over a couple of wives. But they keep the magazines in print, I suppose."

The two waited for the boy who brought them

their beers to leave, and then Marge got down to brass tacks.

"I guess Mango really must be something for you to pull that old scribble and talk trick back in your office. Do the people listening in still buy that one?" Marge began.

"Oh, hell, I don't know," Jespersen said. "And I doubt they listen in. They probably had Hollywood come in and fix me up in high definition. If anything, they watch me..."

"You don't really..."

"No, Marge. It is my wry Danish humor getting the best of you. We're okay, my dear."

"Jens, if I didn't like pussy so much I'd be all up in your business! All over that shit!" Marge joked.

"Oh, you'd get tired of me like my other three wives and I'd be back spending my days at the strip club! You're too good for me!"

"After this mess is scrubbed up I'll hang out with you at the strip club. I might even do a little strippin' myself!"

"It's a date! I'm serious!" Jespersen chuckled.

"In the meantime, there's Mango."

"Mango, yes. Well, I can tell you that there are a bunch of power hungry gas bags in Moscow who are very concerned about Iran keeping their promises about making nice with your government," he began. "They have a vested interest in keeping the relationship a rocky one because they know that if oil prices stabilize and the U.N. sanctions are ended, they not only become minor players at the table..."

"Their own energy exports become irrelevant," Marge deduced. "So what is Mango exactly?"

"You have an asset that is buried well within the FSB who was to be pulled out of Russia completely and see to it that a planned assassination of the Iranian ambassador to Brazil is thwarted."

"What does that have to do with nuclear agreements with the Iranians?" she asked.

"Their man in Brasilia has been the primary back channel guy with your people, and the Kremlin stooges have designed it to look like the hit will come from official U.S. government policy. They plan to carry it out in a way that leaves no doubt," Jespersen explained.

"How?"

"There's a car being shipped aboard the auto carrier that your guy was supposed to sail on tonight. It's an exact duplicate from what I understand," he said. "The idea was to switch out the cars and sit back and watch it go boom. Forensics would prove that it was an official American hit and the agreement will die. Might even start a war, from which the Ruskies would benefit greatly."

"So our guy was supposed to, what, compromise the car?"

"Not only the car, but the guys turning it into a bomb. They were going to arm it during the crossing, and then some local talent would do the switchout once it got to Brazil."

"So do you know who made our guy?"

"Your guess is as good as mine on that, but I agree that it has to be somebody on your side who is exceptionally well placed. And what you surmised about the one who sent you the photo seems more than reasonable to me. But of course, I don't know for sure."

"My field transport doesn't have much time before he gets the stand-in to the ship. I guess it's time to shit or get off the pot," she said.

"You say this is your driver's first trip?"

"Yep. It's his cherry popper. I'm lying if I tell you that I'm not worried," Marge said.

"If you can't get your bearings on this—if you are having trouble with what to do and whom to trust, well, we can scoop them up before they get to the ship and bring them to Denmark and sort it out later," Jespersen offered.

"I'm tempted," Marge said. "But there's still the matter of a powder keg on wheels sitting in the hold of a Grimaldi liner to consider."

"Well, I'll leave it to you. You know where to find me."

The hot lunches landed at the table, and for a brief moment the calm bested what was soon to become a very big storm.

"Are you okay to drive more?" Sander asked me, as we returned to the car. "I can drive for some time if you want me to."

"Do you even have a driving license?"

"Oh no, but I'm such a good driver that you cannot believe. My grandfather have teach me for a long time, and so I'm okay for driving us if you like."

"I think I'm okay. Last thing we need is for the police to pull us over and find the bag of shit in the trunk," I reasoned.

"What will we do when we are in the town and he is being noisy to make people rescue him?" Sander asked.

"That's a good question for Marge, I think."

"May you ask her soon?"

"Yes... Right after we cross the border into Belgium I'll park us somewhere and we'll make the call. If we don't hear from her first."

"Okay, Johnnie."

"Okay, Sandy... Pokey."

"Shut up or I has my boyfriend teach you a great lesson. He is fantastisk spy and he kick ass whit his big gun," Sander joked.

"Big gun, you say?"

"Yes... Wery big gun and it shoots big, too. This I can promise you! So bewares, I am warning you. He is called Bond... Johnnie Bond. And he drive a fuckin' great BMW, so he is wery dangerous."

Sander finally had recovered enough from the ugliness we had endured on the farm road to joke a little and deliver that beautiful smile.

"I'll watch out for him, don't worry," I said.

"Only watch! He is my boyfriend, not yours."

"What does this boyfriend of yours look like?" I asked him.

"He is most beautiful man I ever have seen," he said. "He is very tall and sporty, and he have yellow hair, and his face is wery pleasant and handsome."

"Tell me more," I snickered.

"You like me to tell you about my sexy man?" he

teased.

"Sure! It beats playing slug bug."

"Then I tell you more. Next thing is he is such a smart man. Wery intelligence. And he is kind to me and I think he love me wery much."

"I'm sure he does," I smiled, laying my hand upon his thigh.

"I love it when he touch me. He is wery gentle and you know what I really like best?"

"I don't know... His dick, maybe? Or his balls?"

"Well, yes, of course, there is all of that good things plus a one hundred percent perfect butt. You shall see it; it is the BMW—no, it is Mercedes-Benz of all butts, that I tell you!" he laughed.

"Wow! Sounds like that ass wants to be fucked!"

"Oh yes, but only whit me. But that is not the thing I was going to say..."

"Really? What could be better than that?" I asked.

"I love more than all things his voice. I love when he talk to me and when I hear his voice I feel good inside and outside, you know?" he said, placing his hand on mine. "This I mean."

We drove in silence for a while and savored the moment.

"You know, Pokey, I have a boyfriend, too," I

said.

"Is he some piece of shit asshole who get drunk and poop on the bed and kick the dog?" he laughed.

"Nope!"

"Do he watch the pornos whit donkeys and then fuck the dog after he kick it?

"Nope!"

"Do he... Do he gets his trousers on his ankles on the bus and plays whit his cock when the old dirty men and the nuns are riding the bus to town?"

"Uhmmm... Is there something you need to tell me?"

"Yeah, fuck you!" he laughed. "So are you going to tell me of your boyfriend, then?"

"Well, first I had never really known what love actually is until I met and fell in love with him," I began. "And I had to come exactly half way around the world to be with him."

"Is he handsome or do he look like a wet duck?"

"He is the most beautiful man I have seen or will ever see, do you understand me?"

"He can't be so good. I think you masturbates too much because you go blind, I think. You shall stop or you will be blind and has hairy hands. I learn this at the google, so it have to be true," he chirped.

"No. He really is that beautiful. But that's the

very least thing I even think about whenever I think of him," I explained. "You see, he is the first person in my whole life that I ever met who has a heart that is truly pure."

"What? How do you mean?"

"He only can be sweet and kind. I've never met anyone who doesn't always want something from somebody. You're not like that. You're not like that at all, and even after all the time I've known you I'm still amazed that I've never seen an unkind word pass your lips," I told him.

"I see..." he said, contemplating what I had just expressed in heartfelt earnestness. "But I wonder something..."

I nodded, urging him to continue in this vein of honesty we had established.

"What is it, Sander?"

"Well... Do he..."

"Yes?"

"Do he have a big dick?" Then he broke into peals of laughter. He'd obviously taken great pleasure in winding me up. "He sound like a nice guy. Maybe I get his number and dump you for this guy!"

"Hey, faggots! Shut the fuck up!" came the muted burp from the trunk. The creature of the trunk king-

dom kicked the side of the boot so I replied by ducking the wheel a couple of times, which head planted him against the hard metal liner. We heard the satisfying clunk, and then I gave the brakes a little tap and then gunned it. He definitely was bounced around—if not to, then definitely fro.

"Think that'll shut his gob for a bit?" I asked Sander.

"If I am in Las Vegas and you ask me this I will bet no," he replied.

"You cannot keep me in here forever! I will hurt you! Both of you!" he threatened.

"Tell us where you take the man you kidnap and we let you go!" Sander demanded.

"Fuck you, faggots!"

Sander shot me an exasperated look. "Aren't you glad you're gay?" he asked. "Think of the ladies of the world that has to put up whit that shit."

"Christ almighty, what's he gonna do for a face when the baboon wants his ass back?"

"I can hear everything you cocksuckers say!"

"Save your air!" Sander yelled. "You'll need it later to blow up your date!"

"Good one, Pokey!"

The sat phone buzzed to life. Marge. I switched it on and handed it to Sander to hold as I pulled the car off the motorway. "Hold on, Marge. I'm pulling over."

Once we were safely stopped I hopped out and came over to the passenger side. "Come with me," I whispered to Sander. Taking the phone I greeted Marge with relief. "What's the latest?" I asked her.

"How tall are you again?"

"Six-two," I told her. "Why?"

"Our necks are in deep shit, kiddo. I just wondered how much neck you have left before it gets to yours."

"That bad huh? So what's the plan?"

"What's the status of your imposter?"

"He's detained. He knows we know. Got'em in the trunk," I reported. "I had to shoot him in the foot."

"Really? Damn, boy! Listen, I'm on my way to your delivery point right now. I'm riding in a PET helicopter so I'll probably be there before you are. In case I'm not, do not—repeat—do not go near the ship. I'll explain later."

"What do we do with him when we get there?" I asked.

"There's a big hospital—Antwerp University Hospital; they call it the U.Z.A.—it's off the E19, Edegem. You can see it off the motorway. Be there, but leave him where he is until we land. Park by the

294

landing pad, you copy?"

"Loud and clear," I replied. "What's your ETA?"

"About a ninety minutes, maybe a little more."

"Look for the dark blue BMW five hundred series. It'll be the one with the asshole in the trunk," I said. I heard her laugh as she ended the call, so maybe I still have a job. I really don't care about that anymore. The only thing I care about is five foot ten inches of Dane who has been at too much risk for far too long, ever since this ill-fated voyage left Malmö. I owed it to Sander to be done with this as soon as possible.

"What did she say?" Sander asked.

"Not too much, other than this is a really big problem. But at least I know where we're meeting her," I said.

"She is coming there?"

"Yep. She's in a helicopter right now, and she'll probably get there before we do."

"And then?"

"And then we deliver Fake Fuck into the waiting arms of my lesbian boss who don't take no shit," I told him.

"Maybe she shoots him in the other foot."

"I don't think it'd be the foot. She'd likely have other ideas."

"I kind of feel sorry for him..."

"What?"

"Just fucking whit you," he smiled. "I want him to get all he deserve plus more."

And that's when we saw the BMW speed past us, Fake Petrenko securely behind the wheel.

27

"**S**hit!" was the visceral reaction from my shocked mouth. "Oh my fucking God! We've lost him!"

"We has the phone! Call the boss!" Sander was as surprised as me by the sudden turn of events. If there were any doubts at all about how massive a fuck up this assignment had been since I'd been a part of it, they were erased in that instant. My confidence in whatever abilities I thought I may have had until then were completely and totally deflated. I was stuck on the side of a European motorway—not the most appealing of places for pedestrian activity— with my man. I guess Take Your Lover to Work Day was a confirmed failure, too, just like every other piece of this shitty puzzle. At least Marge answered the sat phone.

"Marge, we've got a real big problem. He got out and he took the car. He's headed west on the A-2, about two minutes ago."

"Shit! All right, I'll ask later! Right now, can you get yourself out of there?"

"Yeah, don't worry about that. I'll get to the central station in Antwerp somehow. What are you gonna do?" I asked.

"Find the fucker, that's what. Worst mistake he's made all day. The car's got LoJack, so we'll find him from up here. Meantime, get yourself gone and we'll hook up later," she said.

I turned to Sander and popped him on the shoulder. "Well, matey, it's just you and me. How's your thumb?"

"My thumb?"

"Yeah. Get it warmed up." Then I stuck my thumb out in the universal sign of hitchhikers the world over. Sander did what Sander does... He laughed. With the absurdity of the situation, what else was there to do.

"Wait minute," Sander paused. "If we is thumbing for a ride, we has to experience it the right way, yes?"

"Sure. But what do you mean?"

To which he pulled the fattest doob from his wallet I'd seen until then.

"Fuck!" I said, wide eyed and truly shocked by this new development. "Awesome! Dude, why didn't you tell me before?!"

"Well, I think because you're not drinking the beers or alcohols that maybe you are upset if you see the cannabis, maybe," he said.

"So, wow, know this from now on... You never have to think that you can't tell me anything, okay?"

"Yes, okay," he said.

"You big fucking stoner!"

He pantomimed taking a hit and offering me one, and of course I replied in the affirmative. But, remember, this was happening on this fucking particular day. So...

"Och! For helvede!" Sander spat in Danish; the loose translation: Fucking hell! "My lighter is in my fucking backpack, man!"

Goddamn it. Naturally! "Well, I guess we have something to look forward to when this shit is all over," I reckoned. "Where'd you get the shit, anyways?" I asked him.

"Well, I has a friend who work at Bongland and

he grow it. It really is wery, wery, *wery* good, you know?"

"What the heck is Bongland, and why don't I know about it?"

"It not by Odense... It is over Lillebælts Bridge in Lunderskov next to Kolding. So ever now and again I ride the train to there and my friend give me a little bag and I gives my friend a little *penge*—er, monies—and everybody happy, specially me!" he explained.

"You know, you surprise me every single day," I said. "Every frickin' day!"

"This is good, yes?"

"Yes, Sandy Boy. Fucking awesome."

"Just like this grass, man... Fucking awesome!"

Soon we were hoofing it down the shoulder of the A-2 as car after smelly car whooshed past. And God, were the trucks ever loud! It was impossible to carry on a conversation, and we had to walk single file anyway for even a semblance of safety. But there we were, with our little thumbs stuck out like hippies bound for San Francisco, or failed spies on the way to Antwerp, and the certain and sudden offer of unemployment.

At least the rain had let up, which was one good thing that had happened in recent hours. Oh, and since I was walking behind Sander, I got to watch his ass and his legs, and I noticed for the very first time how—you're gonna think this is stupid, but hear me out—I noticed how adorable his walk is. He kind of leans forward, and he has this little bounce to his step. His shoulders kind of roll with it on each upward lift, and there's this cute, choppy little one-two-one-two motion that is just so fucking endearing. Christ, how many times can you fall in love with someone all over again! I'm pathetic!

To really make it worse, and you're gonna think I'm making this up so go ahead and judge me, but, seriously, right at the time I'm falling all gooey-back-in-love-all-over-again with the guy, he looks back at me over his shoulder and just tosses me the biggest smile—doesn't even miss a beat. Then he just keeps on walkin'. And there's that pretty ass in those perfect jeans just doin' its thang! Give me strength, Oh Lord!

We were twenty minutes on when our luck appeared to change for the better. A Volkswagen Euro-Maxi-Van pulled off the road and braked to a stop just in front of us. The driver, kind of a chunky but very good looking guy in his early thirties, hopped out of the van and met us half way. He said something in German, but he quickly determined that English was the common language amongst us.

"What's the story, guys?" he asked. "Funny place for a walk in the rain, don't you think?"

We told him that our car was stolen and that my boss was on her way to Antwerp to fetch us, which was technically true. He offered to give us a lift all the way, and so we gladly accepted his kindness. And we knew we were in safe hands when we saw that his entire family occupied the caravan.

"What are your names?"

"I'm Johnnie, and this is..."

"I'm Sander Lars Hansen, happy to meet you."

His wife moved the kids onto a side seat and back bench which freed up a comfortable back seat for Sander and me that was directly behind the couple.

"Get comfortable, guys," he said. "This is my wife, Kira; I'm Angelo; and tall to small there in the back are Gabriel, Helen, Emma, and the one strapped into the torture chair is Joseph."

"Hello, everybody!" Sander smiled. "Your father is a lifesaver today."

"And this is the lifeboat!" I added.

Angelo's wife, Kira, a rail thin German girl whose presence was so calming and Zen-like, offered us a baggy of veggies, and asked us details about our very trying day. We took turns answering while naturally omitting the bits that featured the spy treachery, dark alley meetings in Polish cathedrals, gunplay, foreplay, ass play, and zip-tied guys in car trunks. "How did you come to lose your car?" she asked. I explained that someone I was working with on a job in Antwerp just hopped into the driver's seat and took off when we pulled over to relieve ourselves. I said that we'd already reported the incident to our boss, and she said she would meet us at the central railway station in Antwerp. Field Rule Training 101: Always stay as close to the truth as possible without compromising the situation at hand. At least I got to get one thing right today.

"That's very disappointing," Kira said. "It would make me very sad, I think, if someone I trusted did something like that."

"Until you stopped and helped us, we were both feeling pretty much that way," I said.

"People can surprise you in good ways, and in bad ways, too," Angelo added. "It's a real bummer when they surprise you in a bad way."

The children were very quiet and exceptionally well mannered, especially for kids on a road trip. Sander made a comment about how well they got along with each other and how much he appreciated them for giving up their comfortable seats for a couple of hobos like us.

"Papa, are they real hobos?" the girl, Helen, asked.

"I don't think so, baby; they don't look like any hobos I've seen—how about you?"

"I've never seen a hobo."

"I'm sure our friends are not hobos," Kira said. "And even if they are, they are very nice hobos."

"Hear that, Sander? We're nice hobos!"

"What kind of work do you guys do?" Angelo asked, changing the subject of hobos to gainful employment.

"I work for the American government transporting other government workers to whatever their assignments are. Sander is my mate and he just came with me on this job to enjoy the trip and keep me company," I said.

"Bet you didn't expect to be stuck walking down a motorway minus a car, did you?" Angelo asked Sander.

"No way. When the man took the car me and Johnnie just look at each other like what the fu... Uh, like what is goes on! It was a shock!" Sander said. "I never even know anyone who have a car stolen, but specially me," he laughed. "So all we can do is hold out our thumbs and start walking."

The sat phone came to life and I quickly answered it. "Johnnie here," I said.

"Johnnie, what's your current status?" Marge asked.

"We caught a ride and will be at the meeting point you suggested in about an hour maybe. Angelo?" I said, catching his eyes in the rear view mirror. "An hour, would you say?"

"Yeah. Maybe less even."

"Yeah, Ma'am. No more than an hour. Central ticket kiosk off the main platform. We'll be there."

That bit of business completed, I vowed to enjoy this interlude with the travelling family for as long as it lasted.

"You next, Angelo. I told you, so what do you do for a living," I asked.

"Music," he replied. "Been at it since I was Joseph's age, basically. Kind of a family thing. All my brothers and sisters—well, most of'em, anyways—are in it.

"Cool. What is it that you do? Produce, or perform, or what?"

"Perform. And just about all else, yes, Angelo?" Sander said. *Sander said.* What does he know about it?

"That's right. Started as a performer—well, you

know, Sander. Then when I got older I crossed over into about every kind of job there is in the music business. In fact, we're on the way back from checking out a recording studio. We're looking to get some recording done before we tour in the fall," he said.

"When you is doing the tour you must make sure nobody steal your car," Sander joked.

"True that," Angelo said. "If that ever happened I'd send Kira after them, though. They wouldn't stand a chance."

We made great time getting down the road considering we were in a family van stuffed to the tailpipe with kids, coloring books, and juice boxes. I also found it intriguing that Sander seemed to know about Angelo's music work. I couldn't wait to ask him about that.

Minutes later we were seeing signs for Antwerp and the train station exit. And almost as quickly as it had begun, the ride ended at the passenger drop-off zone at the Central Station.

"Will you let us give you this for petrol?" I asked Angelo, pressing a 50 Euro bill into his hand.

"Absolutely not. We enjoyed having you and are glad we could help you," he said. "You can help somebody the same way or better someday, okay?"

"Okay. Well, thank you again. You were wonderful to help us like you did," I said, giving him a hearty handshake.

"Good-bye, young ones!" said Sander. "Bye Kira, bye Angelo. I will tell my family about you. They will be so happy to know that you help us like this. It's like your song, yes?"

"Song?" Angelo said.

"An angel..."

"Ahhh! Well, I wouldn't go that far, but thank you. Hope we see each other again. We've got a ferry to catch."

With farewells exchanged, and selfies snapped all around, the sweet little family drove away and we headed into the station to wait for Marge and whatever else would come our way before this day was done.

Sander and I settled onto a circular bench where we could see anyone entering the concourse. The loss of the BMW had inspired a new and improved heightening of awareness that would be a part of me from now on. After a good scan of the surroundings I cornered Sander on the travelling minstrels we'd just spent the afternoon with.

"So, Pokey... How'd you know they were musicians, and what was all that song stuff you guys were talking about there at the end?" I was bursting to know the scoop.

"Just a minute," he replied. He pulled out his phone and shoved the earbuds in his head. After a bit of finagling he pulled out the buds and stuck them in my ears. "Here, listen..."

Oh, I've heard that song, I thought. Yeah, I remember that I kept repeating it when I listened to it on the plane to Denmark.

"Yeah... I've heard that before. A lot of times on the radio, too," I said.

"Well..."

"What?"

"The one singing—well, one of the ones—is Angelo," Sander said.

"That exact song? That one there?"

"Yes. That family is world famous. When they goes to the tour they play in the big stadions and big places where they are giving concerts," he explained.

"That family that we were riding with?"

"Yes, well, I tell you... There is world famous band called Kelly Family. They has maybe ten or twelve kids, all of them are musicians, okay?" he began. "Now, Angelo is one of those kids. When I am really small my family see their concert when they come to Roskilde. But at that time, the first most famous Kelly Family is all growed up, so it was just some of them and the new kids that are younger.

"Anyways, now Angelo have songs on the radio and he do tours whit his family that we are whit today," Sander said.

"You're shittin' me..."

"No, I promise, I won't lie to you ever, Johnnie. This you know..."

"So when did you know who he was?" I asked.

"When he get out of the van and say hello to us."

"No way!"

"Yes way. I promise."

So according to Sander, after losing our package, shooting the Fake in the foot, getting our car swiped, and thumbing it down the highway, we got rescued by a European pop star and his brood.

"And how many people come to see them? Like at the concert you saw them at..."

"Fifteen, maybe twenty thousand," Sander said, as though it's every day that you hitch a ride with somebody you read about in weekly picture magazines. "I think they were very nice to stop and help us, don't you?" he said. And then he leaned against my shoulder and fell asleep. As fucked up as this day had started, there was no law that said it couldn't end like this.

> *But there's danger in the air*
> *Tryin' so hard to be unfair*
> *Danger's in the air*
> *Tryin' so hard to give us a scare*
> *But we're not afraid*
> *Sometimes I wish I were an angel...*
> *Sometimes I wish I were you.*

Yes, Sander, sometimes I wonder what it's like to be you. Sometimes I wish I were you. For if I were, I'd be an angel too...

28

A gain, with the sat phone. Busy workout for the orbiting satellite Skynet 4F today.

"Marge?"

"Where are you?!" she shouted.

"Uhm, where you said to be," I stammered. "We got here just a..."

"Get out, now! Wherever you have to go, get the hell out!"

"But what..."

"Now, fucker! No time!"

Sander woke with a start the second the phone went off, and he could obviously overhear what was being said. His face flashed fear for a moment, but quickly changed to one of resolve.

"We go now?" he asked, though the tone bespoke statement rather than question. He lifted me by my shoulder—I was still recovering from the call—and we aimed for the street exit. "Your boss is not angry," Sander declared. "She is afraid for you. We find out why soon, okay? But we goes from here now."

"I'm so sorry how this has been, Sander," I said. "We were supposed to be together and do a simple job. That's all!"

"Den, som er en gang til søs, skal enten sejle eller vask, Johnnie!" Sander said. "He that is once at sea, must either sail or sink! Danes are smart. Listen to us whit our old sayings," he laughed as we rounded the last corner and came out into the open cobblestoned promenade in front of the station.

The rain had stopped again and the striking deep blue of the darkening sky was punctuated by cotton white clouds teasing the wind.

"Marge didn't say exactly where to go, but I vote for somewhere very public," I suggested. "What say the Dane?"

"I goes where you do!"

"There's a park over there and it looks like there

might be something going on where we can blend in. Look at the crowd," I said.

"Look to the sky," Sander pointed, wearing the expression of a kid at a circus. "They fly the kites! They is so pretty, you know?"

That's when he was felled by the bullet.

"Sander! Oh, God, please!!! HELP! HILFE! HILFE!!! Aidez-moi! *aidez-moi!*"

Many around us scattered and ran, but a little knot of good samaritans formed a human halo and were at once on their mobile phones summoning aid.

One lady in her mid forties rolled Sander on his back and pressed hard against the blood spot that was growing on his shirt and jacket. He was crying out in pain and I wished more than anything that it was me instead of him.

"Don't let him die, please! You can't let him die! Oh, God! No no no no no....."

"You! Go there now! Take him!" the lady said to a couple who were standing over us. The girl leaned down and told me—promised me—that Sander would be fine. That I could help my friend more by going with her and letting them help him. Of course! That makes sense to me! I remembered thinking. Pokey will be fine because we have to go home to Denmark tomorrow, and how can he go if he is sick?

So he will be just fine!

And the warmest feeling descended upon me, almost one of comfort, and I went to sleep. Very fast, I was asleep. My head and shoulder and my right kneecap stung. Why is that so? How come things are sideways, and did you know that cobblestones are very cool to the touch, and they make your cheeks wet.

We oh we oh we oh we oh... Wait, it's not the song that goes we-oh-we. See, that's Sander's song. No, this was an odd sound. I could hear it in the cobblestones. We-oh-we-oh-we-oh... I KNOW! It's the sirens that have come to fix poor Sander. Why did Sander fall down? Did somebody push him? I am sleeping. It is nighttime now. Do you know how I know? It's because it is very, very dark.

They had picked up the stolen car just as it left the A-2 and neared the city exits. All they could do for the time being was to follow its progress from their perch in the helicopter overhead.

There were assets on the ground that could affect an arrest if needed, and to Marge's eye they definitely would be. Landing a chopper in a town square is not an everyday occurrence.

"Get the takedown crew on his tail," Marge relayed to the tracking vehicle via her David Clark headset. "And I want somebody on both sides of him," she said.

Either the target was completely unaware that the helicopter was monitoring his every move, or he was as cool as a Nordic February night. His driving never belied that he was under stress in any way. He even stopped for the traffic signals.

Marge noted that he seemed to know where he was going, though that wasn't much of a problem these days with the proliferation of GPS systems so prevalent—especially in a new BMW. Still, she was well aware of the confident behavior of the driver. She could see his gloved hands on the wheel and he never seemed to waver.

"Where do you suppose he's headed?" Marge asked Maarten, the Belgian liaison officer sitting opposite her in the sleek passenger cabin aboard the aircraft.

"Where's your consulate located in Antwerp?" he asked.

"Don't have one here. Everything's out of Brussels. What about the Russians? Do they have a mission here?"

"No. And he's not headed for the airport. Not from where he's at, anyway," he said. "Look there! He's turned onto the N-12."

"What's there?"

"Huh... Well, the only thing really that way other than tourist shops and hotels is the zoo," Maarten said.

"Really! The day before he took our agent he was at the Warsaw Zoo!" Marge exclaimed. "What's his deal about zoos?"

The car did slow, but it passed by the zoo entrance and appeared bound for the N-1 T-junction. To the left would be the Stadspark, a probable setting for espionage activity; to the right, not much. Marge spoke to ground support: "Get your team headed to Stadspark. Good chance our pigeon's gonna land there," she said.

"Wait! He's in a turn pocket!" Maarten observed. "Yes, he is definitely turning."

"Damn!" Marge cried, lighting up the sat phone. "Damn! Pick up, kid!"

Maarten noticed her marked relief when the call was answered.

"Where are you?!" she barked into the receiver. "Get out, now! Wherever you have to go, get the hell out! . . . *Now, fucker! No time!*"

Maarten couldn't suppress the laughter that welled up when he overheard the quick exchange.

"Now, fucker? I will remember that at our next employee relations seminar!"

"My asset's waiting for my word at the train station that asshole's going to. Can we land this thing anywhere near it?" Marge pressed. Maarten relayed the question to the pilot, who then banked the chopper to the right and went into a hover over a little park by the tram turn, the train station, and the Radisson Hotel.

The chopper began to settle, the pilot paying close attention to the electrical catenaries above the tram tracks. Marge kept her focus on the BMW. It slowed to a crawl to the right of the terminal entrance. Events took a quick turn. There's Johnnie! The car made a hard right. Now it faced the station. Arm extends from the driver side. Gun! Flash! Bystander goes down. He didn't get Johnnie. Car slowly backs away from station, heads right, then comes up the Koningin Astridplein facing the helicopter.

The car drove the speed limit right past the chopper as it was about fifty feet before touchdown. It looked no different than any other family car out on a shopping trip.

"At least one shot fired! Tactical, descend and arrest the driver of the target car. Any force necessary. Repeat! Shot fired! Detain the target driver!" Marge shouted into the headset. In seconds she hit the ground running, trying to get ahead of the BMW. She took advantage of the fact that her prey was committed to a one way street that thankfully required traffic to move at a snail's pace. It didn't hurt that he was caught behind a city bus.

Marge saw at least three hot shots from the team casually approaching the vehicle from different directions. She heard sirens approaching, too—likely for the shooting victim; her support guys would never announce themselves for any reason. No, it had to be civilian response.

Marge spoke over the Q-com: "Whatever you have to do to get this guy into our hands, you do—dead or alive."

She immediately heard the double click responses from each team member. Okay, he was getting ready to make a left turn onto Carnotstraat. All according to plan, she would come face-to-face with him at the corner of Van Wesenbekestraat where he would get one, and only one, opportunity to give up quietly. One move; one look; one breath wrong and she would end him from right where she stood. This had gone on long enough.

He was three cars and a city bus away from her. The bus would have to stop for riders. She planned to walk in front of the bus when it paused, turn left and walk along the outboard side. Draw her weapon. And emerge from behind the bus on the driver's side of the BMW. She would announce and demand compliance, then it would all play out as the universe intends. She knew she would have a clear shot, and she'd have the bus there to duck behind if things got testy. Well, it would be there long enough, anyway.

There it was, the heady rush of adrenaline, right on time! Her old friend never let her down in times like this.

29

I am feeling very funny. It feels like once at Lars Bo's birthday party when we were all drinking too many beers. I am like the slow motion in a action movie. Like when there are big fires chasing the big star but he always can run faster than the fire. I think I maybe do not run as fast as the Terminator.

Johnnie was saying something and then somebody pushed me really, really hard and I fell to the ground; and I think I took a nap. What a stupid time to be tired and take a nap! Sander, you are really an idiot for doing that!

Where is this place? Where is Johnnie, anyway?

This is not a hotel—hospital! I am in hospital! What. The. Fuck!

I have to sit up now and ask somebody what happened. Wait, here's a button I can push. "Hello?" *Beep.* "Can you help me, please?" *Beep. Beep.* Shit! Why don't they talk back on the speaker?

"Be there in a minute," says the speaker. Okay, now we're getting someplace!

When I woke up I was in an ambulance and kept feeling like I was going to roll over and fall off the gurney, even though they had me strapped into it. Also, I'll bet that you don't know how loud it is inside an ambulance. The motor was loud, the machines were loud, and the siren was a lot funnier in the old *Pink Panther* movies on cable than here. Frickin' loud, man! *Neener-neener-neener-neener* all the way down the road.

Oh, God! Sander was hurt! He was shot!

"Where's my boyfriend?" I shouted at the three techs who were riding with me. "Where's Sander? Is he dead?!"

The oxygen mask dulled what I said to a point, but they could hear me. But nobody would look me in the eye. I struggled against the straps, and at the same time during the horrible fear and grief I was living, I had to pee! God damn it, it never fucking stops! And at that second I really didn't know if my primary reason to even want to live was alive or...

Now I was crying. And it wasn't from my torn up face or beat up leg. This is how mourning must start, and there is no feeling quite as bad. I was completely helpless and there was no one who could conceive of the pain in my soul. The utter darkness and dearth of hope. If I never knew before how much I loved Sander Lars Hansen, I knew it then.

"We'll be at hospital soon, my friend. Then we'll find out everything for you, okay?" said the kind, college-age girl with the bobtail hairdo. "We'll see that you and your friend are cared for first class!" She smiled at me and turned to her colleagues and jotted down the relevant numbers and readings they would soon give the doctors.

"We're almost there," said the older fellow. Gray hair, but very fit, he moved to the rear, his back to the doors. I felt the truck stop, and then quickly back up. On cue he hit a release with his elbow and backed out of the ambulance with the foot end of the gurney in his hands, never missing a step. In seconds I was being wheeled into the emergency entrance.

I was fine. I knew that. But at the time I still didn't know anything about Sander's condition, or even what had happened to us.

One of the hospital ladies approached my gurney carrying a clipboard. Some things around the world are truly universal, I guess. She started jabbering to me in Dutch.

"Ma'am, I'm sorry, I don't speak Dutch. Can you..."

"Yes, young man, of course I can speak English. Yes, well, there's been trouble at the central station, I am told," she said. "You're the one with the facial and leg injuries. We'll get to you soon, I promise."

I thanked her and asked her about Sander. Did she know if he's okay? Is he alive?

"Yes, yes... He's with the surgeons right now. It was a gunshot that hit him in the left arm, just below his shoulder—right about here," she demonstrated. "It pierced a few layers of his Integumentary System—mainly the Dermis. Some subcutaneous, but not so much. The Dermis is the thick part under the outer Epidermis..."

"Ma'am, I'm sorry, I have to go pee really bad!"

"Wait here," she said, like I had a choice. In a flash she returned with a plastic urinal and tossed the blanket off me. I was still strapped to the gurney, and when she saw that, she just undid my pants and pulled them down right there in front of God and country!

"Sorry... Turn as much as you can. I hold it for you because it will take much too long to fiddle with the belts."

Then she actually grabbed my dick and plopped it into the plastic container. And as bad as I had to go, I couldn't.

"It's okay," she said. "Just close your eyes and it will come soon."

"You do know that I'm just trying to pee at the moment, right?" I joked.

"Aaacchh!" she cried, totally embarrassed now that she realized what she'd said. "I apologize!"

"For what? You just made my life wonderful again," I told her.

"How so?"

"You told me that my boyfriend is gonna be okay. I thought I maybe lost him," and then both the pee and the tears started to flow. "Now, I'm the one to apologize," I said. "Look at me, I'm a mess! Pissing and bawling like a two-year-old."

"Don't feel bad," she said. "Every one of us is a two-year-old. We are human, is all. And your day has been a difficult one."

I was dribbling the last bit of pee and she shook it off and squeezed out the last drop. Her cool touch actually felt pretty good, and her kind way erased any embarrassment that I felt by being as exposed as I was.

"There! All done," she declared, as she helped me get everything back into place. "And you can tell your boyfriend that I am extremely jealous of him!"

While she unbuckled me from the gurney I learned her name was Rita, and that she was not even a nurse, but an intake administrator. "We help wherever we're needed," she said, "and everybody here, even the kitchen and cleaning staff, have medical training. I was a nurse for twenty years before I got the job I have now," she said. She should be head trainer of bedside manner, I'll tell you.

"When can I see Sander?"

"See the orange light that is over that door?" she said, pointing to a set of double doors off of a little annex. "When that goes off, they will move him to a room. I will make it so you are both in the same one, so either he will get there first, or you."

"Why do I get a room?" I asked.

"The doctors have to fix you up! You don't know it, but actually you are worse off than Mr. Hansen.

They have to treat your leg, and your face is really banged up," she said.

"Nothing really hurts."

"That's because your friends in the ambulance pumped you full of the good stuff," she chuckled. "Let's see how you feel three hours from now!"

Two orderlies arrived and pushed me into one of the exam rooms where a doctor and two nurses awaited. One of the nurses took pictures of my face with a digital camera, and the other one examined my leg and knee. The doctor scribbled a few notes, and then the nurse plugged the camera into a large HD monitor.

"Mr. Allen, I'm Dr. Maastricht, and this is Bleva and Bente. We're going to repair you just like a car in the shop. You have a few dents! Look here," he said, flicking the monitor on.

Shit! I looked like a regurgitated bowl of tikka masala! God, it was sickening!

"Oh, that's awful," I said. "Am I going to look different now?" I was worried—actually and stupidly worried—that Sander might now rethink being with me. I blame it on the drugs. Later I thought back and wanted to kick my own ass for even giving that ridiculous idea any credence at all. Sander wasn't some vacant, self-absorbed twink. I was actually ashamed of myself. As long as I live I'll never tell Sander that such a thought ever crossed my dumbass mind. I just wanted them to get done with me so I could be with him again.

"This procedure will hurt a lot, so I'm going to give you an injection of a painkiller in each side of your face," the doctor explained. "Then we can do kind of an advance debridement that will make sure the no infection makes it into that handsome face, yes?"

"You're the expert," I said.

"After we've given you your makeover, we'll take a look at that knee. Okay, close your eyes and I'll be very quick."

FUCK! They need a painkiller for giving you the painkiller. Good thing was that it took real fast. The hilarious part was that I couldn't talk at all. My words were like mashed potatoes. But we were both going to be fine, and we're both still residents of the planet earth. Thankful. That's what I was that Monday afternoon.

30

Glances to the support team. Timing of the curb to rear of the bus movement. Nod to the shooter bearing east. He nods to the west shooter, and she counts three with her head. Like a jump from a cliff, once started, a takedown doesn't end until it ends.

In this order: she caught sight of the driver's side mirror, a young mother pushing a carriage across the road in the park where the chopper had touched down, the windscreen—shit! There's glare!—and then the target's arm spread the length of the door window. She saw his head and the left side of his face last, and thankfully he was looking toward the curb. He must have caught movement in a reflection on a shop window, but by then it was over for him.

Marge grabbed the door handle, which locked, just as the west shooter put two rounds into the right rear tire. Still, the target wasn't ready to toss in the towel. How had they made him, he wondered. But he didn't muse for long; without any demonstrable panic he threw the gear into reverse and slammed into the car behind.

East shot approached the left rear quarter panel and blew that tire out. Marge had already announced and had flashed her ID at the freak, who returned her demands with an arrogant smile. The instant he began turning the steering wheel to the left, she blew his head off.

The entire length of the right side windows and door panels were painted in blood and brain matter that, until seconds ago, maintained the person known as Kolya I. Minkov—a husband, father, citizen of the Russian Federation, and career FSB man. He was also an unbridled killer, kidnapper, extortionist, and true believer in the oppression of others that he and his cronies deemed unworthy of life, liberty, or the pursuit of anything.

In another outcome he would have murdered two young men this day, who would never wish to see the past sixty seconds befall him as they had.

"All on frequency, this is Roadmap. Target has been neutralized. Repeat, target is dead," Marge spoke into the Q-com. The local cops descended on the scene immediately, and the street cops parked three trams end to end to block and preserve the area as best they could.

Marge transferred command to the Dutchman and corralled a traffic officer for a ride to the hospital.

Sander got to the room first after all, and chose to sit in the cushy chair rather than to plant himself on the bed. He asked the nurse to help him call home, and after a bit of fussing with all of the steps required to place a call to Denmark, he leaned back and hoped someone at home would answer.

"Den Hansen hus," came the sweet, unassuming voice on the line.

"Jannik? Det er Sander!" He greeted his little brother warmly. The soft, squeaky voice melted his heart and, for him, presented everything in a clearer perspective.

"How's the cowboy?" he said in Danish.

"I'm good," Jannik replied. "We lost the game today, but we'll kick their butts another day. We will go all Sons of Anarchy on them the next time!" he promised. "Will you come?"

"Of course I will!"

"Will you bring Johnnie, too?"

"Yeah, yeah. Always!"

"Where are you?" Jannik asked. "Mom is making steaks tonight. We were supposed to barbecue them on Saturday, but it rained really hard so we didn't do it. We went to McDonald's instead."

"Oh?" Sander teased. "And whose big idea was that, I wonder?"

"Mine. Maybe. I'm not saying!" he laughed. "So will you and Johnnie come over for steaks?"

"No, Spiderman! We're in Belgien. But I think we'll start home tomorrow or the next day. Will you tell everybody we're doing fine, and—listen, Jannik— tell mom I lost my phone," Sander said.

"Okay."

"What did I just say? Tell it back to me..."

"Big gorillas escaped from the zoo and took your phone and are calling the Congo to see if their wives want them to bring bananas home from the supermarket!"

"Fuck you, little shit!" Sander laughed.

"Fuck you back, bigger shit!"

"Okay, see you soon!"

"Bring me something from Belgien!" Jannik laughed. "Chocolate! Bring me chocolate! I want lots of pimples like you!" And then he hung up.

Sander held the phone tightly, gazing at the tiny holes in the receiver that had brought his brother's voice to him. Sander thought about his short life, and wondered if he had done anything in it that mattered. Had he ever hurt anyone unintentionally? Had he been kind enough? What was he even here for? He wondered if, all things considered, his family was disappointed in him for being unconventional. That's how his grandfather put it. *Sander, you are the most unconventional person I have ever met in my life*, he had told him on more than one occasion.

He always understood it to be kind of a compliment. But what if he was just being nice. That's what grandparents do, right?

I'm a queer, Sander thought. *I'll be seventeen in two weeks and I'll still be a queer.*

But what did that word even mean? *Queer.* It means strange. Different is good; strange is at best tolerated. But his friends have been cool about it. They seem to like him. He'd never really been bullied—well, except... He couldn't ever recall being left out or ostracized, except for that time... But if they were given a choice—anonymously—to choose a gay Sander or a straight Sander, which would his parents pick? That said, what would *he* have picked for himself? Even in Denmark there were those who despised any- and everything even remotely gay. They could even exhibit violence on occasion. It was in the news sometimes. And there was that time...

"Knock knock!"

"JOHNNIE!" Sander jumped up from the chair, his sling catching on the arm. "Ouch! That hurt!" he laughed, meeting me at the door as the nurse guided my wheelchair to my bed. "Can I gives a big hug for you?" he said.

"Sure!"

"It have to be a one arm hug because the other one is getting well." His touch was electricity for me. And in spite of everything we'd gone through that very long and shitty day, *he smelled fucking awesome!* God damn, how does he do that?!

"I love you, boyfriend!" I told him as I hopped onto the bed.

"Me too! I was so scared, Johnnie," he began. "I didn't know what even happened. And then when I got here, they couldn't tell me what happened with you. Then I went to the surgery."

"Same here! I thought you— I thought, maybe you were..."

"You mean...?" He made a slicing motion across his neck.

"Yep. I was never so scared in all my life," I confessed. "Remember, my boss said for us to get out of the train station... And next thing you're shot and I saw blood and then everything went crazy and..."

"We're here," he said.

"Yeah, we're here."

"No. Listen, Johnnie... I mean, *we're here*. Okay? That's the main thing we shall think because, well, maybe the day could be much different, yes?"

"Yes."

"So have they catch who do it?"

"Don't know. But I think we both know, right?"

"Yes. It's what I think," Sander agreed.

"I bet he ran."

"Like a little bitch!" the cute guy with the sling exclaimed. Then we laughed so much it hurt. Seriously, it hurt my face, and it hurt his arm. Damned laughter!

When I awoke the next day Sander was fast asleep, perched on his chair, with his head lying on my bed. I didn't have the heart to disturb him, but it was either that or wet the bed.

"Hey," he said, with a load of sleepies in his eyes. "What's the time?"

"Time for piss! Move your buns, fella."

"Last time I do that, you gets a boner," he smiled.

"Every time you do that I get a boner! Now move it!"

"Here, old man, you forget your cane," he joked, handing me the walking stick the nurse brought in last night. "Shall I paint it white, too?"

"Thanks, sonny! Now outta my way!"

I'm pissing like Niagara Falls when I hear the voice of my favorite lezbo enter.

"Excuse me, do you know Johnnie Allen?" she asked Sander.

"I never hear of him before," Sander replied.

"Oh, I must have the wrong room," she said, turning toward the hallway. "So sorry..."

"Wait, I play whit you! Johnnie is in the toilet," Sander grinned. "I think you are Marge."

"Who the hell are you?"

"I'm the hell Sander, that's who!" he laughed while I kicked the flusher. I emerged from the water closet with a hearty, "Hey, Pokey, if you see a mean lookin' dyke wanting to know where I am you can just tell her to go eat a carpet—*Why, Marge! What a pleasant surprise!"*

"Oh, so that's what they mean by *gay!* You so funny! Not!"

"Why if it aren't Mizzz Marguax Stuplemann, as ah live an' bree-athe," I mocked in my best southern plantation debutante voice. "Ah do declare...ah believe it is time for mint juleps on the ver-aaaannnnn-da, do you not agree, Mizzz Stuplemann?"

"Can you shut it off?" she asked Sander. He just slowly shook his head, pity in his eyes.

"So, Allen, how was your first day on the job? Learn anything?"

"Fuck."

"Tell me about it. I just blew a guy's head off yesterday. Think they'll give me a raise?"

"Uhm, are we supposed to talk when someone is..."

"Oh! Tradecraft Protocols! Yes! They teach those at Camp Peary *before* your first day on the job! I remember!"

The conversation was morphing from playful to pointed in record speed.

"Uhm..."

"Oh, him? You mean *him?* Your 'Friendly' with the intelligence that first made us aware of what could have been such a complete and total ass fuck—

sorry about that, guys...wrong example—you know what the fuck I mean," she said.

"I—it was supposed to be—"

"Supposed to be doesn't exist in this line of work, pal. You're not stupid, right?"

"Miss Marge?" Sander interjected, "he's in love. That's all. And I am, too."

"You know, I get it. I really do. But how many honey trap tales did you hear in training? Those nearly brought down our entire operation back in the cold war. Who's to say that..." She stopped short of saying Sander's name. And I couldn't argue with her.

"You're right, Marge. I can't say a thing to defend myself, and Pokey'll tell you that we know I'm fired. I'm okay with that. I fucked up and ignored every rule and piece of tradecraft I was taught. So... I get it, too," I said.

"I really like you, Johnnie. Have since the day I met you. You're smarter than Einstein, and you're one of the nicest people I have ever known. That's why this whole mess has really fucked with me," she said. "I came and checked on you and I thought I would lose it."

"I'm sorry."

"I know you are. But what am I supposed to do, right? I mean, you take your boyfriend with you on your first gig like it's fuckin' National Lampoon's Fucked Up Espionage Transport Vay-fuckin-cation, and you leave me to clean up the shit, kill a guy, and worry if you got a bullet in your ass! How nice is that?"

"Not very," I admitted.

"Not to mention," she turned to Sander... "Does he love you, *really?*" Sander nodded and shot me a supportive glance. "Not to mention that you put the guy you love, and who loves you back, in harm's motherfucking way! What an *asshole!*"

"I know."

Sander, who was sitting safely behind Marge's Tirade of Doom, looked directly at me and mouthed 'assss hoooole'. The little fucker! I can't tell you how much physical pain was caused from stifling the giggles. It almost hurt as much as the face repair job.

"Can I say something, Marge?"

"Yeah, go for it. I'm fucking tired." Then she sat on the bed next to Sander's chair and shot me the *'Hurry the fuck up; get started already!'* wave.

"I guess since it's all over, I want to tell you that you have no idea what it was like when we found out that our man was kidnapped," I began.

"Sure I do. Panama, 1988. Go on..."

"Well, if Sander hadn't been there, I would've dropped the guy at the dock and who knows what would have happened?" I argued. "I know officially it was wrong, but whatever happens I'm glad he was there.

"Yeah, that was a lucky break," she admitted, "but that doesn't mean you bust regs and act the fool because we got lucky this time. You can't plan for lucky, Johnnie. So however good it turned out you can never, never do that again."

Halfway through the last harangue Sander quietly took her hand in his. He's the Marge Whisperer! He did it out of purity; he did it to make her feel better. And tough ol' Marge didn't even flinch when he softly placed his hand on hers. In fact, she welcomed it. Wait a minute! Did she say 'never do that *again*'? Again? As in there might be a next time?

"I will never do anything like that again, I promise! Never!" I could barely contain the joy. Then she dropped the bomb.

"All right. So, I need you to sign these papers before I leave," she said dourly. Like at every job when you get canned, they make you fill out the separation paperwork before you can collect your last check. Oh well, three days in a brand new

BMW with Sander was a good enough tradeoff I suppose.

"These are your permanent status documents. So you're no longer considered to be a probationary employee. Sign here, here, and here and I'll get it put into the diplomatic pouch when I get back to Copenhagen," she said.

"So I'm not fired?"

"Not today, friend," she said.

"Awesome! Thanks! Thank you so much, Marge!"

"Just don't make me regret it," she cautioned. "And next time leave the boyfriend at home." She turned to Sander and with a smile added, "I'll make sure he gets home to you safe and sound, handsome."

Marge visited with us for most of the day. She confirmed that the fake did indeed try and kill us, and she described the takedown and his eventual death. I'd like to say that I took the high road and felt bad for him. I did not. Just an inch or two and Sander could be in the morgue right now instead of holding my hand.

We learned Marge's story; how her family had completely disavowed her when she had the courage to declare her love for her girlfriend, hoping that her mother and father would see the truth and accept her for who she was. They didn't.

Her partner, Gloria, who worked for the State Department died of breast cancer about five years before we met, and she said that worrying about her "chickadees in the field" kept her sane during the initial loss. She felt watching over her field transport specialists gave her a purpose. It still does, she said, which is why I continue to be on the U.S. Government payroll—though I don't deserve it. I thank the universe for Marge Stuplemann every day.

She really took to Sander—who wouldn't? And we played some trivia games and then Marge scared up a Monopoly game from one of our nurses. Belgian Monopoly was a blast, and the streets were from Brussels and Bruges. The money is Euros, and the little tokens are different except for the hat. You should know that Park Place and Boardwalk are known as Place De Meir and Rue Neuve/ Nieuwstraat.

Hugs and were exchanged all around when Marge got ready to leave.

"I'm so happy that you're both going to be okay,"

she said. "Just get better and go home when you're up to it. The hospital bill is taken care of for you, Johnnie, and Sander just has to give them his Danish CPR number and he's covered."

Both of us thanked her profusely, and of course Sander had to melt her a little more when he laid his head on her shoulder while giving her a final good-bye hug. She actually kissed the top of his head! I swear, that guy...

"Last thing," she said, digging into her shoulder bag, "here's your rail cards to get yourselves home. Get to Amsterdam and take the City Night Line from there to Odense. There's enough on the cards for a sleeping compartment and the restaurant car. Safe trip!"

"You, too."

"And make sure you get some *sleep* in that compartment, too, you walking hormones!"

"*Bye,* Marge..." I joked.

"I'll call you next week for a full debrief. Keep your calendar open, kid. Bye!" and she was away.

31

On Thursday we both felt up for the trip home. A quick visit to the railway website secured a bedroom compartment on the night train leaving at 11:07. It would put us in Odense a little past 1:30 on Friday afternoon. The weekend! YAY!

We checked out of the hospital at three o'clock and were on a train a little past four. Sander sat next to me and held my hand, giving it a squeeze every few minutes, his I Love You code—three quick squeezes.

We gazed out at the passing scenery oblivious to anything or anyone but us. This was our time to reboot and move toward getting over the traumatic experiences of the week. It felt like we had been caught in a loop that was only broken when Sander was felled by that horrible attack outside the central station.

I was healing just like the doctor said, and last night Sander slept well for the first time since the incident.

"You know what I want to do when we are home?" Sander asked.

"What, Pokes?"

"I want to go to a movie."

"Fuckin' A, I'm there. Pick one, dude," I said.

"You pick."

"You."

"Maybe. But if you don't like what I pick, you can't be angry, yes?" he warned. "This happen every time whit Jannik, so I tell you now!" he smiled.

"I don't go to watch a film. I go to sit beside you for two hours," I told him.

"Nooo... You goes for popcorn, this I know!"

"No!"

"Yes!"

"Okay, for you *and* for popcorn. Happy?"

"Very much."

The train rolled to a stop and since we had a few

hours to kill, we hunted for a place to grab a bite. Our noses led us to an Indian restaurant and I didn't know if Sander had ever been to one before.

"What do you think?"

"Smells nice, shall we try it?" he said.

"Have you ever had Indian before?" I asked him.

"No. So you shall show me what is good, yes?" he said, pushing the door open. "If it taste good as it smells this can be fantastisk!"

Dinner was fantastic—fantastisk! as Sander says—and we relaxed in the booth full as ticks. Chicken Makhani, pilau rice, keema nans, papadum, and soda pop! That's what I'm talkin' 'bout! Sander dug it, and since he was an Indian virgin, I made sure we ordered everything mild.

"Johnnie, may I ask you something?"

"No. Sorry. We're closed now."

"Fuck you, dick of dickholes!" he laughed.

"So then stop asking dumb questions. You can ask me anything, always."

"Okay, okay... So I want to know something and you have never tell me this," Sander began. "So can we talk about your family? Your mom and dad, uhm, and perhaps when can I meet them?"

"Yeah, well..."

"What?"

"My mother is a Bible thumper. To her, you and me should be in Hell forever and ever. I don't want you to feel bad, ever. And she's the kind of person that every time I'm around her I feel bad," I explained.

"But don't she want that you're happy and whit somebody who love you?"

"I would hope so. But, no, she thinks that Jesus is real, and that gays go to Hell, and she'll want to pray for us because we're of the devil..."

"What means of the devil?" he asked.

"That because of what we do, who we love, who we are, that the devil controls us. She thinks that if only we stop being gay and love Jesus, well, then we can go to Heaven and be with Jesus forever and ever instead of burning in Hell with the devil. Real intelligent, right?" I said.

"Strange, I think. I don't understand why people believe such thing, you know? And I think she must be good because you are so good. How can she be a bad mother when you are like you are?" he wondered.

"She thinks she's a terrible mother because I just

don't believe in stupid Jesus stories and like men," I said. "She'll never change, and I really don't want the grief that will happen if she's a part of our lives."

"What is grief?"

"It means trouble and bother; sadness maybe. Anyway, I'm happily halfway around the world away from her and her husband, and I don't need to have them shame us and think less of us. If it was only me, well, I'm used to that. But for her and any of them to think anything bad about you—that's never gonna happen."

Sander got quiet, maybe even a bit pensive. This meant a lot to him, I could tell. But it's true—there was no way in Hell I would ever subject him to anything hurtful if I could help it. And this I could help.

"So... Johnnie... I will say something that I think, and please tell me if I am right, okay?"

"Yeah, of course!"

"I think that you have not tell anybody in your family that you are gay, and I think you will not have me to your family because you will not be able to treat me like you do. Like we love each other," he said. As usual, he'd gotten it right.

"Yes."

"Yes," he said as he collected his thoughts. "Are

you not happy whit yourself? Do you hope that you're not gay, Johnnie?"

He doesn't mince words. It's definitely a Danish trait, but in Sander's case he proffers his opinions and ideas so kindly and with such logic that there's no way to refute anything he says. And when he is as right as he was being right then, what's left to say?

"I'm very happy with who I am and who I'm becoming, Sandy. But I can believe all I want that I'm okay and there's nothing wrong with being gay, yet there's nothing in the world that will change somebody's mind when they think like my mom does. I was raised in her ridiculous, idiotic church and I can tell you for a fact that they truly believe what they do. And so I just don't say anything, because why give her the chance to say horrible things to me that she can't take back?" I said.

"I can't imagine what that must feel like."

"I guess you can't," I agreed. "And you wanna know what hurts the most?" Sander nodded, and reached for my hand. "It's that she's missing out on knowing you; on knowing who her own son loves more than life," I told him. "She won't ever get to share in my happiness, the complete happiness that you give me. And that makes me want to cry, Sandy. It really does."

"Well, ever is a long time. Maybe she will open up her thoughts to be a little bigger someday," he said. "But for now you has me, my brother and sister, my mom and dad—even my crazy relatives. You can share them all whit me. And I promise they will love you, okay?"

"Okay. You don't know what that means to me," I said.

"I think I do. Because I know you pretty good."

Sander leaned over and kissed me, and then we traded the warmth of the aromatic Punjabi dining saloon for the brisk, clear evening chill.

32

Luxury and speed are the calling card of the City Night Line express trains that link all of Europe as they roar through the night.

The lights in our cabin were dimmed to the max, and we laid together on the double bed watching the glow of the towns as we whizzed through toward home.

The coolness of the room and the soft bed linen felt so good against our naked bodies. We smiled at each other when we heard the couple next door heat up to a fever pitch, the girl writhing and yelping in ecstasy as her man kept the *thunk thunk thunk* of his rhythm going strong. He really played the 'He Man' with his little shouts of *Take that!* and *You like it, don't you, bitch!* Straight guys and their worn out porn dialogue is just so funny to me. The screwed part is that not only was the pap he spewed extremely silly, it's that we had to hear it in German.

"Know what I think?" Sander asked.

"What?"

"I think we should have a contest whit next door and see who is better at the sex, yes?"

"You mean something like this?" I said, as I reached for his half hard cock. I slowly stroked him into full mast; I was already there the second I felt him in my hand.

"That's wery nice, Johnnie."

"So's this," I said, and then I went down on him and he became completely lost in the wonderfully intense feeling of my lips grasping the tip of his dick, while alternately retracting his foreskin from the base of his shaft. Each time I made the move, my entire tongue and upper mouth would stimulate the head and surrounding corona.

True to his word he started to moan, but in no way was he faking it for the benefit of our neighbors. He was being carried away by the electric feelings firing throughout his beautiful body.

"I want to kiss you right now, Johnnie!"

We rolled to face one another—he lying on his good arm, me taking the pressure off my sore knee—and filled ourselves with sensuous, deep love as our tongues entwined.

Sander took my cock into his hand and began to stroke it slowly, putting pressure from his forefinger on the back side of the head while using his thumb to scurry around the other side. He also would brush his fingertips around my ball sack while I jacked his engorged dick from stem to stern. This we did for nearly an hour.

I laid on my back and his chest melded with mine. Soon he was on top, our dicks touching and throbbing in tandem while he positioned himself to enter me.

I spread and lifted my legs while he slid toward my waiting ass. I could feel my steady, elevated pulse as I prepared myself for the incredible state of worshipful love I would soon experience. His breath warmed my neck, and my tits were as hard as my cock.

The wonderful aroma of Sander's hair mixed with his usual pleasant smell made me even harder, if that was possible! I opened myself to him and his perfect manhood joined with me, his gentle and considerate movement totally contrasting the animal nature of the lovers next door.

Let's talk gay sex. What's the attraction? Why does fucking an ass, or getting fucked; or blowing a cock and swallowing the jizz, or tonguing a hole, kissing a guy, or jacking each other off mean so much?

The ass action: The idea that someone like you, who has the same physical equipment, knows— because of this fact—how to pleasure you is a very big turn on.

Wondering and fantasizing about the unveiling—what does he look like nude; how big is the dick? — Is he cut or uncut? Does he have big, hanging balls, or a tight little nut sack that sucks up against him? Is he smooth or hairy? These are attractions because nothing is sexier than mystery.

One guy taking another guy's cock into his mouth to suck on it and manipulate it to pure orgasmic explosion? Of course, getting your dick sucked feels really nice in any circumstance. But guys know what other guys want. They understand the parts of the penis and know what—and especially what not—to do to achieve the most pleasure for the partner. But the biggest and most erotic turn on for me is the trust involved in trusting your most prized member to someone else's mouth. A real, live mouth with *teeth.*

Why lick and suck on a butt crack and asshole? Well, first off, that doesn't happen unless the area is as fresh as a daisy. No residue. No bad odors. So this becomes—because of those prerequisites—a huge expression of love and esteem for your partner. Face it, nobody tongues the hole of someone they don't absolutely worship. And worship is what it is.

There is no feeling like having your ass eaten out. There are nerve endings there that rival those of the foreskin. And there is no sex act that will relax and ready an ass for a good fuck like a rim job.

Then, to feel your lover inside of you when he mounts you is again the ultimate expression of love.

Each of these acts will bring amazing orgasms, and unlike sex with chicks there can never be a fake one—either you cum or you don't!

But let's say you're not into guy on guy sex. That's cool. Personally I am repulsed by the pussy. They always stink, they're runny, whatever it is that women's cum is made of is just gross to me, and above all *there's nothing there!* Nothing to play with! Nothing to grab hold of. When they walk naked across a room there's just a v-shaped patch of hair, and an odd shaped ass. Grosses me out!

But here's the thing: I would never mount an all

out campaign to hate, discriminate against, deny housing or employment to, or beat anyone up—or even kill them—because they are attracted to the opposite sex.

So why has it always been in vogue to marginalize the gay person? Why is my love for Sander, and his for me, any less important than those two apes bonking in the next compartment? Is it because some farty old men who wrote a very badly written book called The Bible said so? Who the fuck are they?

Well, that's my take on gay sex. I hope if anyone reads this who has never understood our attraction to each other, that they can generate even a modicum of compassion and understanding. After all, we've put up with you and your drama since Noah and the flood.

Speaking of floods, Sander's cock was brushing against my prostate—I know, there's no way to make that sound sexy, but *fuuuccckkkk!*—and I was seriously getting ready to blow my wad. The only thing holding me back was that I wanted to make sure Sander came before I opened my floodgate. But it was getting very difficult to delay the inevitable. Then something happened that I had dreamed about since the very first time I had sex...

"Johnnie, I'm gonna cum! I'm gonna—oh, God! *Fuck!*—Johnnie, I'm cumming! *I'm cumming!*"

And right when I felt the warmth of his load enter me, my cock exploded in a geyser of cum unlike any I'd ever seen. I spurted at least eight times, but what was incredible is that we actually came at the same time! It wasn't planned at all; we just released our cum at exactly the same moment and it was awesome!

When he had filled me with his cum, he slowly pulled out and rolled onto his back. We lay there for the longest time, our heartbeats slowing while we recovered from our special time together.

The entire session happened against the backdrop of the Dutch countryside at night, the sleeping hamlets marked only by the quick red flashes of crossing signals the flew past at speed.

I think I'm the one who fell asleep first. I was safe, my head resting quietly against my lover's chest, knowing he would be there in the morning time.

33

A soft knock at the compartment door ended our slumber. The morning dawned gray as we sped across Northern Germany, not too long now to the Danish border.

"Breakfast time, gentlemen," the car porter said. "May I come in?"

The door slid open revealing a silver cart loaded with baskets of bread, cereal, heaps of butter, coffee, citrus tea, and creamy milk. It officially smelled like morning.

The porter paid no mind at all that two young men had occupied the same bed. It was obvious to a blind man what we'd been up to, and neither of us cared. Nor did he. I could get used to this, I remember thinking. As advanced as the good ol' U. S. of A. can be in many ways, when it comes to sexual Puritanism there are only a few places in the world that can rival that same kind of backwards thinking—and most of those countries are run by Muslim fundamentalists or that biggest herd of hypocrites ever, the Catholic Church.

"Soon to be home again," Sander said, yawning while pouring a glass of orange juice. "Here, Mr. Bond. Shaky, not stirred." He handed the chilled glass to me then he began buttering bread. "You wanting Corn Flakes this morning?" he asked.

"You're not my slave, Pokey. I can do it."

"Ah! But I want to do it for you, see? So Corn Flakes?"

"Sure. You know how to make'em? Need my recipe?"

"I struggle whit it, but no worries. I try not to burn them," he chuckled.

The bread was warm and tasted so good, and it was so relaxing to sit there in the buff having breakfast with the love of my life while the world swept by.

Sander set the cereal bowls of the little table by the window, and ate his sitting naked on the floor. I remembered the first time we ever rode a train together. He was sitting across from me and I would snatch little peeks at the shape under his trousers, and gaze longingly at his cute ass.

Today he was totally nude, that ass planted on the floor revealing his beauty in all its perfection. His cock softly dangled over his balls, his knees up, with his back leaning against the leg rests of the couchette.

"Look whit your hands, not whit your eyes," he joked.

"I think you got the saying backwards."

"No, not in this case," he smiled. "Hurry up and finish your Corn Flakes."

"Whatever do you have in mind?" I joked seductively. "Most guys buy me dinner first."

"Yes, well, I makes you Corn Flakes. It's all you are getting until you fuck this ass."

"Oh, really?"

He nodded, sexily shoving a spoonful of cereal into his mouth and licking the spoon like a dick. I was already hard from just looking at him, and now he goes and gets me all horny and stuff. Oh, well. It's a hard job, but somebody has to do it.

"I think this cock wants to visit that ass," I said. "So come over here and sit on it."

"It's wery big. It looks wery happy."

"It will be much happier when it's making you shiver all over when I'm fucking you," I told him. "So you better eat your Wheaties because I'm ready to plow you from here to Helsinki!"

"Put your mouth where your money is!"

"I'll put my mouth on *you*, fucker! Come get some lovin'!"

The first thing he did was hug me for about half a minute. Then he straddled me butterfly style and slipped my dick right into his hole. We kissed as he took over the motion and soon found ourselves in a perfect, rhythmic four-four time. You could write a song to it.

His moans escalated and he grabbed his cock and stroked himself to the tempo we'd established. Then the train stopped at Flensburg in preparation of crossing the border into Denmark.

Ever been in one of those sexual situations where you were knee deep into it, close to cumming, and something or someone gets in the way of it? Imagine Sander and me fucking like pornstars when the brakes on the train triggered us to a stop at a station platform full of people. Sander was bouncing on my lap and I was just as involved when the platform appeared.

"The floor!" Sander breathlessly said.

"Let me hold you and just lean back," I told him. My hands were against his upper back and in one move we made for the floor. It was a great idea until a shooting, stabbing, killing pain reminded me of my injured leg—which is what I had landed on with our entire weight.

"Ouch!" I cried.

"Your leg!"

"It's okay, it's okay!" I said. Funny thing, even throughout the painful landing I never missed a thrust. "I've got a cute ass to fuck, so nothing's gonna stop me!" I said.

"I will not disagree whit you!" He laughed. "Here, I raise my legs onto your shoulders, yes?"

When he did that, my cock drove even deeper into his tight, warm asshole. I was fucking like a banshee—I guess this is how banshees fuck—and was nearing the end when Sander's moan brought forth a gusher of cum that landed all over our bellies. The warmth and the smell of his cum completely blew my senses and I nearly passed out from sheer pleasure as I filled him with my load. I was surprised how much came out considering I had blasted only a few hours before.

I laid on top of him for a little while, kissing his neck and chest as we recovered and calmed down from our little aerobics session.

"That was awesome!" I told him. "Is this what we both have to look forward to for the rest of our lives?"

"Until I am an old man who take Viagras for my wrinkled old boner," Sander said. "Maybe I have to tape a ice cream stick under my dick someday to make it be hard."

"As long as it's chocolate or strawberry, I'm okay with it," I said.

"You think it smell like teen spirit in here?" he chuckled.

"I think it smells like teen orgy!" I replied. "The poor steward is gonna wonder what hit this cabin!"

"Our big dicks, that's what!"

A half hour after the stop at Flensburg we were on our way again, crossing into Denmark about ten minutes later.

The customs and immigration folks cleared our train into the country, and less than an two and a half hours after that we were standing on the platform at Odense station. Walking to the station exit, I took note of the benches on the platform across the tracks.

The last time Sander and I sat on that bench I had no clue that he was gay, and that I would be returning to the same place with the man I would be spending the rest of my life with. I've always been a believer in trusting where the day takes you, and I'm so glad I believed it last Thursday.

As the weeks passed I learned from Marge that Dimitri Petrenko was safe and that he'd been sent to the States. He deserved that after all he'd been through. They'd held him at the U.S. Embassy in Warsaw. It was like Marge expected; the CIA station chief was the turncoat and he had been colluding with the SVR and the FSB for years. So in effect, Sander broke a major spy ring and no one was the wiser. Marge promised that she'd take it to the grave—as long as I never did anything that stupid again. But between you and me (and Sander), I'm glad I broke the rules. At least this time.

Sander was right about his family and how they'd receive me. It was such a blessing and an honor to be a part of a family so loving and close. Magda and Niels worship their kids, and they love me too. They are proud of their Sander. They have raised a good, kind, and honorable man. I cannot wait to see what he does in life, and to actually get to be there as it happens is more than I could ever hope.

Jannik took a very special liking to me. He said he is happy to have two brothers and he loves to tell me Sander stories. I'm happy to report that there aren't any bad ones to tell. They mostly center around Jannik's penchant for practical jokes he likes to play on his big brother—the one who is his hero.

Ingrid is smart. God, is that girl smart. She converts anywhere she is into a zone of joy. People flock to Ingrid like kids to an online gaming site. I gotta tell ya, if I didn't like men, and a particular one called Sander, I would definitely window shop that girl. She is my sister now, and she treats me like I've been there since the beginning.

Marge Stuplemann has grown from being a great boss—something that I swear I'll never take for granted—to an aunt to Sander and me. She likes to talk a hard ball, but that lady loves us. About once a month we manage to get together for dinner or a show of some kind. She'd never been to Tivoli Gardens even though she lives four miles away from it. Marge, Sander, Jannik, Ingrid and I took the old girl out for a hell of a day. She's not seeing anyone yet, she's still broken up over the loss of her soul mate. I've often asked myself if I had lost Sander that awful day, would I have been so keen to find someone else? I don't think I would, actually.

The day we came home we'd planned to hail a cab to Sander's house, but the day had turned chamber of commerce lovely; puffy cotton clouds blanched against a cerulean sky. So we decided to walk.

We crossed Øster Stationsvej and landed in the park in front of Odense Slot—that's a pretty palace that's become a town landmark. With crisscrossing walkways, gorgeous trees, and the most manicured lawn in all the town, the Odense Palace is a beautiful part of the local scenery.

"Johnnie, can we sit for a little time?" Sander asked suddenly. We planted ourselves on a bench and listened to the birdsong, enjoying the cool breeze against our skin. This time of day the place was fairly deserted, so it provided a peaceful respite.

"You shall listen for what I has to say because it is wery important and it is just fair that I tell you this, okay?" he began. *Oh shit!* was my first thought. Maybe now that we were safely home he planned to lower the boom on our relationship. Fuck! What now? I love him so much, and I thought he loves me. So why is this happening?

"Please listen for everything and wait until I am finish, okay, Johnnie?"

Could it get any worse?

"Do you see this?" He placed his finger on the brown beauty mark on his neck. "I must tell you how this comes here," he said. "I always want to be fair whit you because I love you so much. So here it is..." He took a breath. "Remember when I tell you about my last boyfriend I have three years ago?"

"Yeah. Uhmm... Torben, right?"

"See, I tell you that you are smart. You can remember that?" he commented. "But there is something I don't tell you until now," he continued.

"Did he hurt you there?" I asked him.

"Just listen... When I tell you that we break up and it's no big deal at the time, well, it was a wery big deal," Sander explained. "We have it good for that year, but after a while he says he is not gay and that he don't want anything to do whit me forever."

"What happened?"

Sander paused, took a deep breath. It was the first conversation we'd ever had over the entire time that I knew him where he wouldn't look me in the eye.

"He goes to the school and write wery mean things about me. He say I'm a faggot, dick licker, all the bad things, you know?"

I nodded.

"So, anyways, he says how I try to touch him

when he is sleeping over, and how I have gay pornos and have pictures of our football team under my bed. And so all the class believes him, and when I am leaving one day to go home, a bunch of them hits me and call me more bad words."

"Is that leftover from when they hit you?" I asked.

"No."

He took a little break to collect his thoughts; maybe to work up some courage. Whatever it was, it was clear that the memory of it all was hurting him to the core.

"So I am at home and I don't ever wish to go to my school again, ever. So I write a letter to my family, and I write a letter to Torben. And I take a belt and put it over the wood on the top of my room."

Oh, no... No, Sander...

"I gets up on a chair and I jump off, you know?"

"Oh, God, what happened?" I asked, practically hysterical by now.

"Right when I kick the chair, Jannik come into my room. I don't know that he is home, but I find out his class have a tour that day, you know, so he is home early. He is only six years, and he scream and run to the neighbor where my mother is," he said.

"I can't believe..."

"So the neighbor and my mother run inside and they put the chair back under me and they take the belt away. The mark on my neck is from the snap on the belt. It make a wound, and this will always be here," he said, again pointing to the scar.

I felt so fucking useless at that moment. I hugged him, and by then he was sobbing uncontrollably, but I had no words. The very idea of a world without Sander Lars Hansen was incomprehensible to me. And if he had succeeded, I never, ever would have known him.

"What happened. Pokey?"

"Well, the worst part of it all wasn't even that I will have died," he said. "I felt like a bad, bad person because Jannik sees what happened."

"He saved your life..."

"Yes, he did. And I don't know what to do to make it up for him," Sander cried. "I feel so awful because he is so good, and he should never have seen what he did," he said through his tears.

"But he loves you... He has you here, and I'm sure you must have told him that it was a mistake, right?"

"Oh, yes. We go to the counseling every week still, and I want to tell you this because you should know if you want to be whit somebody who do such a crazy thing and have to see the psychiatry man," he said.

I contemplated his words for a little while, the birds still going strong. I didn't want to pump him full of stupid platitudes; besides, who the fuck am I to give any advice at all?

But *this* I could do...

"Sander, now it is time for you to listen to me, right?" I said. He nodded, his jacket sleeve doubling for a hanky.

"First, I think that you are the bravest person I've ever known."

"Yes, yes, sure, sure... You should see me on a chair," he snarled to himself. "Some Braveheart that guy is."

"Shut up, yeah?" Again he nodded. "I am so happy that you told me this because it just proves again something that I already know."

"What?"

"Your honesty. And that's everything if we're ever going to be anything together," I said.

"Well, if we are to be married, you have to know. It is only right that you know what a shit I was," he said. "I can still see Jannik screaming. He was terrored, and it wasn't fair to him!"

"So, what—are you never gonna forgive yourself? Do you remember what brought you to that awful place? Everybody hating on you and even beating you up! And that fucking Torben, the person you trusted with basically your whole life... He did and said those rotten things."

"I know, I know. The doctor, he say the same. And so do my family; even Jannik. But I still feeling the same way," he said.

"So then I forgive you."

"What do you mean?"

"I said, I forgive you. I forgive you for making a mistake that would have made sure that my life would never be as good as it is now. If you would have left this world, then what? So because of that, I forgive you," I said.

"Huh."

Huh is what Sander always says when there's nothing else to say.

"And if I ever meet this Torben character, well, I shot a guy in the foot once, don't forget!"

"It's okay," Sander laughed. "Torben made it good again. I forgived him."

"So you forgave your terrorist, but you won't forgive yourself? What kinda shit is that?" I scolded. "Dude, you gotta get past this, I swear!"

"Okay, well there is a big change that I think—I know—is make a difference, I can tell you..."

"Yeah? What?"

"You. I didn't have you before. I don't mean to say that you has to fix my problems—I know the problem is mine. And I am better than three years ago. It's just that I was wery down for a long time, and just knowing you since we meet have make such happiness," he said. "But now, I know things is wery different. It's what I've been waiting for."

"What did Torben do to make things right, as you say?"

"So I tell you not the truth before about how my family learn I am gay," he said. "They reads the letters I leave and that is how. So my father talk whit Torben's father and together they meet whit Torben. And he feel really bad and come to me in hospital all crying and he say he is wery sorry, so I says okay."

"How was it after that?" I asked.

"The school were wery nice, and when I come back Torben is off to another school and the ones who was mean was nice after that."

"And what about when you got home?"

"My whole family was wonderful to me, and Jannik climb onto me and will not let me go. My mother and father, and Ingrid, say that if I am gay it is nobody's business but mine, and they said that I could have tell them and it would've been fine," Sander explained. "So that is when I know for first time how stupid I am to try what I did."

"I thought about it once," I confessed.

"Really?! What happen?"

"They have these fucked up meetings called revivals at my mom's church," I said. "My mom made me go to one when I was twelve. So, anyway, they had this freak up there talking about how the worst thing anyone can do is to be homosexual. That God and Jesus would forgive—get this—would forgive Hitler before forgiving somebody who's gay!"

"Fucking hell!"

"Yeah! Then he says how there's a special Hell— one that's worse than regular Hell, I guess—that's just for homos. Then he said that it's true that parents would rather know that their kid is hooked on heroin, or is a murderer, than to know that he's gay."

"Wow, that man should be sent to the jail," Sander said. "That man is crazy!"

"Yeah! And you should have seen how everybody thought how wonderful and wise that fucker was! So you can imagine how I felt about myself that day," I said.

"What did you do? What made you stop?"

"My grandpa came over. That's the only thing that stopped me. I was gonna sit on the train tracks and act like it was an accident. I didn't plan to leave a note, or anything. Because I knew that if I told them the truth they probably wouldn't care as much that I was dead."

"Did you tell your grandpa?"

"No. I never told anyone in my family. But he was just nice to me and made me feel like I mattered, you know? That was enough to make me stop."

Sander thought for a minute then, choosing his words carefully as he always does, he offered up an idea.

"I was thinking about something, Johnnie."

"That's always good when you do that," I said. "Lay it on me, brother!"

He finally laughed a little, knowing that the worst was over.

"I will make a good deal whit you, right now," he said. "I will forgive myself if you will forgive yourself. And then we will make a promise to each other that we will never think stupid things like that and if we are sad, we will help the other one to not be sad anymore."

"I don't even have to think about it," I told him. "It's a great idea."

He leaned on my shoulder and I kissed him on the top of his sweet head. We sat there for the longest time, secure and happy in each other's presence. Life can get complicated, and when it does it's usually because we choose to complicate it. We care far too much about opinions that do not matter and that oftentimes represent the truest definition of irrelevance.

"You ready to head home?" I asked.

"Sure," he replied. We started down the pathway past the King's Garden, our hands joined.

"Pokey, I don't know about you, but I'd rather get a taxi after all."

"Fuck walking!" he said. "I thought you'd never say it. That was the dumbest idea I ever hear, walking home—especially whit your knee and my poor little arm!"

"Your arm's fine!"

"It could be a big stump right now if that asshole knows how to shoot a gun!"

"Tell it to the Marines, ya big baby!"

"You will see! When I can't jack you off cuz my arm falls off! Then who is laughing..."

"Hey, you still got that joint on you? Bet we can get a light from that cop over there."

"You are so fucked in your head," Sander smiled,

shaking his head in disbelief."

"And that's why you love me."

"Yeah, Johnnie Allen, that's why I love you."

We steer our lives onto roads where they don't belong, craving validation from those who do not deserve the consideration that we are so eager to award them.

We are fragile, sometimes broken. But sitting there on that park bench, Sander consuming my whole world, I felt pure strength. I was stronger than I had ever been, and it was because of a man who loves me and takes me for who and for what I am. There is no greater aspiration in life, to have a relationship like the one I share with Sander, and I had it at the age of twenty-two.

But more important than the love I was gifted by Sander, there was someone leaning on me whom I could love back.

It's said that it is better to give than to receive— I think that when the gift is love, no truer words could ever be spoken.

Will we make it together? I think so. I really do. Sander was the final piece to the very strange puzzle that is Johnnie Allen. I'm happy to be me. But I'm much happier to be us.

about the author

CADE JAY HATHAWAY was born in 1991 near Seattle, Washington and became a U.S. Merchant Mariner at age 18. It was while serving aboard the cargo liners of the Military Sealift Command that he was offered a position at  the Central Intelligence Agency, where he was subsequently posted to Denmark as a field transport specialist in the operations division of the clandestine service. He resides on the Danish island of Funen with his life partner, Lasse, and two very friendly cats named Klaus and Slinky. This is C.J.'s first novel.

He can be reached at:
cadejayhathaway@tutanota.com

Author Photo by Lasse Jørgensen Hathaway

Made in the USA
Monee, IL
14 November 2020